Praise for *Rinsing Mũkami's Soul*

'What a heart wrenching book... I loved the interweaving of Gĩkũyũ mythology, distant, and past history with Mũkami's desperate life. A clever mind with sharp skill is clearly at work here. Events tied together in strange, mysterious ways. The book is both extended metaphor and identifiably Kenyan.'

—Makena Onjerika,
2018 Winner of the Caine Prize for African Writing

'*Rinsing Mũkami's Soul* is an immersive experience. We fall in love with Mũkami from the first page, as she experiences the turbulence and thrill of first love. We stay with Mũkami as her world tumbles and she tries to save herself. McGrath takes us on a gritty yet spirited ride through 1980s Kenya, a society wrestling with corruption and grief in the wake of independence. McGrath is a talented writer. She manages to balance brutal realities with a light humourous touch that make *Rinsing Mũkami's Soul* a meaningful and entertaining read.'

—Isabelle Dupuy, author of *Living the Dream*

Praise for *Through the Leopard's Gaze*

'Beautifully written...'

—*BBC Radio 4* Loose Ends.

'McGrath's book is a courageous contribution...'

—*Big Issue North*

'Britain is traumatised by its history...'

—*The Evening Standard*

Rinsing Mũkami's Soul

Njambi McGrath

JACARANDA

This edition first published in Great Britain 2024
Jacaranda Books Art Music Ltd
27 Old Gloucester Street,
London WC1N 3AX
www.jacarandabooksartmusic.co.uk
Copyright © Njambi McGrath 2023

The right of Njambi McGrath to be identified as the author of this
work has been asserted in accordance with the Copyright, Designs
and Patents Act 1988.

ISBN: 9781914344831
eISBN: 9781914344855

Cover Design: Christina Schweighardt
Typeset by: Kamillah Brandes
Printed and bound by CPI Group (UK) Ltd, Croydon, CR0 4YY

To my daughters Inez and Neve, my proudest achievements.

To my husband Dave, my rock.

To my darling mother Gakarĩ, your spirit keeps my fire burning.

Chapter One

It's the first of September and the prognosis is bleak. Mama still can't raise my school fees. She has trekked the length and breadth of Kīrigiti with the gait of a defeated goat, but in the era of *kitu kidogo* no one has spare money to lend.

I'm on edge, fraught with worry. What if mama can't find my school fees? I'll become like Wa Njūgū. I shudder at the thought. Her only purpose is to spread gossip, crisscrossing doorways, her lactating breasts nourishing yet another mouth. Nor do I want to be like Būi, my school friend, forced to give up school because her mother chose drink over her education. Now Būi is a hustler in town, perming people's hair and clubbing every spare minute she gets.

Mama's avoided the crossway tailor, but she's run out of options. I am about to embark on my final term of middle school and leaving education is too bleak a thought. I shut my eyes tight and pray.

'*Ngai Baba wa matuini*, please help mama find the money.'

I toss. Impatience for what the morning brings gnaws me. I yearn for sleep, but my mind is busy. I've no space to think. The thin corrugated iron walls are unforgiving. Inexhaustible stray dogs squabble outside my door. The dying woman hollers her funeral song. Wa Njūgū screams at her children. There's a wail from the direction of the gate, God knows why.

Amongst the clatter, I think I hear mama weeping. I shrink at her anguish. The thought of her crying cuts like a razor into my soul. I'm guilty of fuelling her woes. I fear the lack of my school fees will break her. She's down on her luck, with a dead husband and a useless boyfriend. She's laden with problems bigger than the pile of mitumba clothes she sells in Gīkomba market. The Nairobi municipal council is threatening to bull-doze kiosks that defaulted on permit renewals, and she fears hers is next.

The long rains are still in our midst. The rains that once sent jubilant gratitude to our supreme mighty Ngai looking down on the Gīkūyū, now leaves us in despair. With no storage, her meagre stock will be ruined. Not only that, but my school shoes have so many tyre patches, I might as well wear one.

I hold my breath, sit up, and listen, but the compound hullaballoo makes it impossible to hear Mama. This place is the purgatory before madness.

'I am the king of this household, no woman tells a man what to do, I-.'

There's a clang, then a bang, silencing the voice mid-sentence. Must be resident of house number five hitting her husband on his head with a pan. Again.

'May the blood of Jesus rinse your sins darling Jane.'

That's Firifo cleansing his wife. Again. Does no one have a clock round here. It's gone midnight and the nightly chorus continues. This orchestra of misfits is inescapable.

Now I hear her. Mama is crying. There's no interconnecting door between her room and the room I share with the kitchen, living room and the occasional rat. To get to her, I must step outside into the sludge and risk the night robbers. I am about to call to her then remember she can't answer without the neighbours joining into the conversations with ridicule. I want to hold her tight, but Kaminde is in her bed. My teeth grind. I can't face him tonight. Mama is saying something, but her voice is muffled and Kaminde responds in an inaudible low tone. I lie back on my bed. Enveloped by the hollowness of darkness, I fall asleep.

A stampede of early risers rush past my window to the communal ablutions. The crow of the resident cock is begrudging. They've sucked his essence too. I guess rousing the residents of the Ministry of Works must be a strife. It says something when even the compound cockcrow is bitter. Firifo and his wife Jane screech their prayers in his place.

My bladder throbs. The queue to the toilet will be a mile long. I lay in my bed and wait. The corrugated iron walls radiate the September sun that once nourished *mwere*, but now, its suffocating. The rush is diminishing, only the occasional voice piercing the air. I hear footsteps stop outside the door and there's a knock. Who can this be? No one visits at this hour and Mama is long gone to fight the municipal council.

I roll to my side and throw off the covers. Kneeling, I reach over to the window and feel for the latch. I slide it to the left and push out the shutters allowing fresh air. Light floods in. There's another knock and I hop onto the armchair wedged against my bed, its tattered leather scratching my thighs. I move our drum coffee table out of the tight living space. The coolness of the unvarnished floor is a contrast to the stifling air.

There's another knock. It's loud and impatient. I jump to the door and slide the top latch. I'm about to slide the bottom latch and there's another knock. I open the door and a large foot in a sandal two sizes too small steps in. The woman attached to the foot enters, closing the door behind her. She stands with her back to the window and all I see is her silhouette which reminds me of our coffee table. Top heavy with thin legs.

'These people have no decorum,' she says.

'Please come in.'

She's already in but I can't think of another greeting. She's bullish and towers over me. She walks to the middle of the room close to me and scans around. Dirty dishes are stacked on our two-ring burner sat on top of the rickety table. She turns to look at the stained curtain, the roll of fat on top of her neckless back making her look like a humpback whale. Her head pivots to our worn leather settees that make up our living space. She's got the scrutiny of a hawk calculating our worth.

'How long have you lived here?'

My throat is dry.

'How long?'

She makes my skin crawl. I don't know who she is or why she's here.

'I was in form 1, four years ago.'

She must be the bailiff.

'Mmm,' she says.

I gulp.

'I've heard you're something else.'

She's studying me as if she's ready to eat me; like the human eating giant *irimũ ria nyakondo*. I can't see her face but imagine, like the giant, she has one eye and two mouths. I'm scared and wish Mama was here. I feel her stare. I'm filled with unease. I am conscious I'm still in my see-through nightdress. Her claw-like fingers reach out, her nails which look as if she scratches the earth for a living, clamp my breasts.

'Nice and juicy.'

I wince and recoil.

'If your mother doesn't pay me back I can put you into good use.'

I swallow hard. I'm cornered by this ogre and won't be able to run out of the door without her squashing me like a fly. She sniffs. There's a smell of urine and our eyes land on the half full bucket I use for bathing and night toilet. Nervousness makes me go to the other window, undo the latch, pushing out the shutters. A breeze refreshes the room. I turn round and the fresh light reveals her face. It takes me a moment to recognise her. It's the crossway tailor. I'm taken aback. I've never seen her outside her kiosk. She sits down, her wide girth filling Kaminde's armchair.

'I'm here because I knew your father.'

I stiffen and stand back.

'My father?' I ask.

I am dismayed. No one here knows about him. How did she know him? No one has ever spoken to me about Baba. Not even Mama. She's still heartbroken by his death. Why is she here? Was she sent here by Baba's employer?

'He was of my brother's *rika*. They were circumcised together.'

With piqued curiosity, I fold my arms and stare at her large oval face, expecting to hear more about Baba. But with her pointed chin raised, she gives me a vacant look.

'Anyhow I told your mother I'll drop the fees for your education, on my way to the kiosk.'

The mention of school fees is heartening. I should thank her but she's dominant and scary. Her breathing like an old engine powering an old tractor.

She slumps back. Stretches her plump hand to her head and scratches. The synthetic wig moves with the movement of her fingers. With her left hand she pulls open the top of her *kitenge* and buries the hand into her bosom. Lifting her large breast, she pulls out a wad of notes. She scrunches her face as if parting with the money aches her and throws them at me scattering them all over the floor.

'Your mother can grovel for the rest.'

I scramble for the notes like a grateful beggar.

'Tell your mother she must pay interest too.'

I nod. I don't know what that means. Her wide nose and slanted eyes make me uneasy.

'I want it back by the end of the month.'

My heart sinks. Where will poor mama find the money by the end of the month? When I'm old enough to have a job, I promise myself, she'll never want for anything.

The crossway tailor gets up and pushes our coffee table out of the way. She walks to the door, and she's gone.

With my ear pinned to the wall, I listen, assessing the queue by the chatter outside. It seems like the morning rush is subsiding. Stray dogs must be basking against my wall because I can hear a dog lick its balls. I must get ready if I'm to make it to school by lunch. I step outside carrying my soap dish and face cloth and head to the ablution area.

Wa Njũgũ's children surround a goat and are debating who should ride it. The tallest child hops onto it's back as it takes off. The enraged goat reverses, gathers momentum, then speeds forward knocking one child to the ground. Others cheer as the goat knocks the others to the ground. I guess they say what your mother doesn't teach you, the world will teach you. In this case the goat taught them.

Chapter Two

Ngai, the purveyor of brightness, stood on the slopes of Mount Kīrīnyaga and beamed with delight at creating the earth and the universe. And when he created Gīkūyū, our supreme elder, granting him all the land his eye could see, he would not have anticipated what Kīrigiti would become. A constellation of hills, one housing our home at the Ministry of Works and the other our school. Built on the cusp of freedom, our government-funded, parent-supplemented school for gifted children is an oasis from the chaos of our compound.

I walk past the familiar gate now wide open for start of term. I hoist my blue tin suitcase onto my shoulder and begin the mile long dusty walk to the school.

I step into the musty smell of the dark dorm. It's obvious it's been deprived of air for the month during the school holidays and the meagre louvre windows do little to freshen the place. I place my suitcase in the centre of my cubicle and take a deep breath. I'm glad to be back.

Būi will not be returning, and I'm gutted. She's my best friend and I've no idea how I'll cope without her. I immerse myself in the silence, enjoying the calm before the storm, as there's only a handful of students scattered around the school. Most tend to arrive later in the day, but I like being organised.

I begin unpacking. I hang my school shirts, their whiteness faded with age, on the wire hangers and drape my spare skirt over the one wooden hanger. My two home dresses, socks, towel, underpants, and ablutions bag, I place beneath the hanging shirts. My toiletries go on the bottom shelf. I hoist my suitcase on top of the lockers. Hooking the small padlock on the locker door, I push it in and head out. My shoes, raised on the platform of tyre replacement, give me extra height.

I stride across the assembly ground and greet some familiar faces. I turn towards the gate where students, laden with boarding paraphernalia, are filing in like safari ants. The school is waking from slumber. To my right is the school kitchen from which the cooks are already firing the stoves. Next to it is the dining hall. To my left is the view from the scenic valley overlooking a few scattered homes. The administration block is set aside from the classrooms and labs with courtyards interspersed in the middle.

I walk past the administration block towards my class. This is the final term, and I can't wait to get started with mock revisions. I go past the courtyard enjoying the breeze. September is my favourite start of term. It's not hot and dry like January or wet like April. I emerge from the corner of Form 2c blinded by the sun reflected on the sandstone pavements that carpet our school.

My eyes squint. There's someone sat on the ledge of the planters outside the science block. He doesn't look familiar. He looks out of place. His faded denims and white shirt, emblazoned with the New York Yankees logo, tells me he can't be a student since students must arrive in uniform. His boyish face is too young to be a teacher. He looks my age, sixteen. I conclude he must be dropping someone off.

I study his dark face, unable to hide my curiosity. He stands out from Kĩambu boys. His aura is supreme, and he oozes a confidence I haven't encountered before. I can't stop staring at him. He doesn't belong in Kĩambu high. He appears too well off. This school is for children whose parents can't afford two thousand shillings in one go. The shoes he's wearing must have cost more than that.

His buttocks rest on one heel of his Nike trainer. I've never seen any that white. Besides, he must have flown here because Kĩambu's red soils stain everything like freedom fighters' tears. Nike trainers are mainly worn by turnboys in *matatũs*, but theirs are dull castoffs from *wazungus* in Europe. His other leg is stretched out on the pavement swinging from side to side like a pendulum. His back is resting on the bougainvillea bush, trimmed for the start of term, its purple blooms reflected on the glass of the classroom windows.

Our eyes meet. His face softens. He moistens his lips with a pink tongue, tucking his bottom lip underneath it. The sides of his mouth peel back, revealing teeth so white they match his gleaming trainers. I gasp, as his gallant smile deepens, wilting my soul. Like village dwellers who stare without shame, my face drops in embarrassment. I've lost focus, forgetting where I'm headed. Sweat seeps from my skin and I think I will faint. Then my body takes over and I continue walking in his direction, my heart drumming like *kĩhembe* dancers in moonlight. I get close.

His lemon-scented fragrance is intoxicating. I'm about to walk past him but he raises his foot a little, catching my foot. I lurch forward, steadying myself before crashing to the ground. Raw with bashful confusion, I stand up, gather my pens, books, and continue walking. I pray I haven't lost my cool. Unable to understand what just happened, something compels me to swagger. I push my bottom out and let one side drop as if in slow motion. I've never done anything this ridiculous before. I disappear from his searing gaze, my skin burning. Finally, out of sight of the science block I approach my classroom 4b, completely thrown off-kilter by the encounter.

Chapter Three

I sense his aura before I can look up. His presence fades the classroom noise into the background. It's been several days since we first met and I've found out he's a new boy in my class. His desk a few rows down from mine. My eyes roll up his creaseless uniform landing on his babyface. He is masculine yet delicate. He's pressed against my desk, and I can feel his breath on my skin. He's standing close. I don't know whether to lean back or move in. He lifts his hand towards my face. I stare at his smooth hands and manicured nails. He's in a league of his own, possessing a finesse I've never seen before.

In his hand, is a picture. He studies my face suspending my curiosity. He turns the picture round like a magician playing a trick. I stare. It is a woman whose skin is the colour of the belly of a frog. Her hair is the colour of dried maize. She's wearing a leather jacket and short floaty skirt. Her legs are covered in bizarre socks that don't cover her feet. What's the point of such socks? The short-sleeved top she's wearing reveals her long arms weighted with multicoloured bracelets. Her low-cut top reveals the mounds of her breasts. I've never seen anyone pose for a picture like that. I wonder what mama would say about the woman in the photo. The washerwomen of the Ministry of Works compound would definitely twist their lips in disdain and call her a prostitute. Her neck is decorated with bright necklaces. Her lips are the colour of a cock's crown. She's smiling with one eye half closed. Confused, I gaze at the picture. Am I supposed to know this woman? Then it hits me. He must suspect how I feel. He's here to warn me of his girlfriend. I am deflated at the thought.

'Who?' My throat croaks as if stuffed with dry earth. I pray he doesn't confirm my suspicion.

'Is that your girlfriend?' I ask before he can respond.

What's wrong with me? I'm a mess. Uncultured and exposed. He laughs and slaps my desk. I'm unable to see the joke.

'No. This is Madonna, she's so cool,' he says.

His American twang detonates my logic. He sounds like the people on TV or radio. I'm thrown off-guard but laugh too. It comes out wrong. We are speaking at cross-purposes. I feel clumsy. Like a shipwrecked sailor, I'm still searching for somewhere to anchor. I don't know the meaning of this. Instead of speaking about us, he is here to speak about this Madonna.

'How do you know her?'

My accent is crude.

'You are cute! Don't ever change.'

My cheeks burn. My school shirt is damp, magnifying the smell of sweat from my armpit. I'm embarrassed by not knowing what to say, by my clothes, my ugly tyre shoes, the way I speak, and not knowing who the woman in the picture is. I have no clue what this conversation is about. It's not what I imagined we'd talk about if we ever spoke.

'She's the singer of "La Isla Bonita". Madonna,' he says, licking his lips.

I'm out of my depth. I am foolish, unable to make a viable contribution to this conversation. I've never seen a picture of Madonna, but of course I know who she is. Besides where would I get such a photograph from. They don't sell such things in the market.

He smiles, his boyish face drawing me in.

'Please excuse my rudeness, I am Kĩmathi,' he says.

'Kĩmathi is a Gĩkũyũ name.' I say, glad to move away from the conversation I know nothing about.

It's not clear if he heard me, because he says nothing. Or maybe the words never left my mouth.

'My name is Mũkami,' I say to fill the awkward silence.

He replies solemnly, 'Mũkami is boring. From today onwards, I will call you Madonna.'

My mind buzzes. He wants to change my name to Madonna. It never occurred to me to change it. No one has ever commented on my name, let alone tried to change it. People here don't change their names because they are boring. But Kĩmathi thinks mine is and prefers Madonna. I'm already out of my depth with him, and if he thinks it will help then what's a name change? Who am I to resist? Nothing about him is conventional. He is so refined. I wonder where did he come from? He is different. I'm the opposite, primitive and uncul-tured. Even my name. Mama says Mũkami means the diligent young maiden who milks. But we don't have cows, so I've never milked. I feel his penetrating eyes on me, and I am about to shrug in agreement, when Mr Onacha, the history teacher, walks in and Kĩmathi disappears.

Chapter Four

It's Saturday, mid-morning, and the weekly cleaning duties are in full swing. It's the one day students can wear home clothes, so we resemble overdressed house cleaners. I'm wearing a lilac skirt and white t-shirt. In my left hand is a clipboard with a duty roster clipped onto it. I have a biro in my right hand. My presence inspecting the dorms causes a hive of activity. Students crisscross with brooms, mops, and buckets. Three girls form a line pushing frothy water towards the door, squeegees in unison. Another one passes me carrying a bin overflowing with period-stained cotton wool on the way to the outside pit latrines. Some students have dusters cleaning the louvre windows.

In the corridor that serves the ablutions, Form 3s and Form 4s dorms are starved of natural light, so I turn on the florescent lighting. The unvarnished bare concrete floor is immaculate. I cross reference it to the list on my clipboard and tick. I walk to the toilets, enter the first cubicle, inspect the bowl. It's clean. I move to the next one. Another tick and move to the third one. There's a full bin. Someone is going to have to answer for this to the duty master. The floors look clean enough, so I head to my dorm.

Shi Shi is by my locker spooning cocoa powder and sugar into a cup. She opens the lid of the Blue Band margarine and scoops a large spoonful adding to the cocoa and sugar. She blends the ingredients.

'Ooh *kamixy*,' I say.

That should stave off my hunger for now. Lunch is still an hour away. I'm about to scoop some with my finger, when a girl appears from behind the lockers of the second cubicle. She walks straight to me.

'Are you Mŭkami?' she asks.

The petite stature of the girl tells me she is a mono.

'Yes. What's wrong?'

I assume she's here to report some cleaning neglect. She is timid and shifts in discomfort. If she's a first former she should have gained more confidence by now. Shi Shi is eating spoonfuls of *kamixy* and I scoop some more with my finger, stuffing it into my mouth.

'Someone wants you by the flagpole.'

And with that she is gone.

Who could that be? Mama? She wouldn't just turn up unless there was a problem. It must be the crossway tailor harassing her. Placing my clipboard on my bed, I hurry out of the dorm, into the corridor and out. I rush past the shrubs marking the pavements, their overgrown branches brushing against me. I turn round to see Shi Shi watching me through the window and I wave.

The assembly ground is dotted with students picking litter, wilting in the overhead sun. I'm scanning round for Mama but she's nowhere. I look towards the administration block and freeze mid-step. Kīmathi stands in white denims, legs apart leaning against the flagpole. He's got one hand in his pocket,

15

posing like the men in the tailoring catalogue in the tailor's kiosk. He holds a carrier bag in his other hand. The sight of him charges me with an electrical surge. My heart is thumping. He smiles from the corner of his mouth and bites his lip. He studies my walk like a leopard stalking prey. Time stands still as I walk in slow motion, bathing in his gaze. The ground beneath me crumbles away. By the time I reach him I am breathless, my forehead littered with sweat beads.

'My beautiful Madonna.'

He steps forward taking my hand into his smooth palms. His touch is electric. A magnetic force draws me close to him. I want to tuck myself into his ribbed chest. His perfume makes my insides go wild.

'You called for me?' I ask with my dry throat.

'Close your eyes, Madonna.'

I close my eyes giving in. His hand locks into mine.

'Come this way.'

Hypnotised, I walk, feeling the crunch of the coarse gravel.

'Stop, lift your leg forward and step.'

I step on to a ledge. This must be the end of the assembly ground.

'Now step down.'

I step onto what feels like grass on a slope. We must be on the scenic valley.

'Sit.'

Like a dog to his master, I lower my bottom on the grassy verge, curious at the rustling noise he is making. My shoulders arch in suspense.

'Open your mouth.'

He places something on my tongue which draws saliva from every corner of my mouth. The smell of batter-fried potatoes with coriander is unmistakable.

'Bhajias? Where did you get them from?' I ask in between chewing.

'I went to town to buy them for you.'

'For me?'

I stop chewing in alarm. I assumed a visitor brought them for him.

'For real? How about the bus fare and money?' I ask, unable to hide my dismay. I barely have money for potato sambusas from Geremani the carpenter from his cabin, let alone to go to Nairobi for bhajias.

'My Ma gives me loads of money, I guess she feels guilty for dragging me here from the States,' he says.

I'm impressed and overcome at his gesture. No one's ever done anything like that for me.

'Are you sick?' I ask, my mouth overflowing with flavour.

'Sick?'

'Yes, sick. Isn't it the only way you can get out of school?'

He laughs. 'That don't matter.'

'So how did you get permission to go?'

'I sneaked out,' he says.

I look at him expecting him to laugh at the joke. No one sneaks out of Wamakũbũ's school.

He is serious.

'Weren't you afraid of getting caught?'

He shrugs looking into the valley. He is defiant and unafraid. I've never seen anyone with that attitude before. I am confused and in awe at the same time.

'My parents are pretty liberal.'

'What? How? Mama would be furious if I sneaked out of school.'

I stuff more bhajias into my mouth.

'It's not the worst thing I have done.'

I gasp.

'What do you mean not the worst thing, I'd say that's very bad.'

He throws his head back and laughs stealing a kiss on my cheek.

'Don't get too serious Madonna.'

Chapter Five

⌒

I'm woken by Tabitha's hippopotamus bottom bellowing like
a tormented giant. I half open my eyes, but my eyelids are
weighted down by exam blues. There's beeping from a revers-
ing lorry. I lie still, cursing her for rousing me with the stench.
A chorus from the tinker birds almost sooth me back to sleep.
I bolt upright.

'It's 7th October 1988' I say, waking everyone up.

Squeals emanate from different corners of the dorm. This is
the day fourth formers have been dreaming of for nine months
and it's finally here. It'll be the most important day of my
life. Tonight, is the school disco. That lorry must be bringing
tonight's delights. The sound of soda bottles tinkling as they
are offloaded, adds to my excitement.

The rickety bunk-bed frame shudders. My head is on a collision course with Tabitha's rear, suspended on the top bunk like
a thief's loot. I curse. There's already a golf ball swelling when
I rub my stinging forehead. I'm convinced the overworked coil
springs bearing her weight will give way one day and she will
come crashing down, squashing my thin limbs. I'd have no
chance. She would suffocate me.

The hard edges of my textbooks poke into my leg as if urging me to leave before the fumes from Tabitha's bottom choke me. My revision torch is next to me where I must have dropped it when I fell asleep. I pull my textbooks from under my blankets. They are still where I put them last night, still unopened. A pang of guilt rises from within. It's six days to the exam but instead of swotting I got carried away fantasising with Shi Shi. She has an eye on a boy and thinks there's a chance they could be an item. It was long after light's out when she sneaked back out to her dorm.

I am aware my nails are digging into my palms. It is Kĩmathi's photograph, which I cradled to sleep, clenched in my fist. I unfurl my fingers, sticky with damp sweat, releasing it. I look but it's too dark to see in the early morning light. I flick the switch of my torch, but the battery is dead. It doesn't matter. His handsome face is imprinted in my brain. When Tabitha eventually crushes me to death, I want to die holding Kĩmathi's photo. I press it onto my chest, willing it to perforate into my hearts cavity where he belongs. I'll keep him there and never let him go.

A sudden waft of hard-boiled eggs and weevil infused porridge invades my dorm like an evil spirit. My stomach churns and rumbles at the same time. I get out of bed. Smidgens of light seeping through from the waking sky are barely enough to see my way. My toes recoil at the feel of the concrete floor as my feet tap around seeking my flip-flops. I find them and slide my feet in.

I think of Bũi's polka dot chiffon dress hanging in my locker. I can't wait to slide my body into it and do up the cream bow under my chin. Bũi loaned it to me when I visited her during half term. Since she left school, I don't get much chance to see her due to lack of bus fare and being in boarding school. Such a shame she'll never get to experience tonight. I'm filled with delight and Bŭi is soon out of my mind. Mama's pumps await my eager feet in my locker. She begged me to only wear them for the disco because she intends on selling them. I think of how I'll strut in those pumps. I feel like a bride on her wedding day. I can't wait to see Kĩmathi's face when he sees me all dressed up. My poor heart cannot contain the love I feel for him. Thrill soaks through my body like a sponge in the long *Njahĩ* rains, dissolving thoughts of the final mock exams. The do-gooder of my brain intervenes yelling the mocks are only a week away. But today is the official day of pleasure the left side of my brain pleads. I feel an impatience as I think of how many hours there are till the evening. It might as well be a million years away.

I decide I'd better get in an hour of revision to appease the do-gooder in my brain. This will kill time and make it go faster. On normal days I rise at dawn. By the time other students stir from their bunk beds, I am all clean ready for early morning revision. But this is not a normal day. I reach into my locker, and pull out the plastic bag containing my toothpaste, toothbrush, flannel and bar of Palmolive soap. I take my towel from the bottom of my bed and head to the ablutions.

The sharp smell of decaying menstrual blood from the overflowing bins and stale urine greets me. Covering the lower part of my face with my nightie, I step in. Stagnant water, frothed with slime and skin residue wraps around my ankles as I make my way through. I am surprised there isn't an infestation of mosquitoes on the water but conclude mosquitoes too have their limits. A shiver ricochets through me as if to taper the joy in my foolish heart. Happiness is not for the likes of me. I hush that thought away into its cage of negativity. I'm letting nothing or no one dampen my mood. Florescent lighting above flickers as if to warn me to stay back but my bladder throbs egging me forward to the toilets.

I walk to the toilet cubicles. Held back by the putrid smell, I peer into the toilet bowls half filled with faeces as if identifying a corpse. Cleaning duties haven't begun as it's still early. Why can't the cleaning be done at night? I'm relieved to be exempt from cleaning duties, a virtue of being a prefect. I gag, and head for the showering space. I look around and it's empty. Give it an hour and the whole place will be heaving. I like the stillness of early mornings. It's the only time when I can enjoy space and silence. I can hear myself think and revise without interruption.

Listening, I hear no one coming. I pull down my pants and hang them with my towel. I turn on the shower and hold the pail underneath the spray. The sharp noise of water hitting the bottom of my steel pail, rings into my ears. The spray of the shower masks the spray of my urine gushing down my clenched thighs. I watch the stream of urine merging with soapy water. It's all liquid anyway. The comforting warmth reminds me of the ice-cold water in my pail, tensing my skin with dread. My body will never get used to it. Some days, I wrap up warm and walk to the back of the school canteen. If I time it well, the cooks gives me the remnant hot water after boiling eggs. Smelling of boiled eggs is a small price to pay for a hot bath. I haven't asked the cook for hot water since meeting Kīmathi for fear of repelling him. I once tried using a rudimentary heating device made by a boy in my class wanting to impress me.

'It mustn't touch the metal pail,' he said.

I was amazed. My life transformed. Then one night, after an all-night revision session, I dozed off whilst heating my water in the pail and the tin cut-out touched the side, throwing me to the floor, causing an electrical outage. That was the last time I accepted gifts from suitors. This morning my resolve almost caved in making me nearly beg the cook for hot water, but the thought of smelling of eggs at the disco made me reconsider.

I place my pail down, throw in my washcloth and rub my bar of Palmolive onto it. Goose pimples erupt from my skin in protest. I lift my hands from the pail and bring my face close. The bitterness of the soap draws tears from my eyes. My clenched eyelids fight the stinging. With my back arched like a cat, I reach into the hollow of my armpits and scrub with vigour careful not to let the cold water touch anywhere else. Bowing out my legs, I scrub in between feeling the sting of the soap. I splash with two handfuls of water from my pail to extinguish the stinging. I am cold but, intoxicated with love, my heart sings with glee. Since meeting Kĩmathi, a kind goddess has breathed life into me, condemning me to eternal joy. The thought of spending tonight with him warms me like a log fire.

I wrap my threadbare towel round my body, which is like a lizard with a wet front and dry back. The wet flip-flops slap my heels as I walk down the corridor to my dorm. The square dorm is divided into quarters by lockers. Each space has four bunk beds, pushed against walls or lockers leaving communal space in the middle. I look around, some students are snoring in their beds, one above the other, like cocoons of butterfly larvae. I tiptoe to my locker and feel around for my Vaseline which I apply all over my body. I pull a P.E. t-shirt and skort out which I wear with my uniform on top. I haven't got time to run to the dorm after lunch to change and would rather utilise the time for revision. Putting my blazer on, I head out to class.

After lunch, we wait at the assembly ground in our P.E. kits, gripping our weather-beaten hockey sticks. Not even the intense sun can quell our enthusiasm as we are discharged to walk to Kĩrigiti fields for hockey. We walk in groups dragging our hockey sticks behind us down the long dusty road to the main gates. Far behind, I see Kīmathi's tall frame walking to the field with a group and my limbs melt in the heat. I walk close to Shi Shi. I am ecstatic at the thought of tonight's dance.

'What are you wearing tonight?' I ask.

'A red off-the-shoulder dress,' she says. 'You?'

'White beige-ish dress with blue polka dots and a big cream bow,' I say.

We congregate by the running track waiting for the P.E. teacher who is making her way to the pitch. Kīrigiti field is deserted other than Form 4 students and a few goats mowing the fresh long grass nourished by the long rains. I shrink back as the P.E. teacher picks out the first team. Shi Shi joins me standing behind Nalisua's broad shoulders. She raises her hand in the air her sixth finger sticking out of her clenched fist like a knife. She has six fingers on each hand and six toes on each foot. She is mimicking stabbing Nalisua and we throw our heads back and laugh. She knows I have hated hockey since Nalisua whacked my face with the hockey stick then claimed it was an accident, but I think Nalisua's just mean. Shi Shi is called forward, but I am crouching lower, obscured by tall girls in front of me.

The whistle goes prompting those not chosen to stand back. The noisy scramble begins. I step away from the pitch, walk to the elevated spectator verge and sit down, placing my hockey stick by my side. The boys' team is playing at the far end but I can't see Kīmathi. There are clusters of clovers. I remember Shi Shi saying the four leaves ones bring luck and I begin hunting for one for tonight's prom. My fingers sweep the three leaf ones out of the way and I lower my head scrutinising. I find one and begin by plucking out a tiny leaf.

'He loves me, he loves me not, he loves me, he loves me not.'

I am engrossed and don't notice how close I am to two elderly men grazing their goats basking in the sun.

'It was only yesterday when the *mzungu* run around this pitch. And now our children are running around wearing *mzungu* clothes playing their game,' says pancake face.

'And we thought they were wasting time running around,' says his friend, whose long scaly legs resemble an aged donkey.

'Kĩrigiti means cricket. Our Gĩkũyũ tongue is too heavy to say cricket,' says pancake cut-out throwing his head back in laughter.

'All that running around came in handy when they decided to flee to their Queen Elizabeth,' says donkey legs.

'Mũkami, you are not in the market. We need a replacement.'

The P.E. teacher interrupts me as I pluck more tiny leaves from four-leaf clovers. I must finish on he loves me otherwise it's bad luck. I pluck the *he loves me not* leaf and the teacher yells with impatience bringing me to my feet. I grab my hockey stick and run to the pitch. I should have just finished plucking. Damn. I hover behind the rounded bottoms covered in skorts scrambling for the ball like a herd of buffaloes. Shi Shi turns round sees me and moves back wiping the sweat off her face.

'I didn't think you'd get to play, you're saving your energy for dancing later,' she says.

We laugh and lean on our hockey sticks. The final whistle goes, and we walk towards the school mimicking the old men moving their goats away.

Chapter Six

The sinking sun raises the tempo amongst fourth formers. Gleeful shrieks are ubiquitous. The corridor to the ablutions is busy with activity as I dash to freshen up. I have no time to queue for the toilets so head to the showers. I stand back waiting for a free shower. Whole pail-loads of cold water are tipped onto bodies lathered and gleaming like hippos in the moonlight. The cold is met with giggles and screeches. Shower loofahs scrub skins with vigour. Nalisua's buttock cheeks clap as she scampers from the end shower. I step into her place. After a slap dash, I dry the cold away with my coarse towel and rush to my locker.

Figures are crisscrossing the space between their beds and the lockers, whose doors are ajar. Someone is asking for help with doing a zip, another is looking for a mirror.

'Can someone lend me mascara?'

A voice says from behind the lockers.

'My bra is still wet, tough luck. Hopefully, it'll dry with my body heat,' says another.

I stuff my soap dish in my locker and pull out my tub of Vaseline. Sitting on my bed, I smear the pomade on my limbs, massaging with care, listening to the hum of excitement. Never did I imagine that I would be attending the fourth form school disco instead of revising. Not only that, but I will also be attending in the arms of the boy I love. I am stepping into a dream. Beautiful things like this happen to others and not me. I am one of the undesirables. The spare wheel in friendship groups. The one that never makes the core of friendship but is always on the peripheral. I'm not rich enough to pay for my school fees upfront, so must suffer the humiliation of being called out in assembly for defaulting on school fees. I am not lucky enough to have a father since mine died and we fled our home in the night from the militia sent by my father's employer. But like Cinderella, I shall go to the ball.

Hanging in my locker is the soft chiffon dress. I've pushed everything out of the way to give the dress space, as if it were a queen. I reach out and stroke the luxurious chiffon, letting its coolness rest on my arm. It sends a thrill through my body like a shooting star.

'Please take care of it, it belongs to my cousin,' Bũi said. 'My aunt must never know I let you borrow it.'

'I promise,' I said giggling with delight.

I spent hours admiring its poker dots masking the faded white background. It's the best dress I have ever seen. I raise the dress and let its smoothness caress my oiled body like a sword in a sheath. I adjust it at the waist and do the zip. There's a band of satin round the neck with frills above it. I fold both ends of the fabric taking my time. Peering into the mirror shard inside my locker, I tie the delicate bow beneath my chin. I throw my mother's pumps from Gĩkomba market onto the floor and slide my feet in. My look is complete.

The excitement in the dorm is reaching fever pitch, girls complementing one another's look. I feel Tabitha's eyes giving me a cold sneer. I ignore her. She looks like she is attending a funeral. She's wearing an awkward frumpy dress which looks like it's been chewed by a cow. Her eyes are emphasised by a kohl pencil which is too thick making her look harsh. The beauty spot drawn on the side of her cheek looks like a pregnant tick.

With the gait of the great Gĩkũyũ matriarch Wangũ Wa Makeri, I walk out of the dorm, my shoes warning the world to stand back. I walk towards the assembly ground. Shi Shi sleeps in another dorm and I am too excited to go find her. In any case I'll have no time to speak to friends as I intend on making the most of the night with my love.

The full moon and the brightest stars are out having a disco of their own. It's illuminating a skyline of distant hills as if to set the mood. A group chats animatedly as they walk towards the hall, leaving a trail of Impulse Body Mist. I hasten to join them reluctant to walk to the dining room alone.

The hall is empty. The lights are dim. Kitchen staff are standing by the serving table, the smell of stale cabbage is masked by roasting potatoes. Dining tables are pushed against the walls leaving an island for the dance floor now flooded by rainbow coloured disco lights. It looks like the room has had an infestation of fireflies which are dazzling in tune with the music. A glitter ball suspended in the ceiling is spinning like a young moon.

I wonder if Kĩmathi is here. My palms moisten in anticipation. My chest is drawing small amounts of air as if there's a ration. I scour the room. No sign of him. Nalisua and Zippy walk into the hall and approach me. Nalisua stares at my dress, her bulging eyes and dromedary eyelashes flatter as if controlled by a puppeteer. She sneers.

'Is that your dress?'

Before I respond, someone taps my shoulder. I spin round expecting Kĩmathi. It's Shi Shi, her eyelids hooded with orange eye shadow. She's wearing an off the shoulder red dress which is clashing with her lipstick and eye shadow.

'You look fabulous,' she says.

I look and feel elegant. I've never had this feeling before. This must be a dream and I never want to wake up.

'You too,' I say.

'The hall looks amazing,' she says.

'The disco lights are something else.'

'I am famished. Shall we grab some food?' she says.

My rumbling tummy answers on my behalf. I'm famished too and full of butterflies. I've barely eaten all day from excitement. We join the food queue. The mood is jovial and romantic. Everyone brought their best manners. This is a big contrast between tonight's etiquette and normal code of eating. People tend to chat with their mouths full and always in a hurry. But tonight, boys are standing tall like gentlemen, exercising chivalry. Girls are giggling and eating small mouthfuls like bashful mice.

There's clashing and banging as the cooks replenish roast potatoes and French beans to keep pace with the students. The hall is filling, and everyone is animated. It's my turn to be served. I stretch my plate out. Roast potatoes and roast chicken. Cook looks proud. He has outdone himself.

Food in hand, we walk to a table. We sit, backs arched, and begin nibbling on our potatoes. I look across the hall and my heart stops. Kĩmathi strides in, his long legs clad in black leather trousers contrasted by white high-top trainers, a sleeveless white t-shirt and curly hair. He looks like a model from the *Ebony* magazine he gave me. By his side is Wambũgũ dressed in a replica outfit. They both look like they are auditioning for a boy band.

'Madonna, the most beautiful girl in the universe,' he

says, exaggerating the twang of his American accent as he approaches me.

His presence blurs everything. With his gaze transfixed on me, I glow. He's smiling. I'm smiling.

'You are so beautiful.'

I have no words. I bask in his flattery.

He steps back and gazes at me from head to toe. It feels joyous.

'I would never let any of my pals lay their filthy hands on you,' he says.

Yet again we are speaking at cross purposes. I don't understand what he means so I giggle.

'Pals, I like how you speak. You don't say friends,' I say.

He smiles, his eyes devouring me.

'Have you eaten?' I ask him, pointing to the food counter.

'I already ate, I popped into town,' he says.

How can he not eat this sumptuous food? Every student looks forward to the fourth form school disco just so they can taste the food. It's the only opportunity we'll get to eat roast potatoes. The dining room has never smelled so good, even the rats must be scrubbing up for the afters.

Shi Shi joins us in the arm of a boy from 4b. He smiles and I smile and nod. She seems infatuated and keeps gazing at him. Kĩmathi leads me away to the dance area. He's whispering in my ear, but the music and his accent makes it difficult to hear, so I simply nod and smile.

The hall is full. It's hard to recognise anyone with their attire. Music is blaring out of the speakers fastened against the pillars. To the right, there's a Rastafari man standing in front of the decks whose voice is beaming out of the speakers. He's dancing to Bob Marley's 'Buffalo Soldier' with exaggerated arm movements. He's encouraging the students crowded on the edge of the dance floor join in. The song comes to an end and it's clear no one is interested in reggae. Madonna blares out of the speakers with 'La Isla Bonita' and everyone squeals in excitement heading to the dance floor.

Kīmathi steps forward and extends his hand to me.

'This is our song Madonna, shall we dance?'

I walk to him hypnotised by his smile. My chiffon dress wraps around my knees as if to stop them from giving way. His fingers connecting to mine ignites my emotions as he leads me to the dance floor. He's turning sideways admiring me. His muscular arm wraps round my back pressing me against him. His heart thuds against mine. His zesty perfume teases my nostrils. I feel his breath on my face, and I inhale to capture his essence. I can taste him, and it is turning my legs into rubber. I'm glad to be leaning against him otherwise I couldn't support my body. I want time to stand still and encapsulate this moment. He is smiling and his muscles are twitching with the rhythm and happiness. He clicks his fingers and sways his hips. I thrust my pelvis forward and gyrate. We are dancing solo lost in the beat. We are in sync.

Next Michael Jackson's 'Thriller' gets everyone scream-ing. I am aware of others filling the floor. We form lines, our bodies wiggling with exaggerated ghoulishness. Someone taps on Kimathi's shoulder, and we turn to see Wambūgū smiling holding the hand of a girl whose name escapes me. We smile and wave and are soon absorbed by the music. The world belongs to us.

As the song ends Kīmathi spins then crouches before rising again. He leans close, his lips brushing mine. He takes my hand, spins me round and I'm straight into his arms. I'm intoxicated by his scent. I look at his lips now mouthing *You don't have to be rich to be my girl*. He draws me closer, pressing himself on me.

He nibbles my ear, with a little help from Prince. I try to contain myself for fear of losing control. There's a bulge of hardness pressing against my belly. He's whispering sweet nothings into my ear and my knees nearly give way. Heaven's doors are open. I'm in. We are swaying on the dance floor. Our limbs entwined; lips glued together.

Lights dim. It's our cue. We stagger behind the dining hall pillar, hungry and impatient for one another. We kiss. He holds onto my face, drinking me like a thirsty traveller in midday sun. Unwilling to break the seal of our lips, we stagger to the darkest corner of the room. He lays me on the bench. His lips plant little parcels of love onto my neck. He undoes the bow on my dress, parting the chiffon fabric and begins caressing the sides of my neck. At the centre of my chest, he glides. Bliss. My skin is rippling with joy. His fingers crawl up my thighs sending miniature bolts of lightning into my soul. He hooks his finger onto my panties and begins to slide them down. I feel the slimy wetness as his penis brushes against my thigh. My chest is heaving. He's pushing, trying to enter me. I spring upright.

'No!'

I'm so loud I fear everyone in the dance hall heard me. My heart is pounding almost in a panic.

'What's the matter?' he asks.

He's breathless.

'I'm a Christian,' I say.

It's the only thing that comes to mind. I have never been so close to a boy and this is uncharted territory. *No one should touch your special place whilst you are still in school, not until you're ready for marriage.* Mama's warning rings in my head.

'What's that got to do with us?'

He is impatient and there's a coarseness in his voice. It's as if he is a different person to the one I danced with a moment ago.

'C'mon Madonna,' he says.

He pushes himself close to my private parts. He's serious and scary. I put my hands on his chest and push him back.

'Please stop I can't do it,' I say.

'You've been teasing me all night,' he says.

I'm confused. Everything I said and did was honest and genuine. I did not tease him.

'C'mon Madonna, what's wrong?'

'It's my mother. She said not to,' I say.

'Your mother isn't here,' he says.

He is pushing me to lay back down. I resist.

'Baby I thought you love me?'

My heart is bursting with love for him. I want him to know how much. I want him to carry on kissing me.

'I love you so much,' I say.

'Then prove it,' he says.

There's a tenseness that's crept in and I want to return to the happiness of a moment ago. The air has been polluted, spoiling our special moment. I never anticipated this being the only way to show him my love. I don't know what to do. Mama never told me how to demonstrate love to a boy.

'You are the only boy I have ever loved,' I say.

'Then show me,' he says.

He leans forward and drags his bottom lip on my cheek, calming my concern. His lips go over to the back of my ear and my body flops, overcome by the loveliness. I want to be in his arms for eternity. I throw my hands around him tight. He drives his fingers down my chest to my thigh and lifts my dress up. His trousers are down. His bare skin rubs on my skin. His blunt hardness pushes onto me. He reaches for the sides of my panties again and this time pulls them down. I let go of his neck and pull them back up. He grunts. He peels his body from mine. My hands flail in the air searching for him. I open my eyes to see the silhouette of his body bend down and pull his trousers up. The interlocking teeth of his trouser zip grind my ears.

'What are you doing?' I whisper.

'Not playing games.'

He stands up and begins to walk away.

'Wait...'

He doesn't hear me, and fades into the sea of dancers who are now chorusing 'Tainted Love'.

My heart deflates. I pull my dress down and feel around for my shoes. Sliding my feet in, I go back to the dance floor squinting to see if he's there. In the dim lighting it's difficult to make out who is who. All couples, intertwined, and there's no sign of a lone person. Uncertain what to do, I walk outside hoping to catch sight of him. He is nowhere.

I return to the hall and slump on a bench hoping he'll come back. Tears well up blurring my vision. I keep expecting him to appear, offer his hand and, with his warmth, evaporate my tears. The doors open and the cold breeze makes goose pimples erupt on my skin, pricking the thin chiffon of my dress. Floodlights illuminate my face drenched in disappointment. Teachers swarm in ordering everyone out of the hall. The fourth form school disco is over.

I stand shivering in the shadows of the administration courtyard convinced he'll come back to me. I yearn his tenderness. Why did I deny his wishes? I never meant to hurt him. If only I knew how to express my love for him. All lights in the education quarters go off, and I head to my dorm, my heart constricted in anguish.

Chapter Seven

The shrill of a distant bell wakes me with a start. I sit upright. Not even the melody of the birds outside the window can thaw the frost that seems to have settled all around me. I am stunned by the silence in the dorm. It's empty. I overslept. Today of all days, the day of my exams. I don't have a watch and have no clue what the time is. I have missed my exams.

Leaping out of bed, I grab my skirt, tripping, whilst sliding it up to my waist. I fling my arms into the sleeves of my white shirt. There's no time to do the buttons. I put on my jumper and blazer. Heels on the back edge of my shoes, I half walk, half run across the assembly ground to the exam hall. I burst the door open causing alarm amongst students already sat behind the desks arranged in rows. In front of them are pencils, erasers, and papers. There's nervous energy emanating from the room. All desks are taken except one. All eyes turn on me.

'Stop. What do you think this is? Your mother's house?'

A large woman sits at the front facing the students, her buttocks overflowing the petite chair. Her greasy forehead hosts a formation of pimples ripe with yellow pus. This must be the invigilator. She wears spectacles which look like moths in flight. There are moths in my stomach. If it wasn't empty, I'd vomit.

'No Miss,' I say.

'Why are you late? She asks.

'I was sick, I am sick.'

She stares at my puffy eyes. The effects of poor sleep and crying are imprinted on them. It's exactly a week since the school disco and Kīmathi has not uttered a word to me.

I've tried my late night torchlight revision under my blankets which now ends in disaster. Last night, whilst preparing for today's afternoon literature exam, I argued whether Michael Henchard could ever be a reformed character after the spectacle of selling his wife Susan in a drunken madness to become the mayor of Casterbridge. She must have been humiliated. Rejected by the man she loved. I felt her anguish merge into mine. I broke into tears and cried myself to sleep still clutching the crumpled soggy mess that is Kīmathi's photograph.

There is no doubt the invigilator will throw me out. I hold my breath and wait. She stares at my prefect's badge pinned to the lapel of my jacket, wriggling her nose as if I was a pile of dog faeces.

'Today is your lucky day because you have one minute to spare. Anymore and you would have been disqualified.'

I walk to the empty desk, sit and await further instructions. At the invigilator's command, I begin. I scribble on the paper, but as if in silent protest the ink refuses to appear. I shake the biro and rub the tip hoping to warm the ink to flow. It obliges but it's messy. My desire to excel seems to have been covered with a heavy curtain that I cannot lift. I want to run back to my dorm and bury myself under my blankets. I have no one to blame but myself for upsetting Kīmathi. I am angry for listening to my mother's advice, *No one should touch your special place whilst you are still in school until you're ready for marriage.* But she didn't tell me what I should do instead.

'Ten minutes gone, thirty minutes left.'

Oh God, I haven't even started. My arm is numb or reluctant. I don't know which. I must start. This is what I have being preparing for, these past few months. I memorised the scramble for Africa, the two world wars, and woes of Katherine the Great. Now I must choose which question to answer. I have scoured for every minute detail of The Great Boer Trek and that will be my main answer. I summon my inner strength squeezing the knowledge stored in the crevices of my brain. My heart refuses to join in but I persist. Oh no, I should have answered the question on the two world wars. I cross out the page and begin again.

'Ten minutes left.'

No! I should have continued with The Great Boer Trek. I know everything about it. I cross out the two world wars and begin with The Great Boer Trek. I am writing as fast as I can.

'Stop. Put your pens down,' says the invigilator.

My heart sinks. I have written a quarter of a page instead of the four pages. The bell goes. The room erupts. I want to kick my desk. The invigilator stops at my desk. She breathes like a dragon about to strike as she stares at the mess on the exam paper.

'Those who sowed the seeds of revision always walk out with broad smiles. Those who wasted their time are clouded with worry,' the invigilator says gathering the papers.

What does she know about revision? I have read all my textbooks from cover to cover. When everyone is sleeping, I am under my blankets revising until my head hurts. Maybe if she'd done her revision, she'd be a top lawyer in Nairobi and not busting her pimples in a classroom waiting to judge us.

The courtyard between the exam hall and dining hall is awash with animated students basking and debating their answers. I want to bang my head against the wall. I should have been one of the exhilarated students because of the ease of the papers. I messed up. Tears well from the pit of my stomach but they don't reach my eyes. I have run out of tears and I am exhausted. There's a cloud of darkness hanging in my heart. A whole week without Kĩmathi is like being condemned to hell. There's an invisible wall in front of me preventing me from seeing joy. My chest contracts. The path to my future once cemented with confidence now seems like a derelict cul-de-sac. Not even my dreams of becoming a geologist can drag me out of this pit of gloominess. I am like a pebble freewheeling into a well.

Musty aromas of fried jaw-cracking maize and weevil infused beans waft into my nostrils reminding me lunch is being served. My stomach constricts. I have no appetite, but I must force myself to eat. *Gĩtheri* is the lunchtime extravaganza whilst supper is a treat of *ugali* and anaemic cabbage. For breakfast, it's a slice of white bread laced with the cook's discontent. Occasionally, breakfast is complemented with an egg. For people with medical problems, the offering is maize and beans without cooking fat, making it just boiled maize and beans.

The queue edges forward. I stare through the counter opening at the kitchen assistant sharpening the knife. He feels for the tip and runs it through the sharpener. A ladle extends out spilling its contents into my plate. I look up to see the cook. Not only does he always give me a bigger portion but also gives me a pail of hot bathing water. I grimace. I am in no mood for conversations. He gives me a look, but I don't want to speak about my broken heart. I am about to walk away.

'Madonna, can I join you for lunch?'

His just-broken voice commands my attention. That

sophisticated American accent is unmistakable. I freeze. My ears must be deceiving me. I turn round. It's Kĩmathi. Standing behind him is Wambũgũ. Blood rushes to my cheeks. Things have been awkward since the fourth form disco to say the least. Kĩmathi pretends I don't exist and walks past me without a glance. But he's here now. He does love me after all. Maybe he's realised how much I mean to him. My shoulders peel back dropping the heaviness I have carried for the past week.

'No, I mean yes, sure,' I say.

My raspy throat makes my voice sound like more of a croak. My plate is tilting, spilling the watery gravy. He points to a table allowing me to go first. It reminds me of how impressed I was with his chivalry. I walk to the empty table and sit down. He sits opposite me and Wambũgũ sits next to him.

'How did the exam go?'

I almost choke on the hard maize at the mess I made of the exam.

'Forget that. See the effects this school is having on me? Students in this school are too boring, they are always talking about books.'

He hasn't mentioned the disco and I don't want to upset him by bringing it up. I should lighten up.

'What do you want to be when you grow up?' I ask.

I am not sure what to talk about. I wish we could go back to the ease of our conversations before the disco. We chatted and laughed about everything and nothing. My tongue is heavy, and my cheeks are burning with discomfort. My brain has been replaced with gloop and it's impossible to find a comprehensible question.

'C'mon Madonna, I just want to have fun and you should do the same. Stop taking life so seriously, we've finished our mocks let's celebrate.'

How can I lighten up when I spent my week feeling like a dead body weighed down by rocks in the bottom of a dirty lake? That my days for the last week have merged into one soggy mess. That when I sit in class and stare at the teacher, words that once caused me wonder, bounce straight back to the teacher. How can I tell him how my heart yearns for his tender touch?

'How shall we celebrate?' I say, sounding like the croak of a giant bull frog after it's swallowed a rat.

I think of how he held me when we danced. That moment I never wanted to end. Perhaps we can recapture that feeling again. There's a glimmer of light and the end of the tunnel. There's a lightness in my heart like the frost is thawing.

'Leave it to the master Madonna, I will show you how. Meet me behind the labs after the last exam.'

Chapter Eight

'Madonna, I knew you would come.'

Kīmathi hugs me pressing his lips on mine. My limbs go limp. Taking my hand, he leads me to the fence. He grabs the metal between the sharp spires of the barbed wire and lifts. He looks at me and nods.

'Go on Madonna, crawl underneath. Be quick before anyone spots us.'

My confusion is surpassed by my need to please him. The incident at the disco is something I never want to repeat. It's been seven days and six hours since the school disco. The day when my world caved in. I was cast out to an emotional wilderness without a map. I never again want to feel such anguish that has left my heart bruised and raw. When not in class, I sat under the covers of my bed wishing someone could sooth the aching. And now Kīmathi is reaching out to me quietening the anguish in my soul. I am not about to push him away when he's here because he's discovered he can't live without me. I mustn't get in the way of our happiness. He wants to make it up to me and I should just let him. I am not about to compromise it.

He nods again. I detect an impatience in his mannerisms. I get on my knees. He senses my anxiety and smiles melting logic out of me.

'Go on Madonna, you want to celebrate the end of the mocks?' he says.

'I do,' I say.

I lower my back underneath the barbed wire and crawl to the other side.

'Hold the barbed wire for me,' he says.

With all my strength, I pull up the wire careful to avoid the spikes in between.

He lowers his body and arches his back as he moves between the spikes. With his body on my side, he draws his other leg in and stands up. I hear footsteps. I'm about to dive behind the coffee bushes but he laughs.

'Wambũgũ is joining us,' he says, leading me away from the fence into the covers of the coffee plantation.

'Where are we going?' I ask.

My voice is a whisper. My heart is racing for all sorts of reasons. I am scared because we've just crossed the line. This feels wrong. The fence is there for a reason. To stop students from leaving the school compound but also to keep intruders out. I want to be on the other side of the fence. Even better I want to be in class. I'm thrilled to be with him again, but there's something about him that's making me on edge. I can't put a finger on it. I want to be in the place where we were before the disco. We'd sit on the slope cushioned by the soft grass looking into the valley across, imbued with love. But now we seem to be in a different space. It's like the haze lifted and we see different things. There's a discomfort deep in me I can't shift. The heavy blanket that weighed my heart down is still there, although a little lighter, and it's stopping me from feeling the ecstatic happiness of a few weeks ago.

'Shhhh don't ruin the surprise, Madonna.' He plants a kiss on my lips.

I let myself absorb the loveliness of his kiss. I am back in the school disco bathing in his aura. He possesses a power to render me helpless. My body aches for more. I close my eyes for too long and when I open them again, he's staring at me. I am embarrassed and straighten up. A rustling in the bushes interrupts the awkwardness. We wait. A tractor roars past. Wambũgũ appears, beaming with a broad smile.

'Are you ready Madonna?' Kĩmathi asks, smiling at me too. 'Come it'll be fun.'

He takes my hand and begins to run. I run with him. Coffee leaves soaked with pesticides slap my face as we tear down the rows of coffee plants. Wambũgũ runs alongside me, his maroon shorts flapping around his long legs. I am getting breathless and want to stop but Kĩmathi tugs my hand to keep moving. There's the noise of the tractor that's spraying the coffee and it's a few rows down. We are silent not wanting to draw attention. We reach a clearing. There's a breeze, easing the nauseous fumes of the insecticide.

Chapter Nine

An old haggard face emerges from a cloud of smoke like an extra-terrestrial being. I step back in fright. My skin crawls as our eyes lock. Hers have a grey silverish sheen and it's not clear if she can see me. They are distant and saturated with pain. At our sight, her wrinkles stretch with scorn. She looks at us. Then she scrutinises me. Her lower eyelids droop low like an old dog. She blinks in slow motion, one eyelid slower at opening than the other. She's frightening and I am ready to run. Her lips are scorched black like an elderly goth, and the inside of her lower lip is crimson from alcohol overconsumption. She lifts her pointed finger, its calcified nail twisted. I think she'll poke my eye and I step back. Instead, she lifts her finger to her face, scratches, and I watch it glide to her skull which is covered with matted dreadlocks. Her hair is dirty, and I am almost certain I can see head lice jumping around.

She steps outside her door which sits on a rickety frame. I look away from her gaze to the walls of her house which are plastered with mud, most of which has fallen off. There are gaping holes from which thick smoke emerges. Old plastic bags are stuffed in between the holes which do little to stop the smoke stinging my eyes. She steps further out of her house, retracts her body, then pounces forward lobbing a big spit which splatters on the dust missing my feet by a few inches. I stare at the splatter now soaking into the earth.

A gasp escapes my mouth. I recognise her. Mama will kill me if she finds out I was at her house. People in Kĩrigiti know her story well. The only people never to have heard of her are the newborns and the dead. She was a Mau Mau freedom fighter. One of few women to survive in the dense bamboo forests of Nyandũrũa. The British dropped tonnes of bombs hoping to wipe out the Gĩkũyũ resistance. The harder their assault, the more determined the fighters became. She, like others, took the war to the forests as Britain littered villages with soldiers to quell the uprising.

She is reputed to have taken seven oaths according to an ancient Gĩkũyũ ritual. For each of the oaths, she swore to slay a British man who had stolen the birth lands of the Gĩkũyũ. At night she sneaked from native reserve to native reserve administering oaths to people, binding them to the cause. Once an oath was given, a Gĩkũyũ cannot turn their back on the ancient custom risking the wrath of our ancestors. An oath made anyone a freedom fighter. She was arrested and taken to Kamĩtĩ prison. Whilst in prison, the British interrogators tortured her night and day believing she knew the whereabouts of the most wanted freedom fighter Dedan Kĩmathi. Not even slamming her breasts between two rocks would break her.

Now I stare at her in horrified awe, my chest heaving up and down. It's as if someone sucked the oxygen from the air. Sweat trickles down the side of my hairline. I look away. I don't want to lock eyes with her again. Instinct tells me to run. Kĩmathi senses this and tightens his hand around mine.

'Have you come for me?' She asks.

She frightens me but I just stare. She turns her head and her bitter eyes stare into mine.

'For nine months, I carried a baby. If you don't believe it look.'

She stretches her lose belly and wobbles it.

'The white man raped me. Many white men raped me. Followed by gatis. They raped their mother.'

This is horrific. This is the first time I've seen her close. I cover my face. I'm haunted by the pain in her eyes. Even in her madness, she speaks of her trauma. People of Kīrigiti know her story well. She once invaded our hockey match running around stark naked with a stick pretending to shoot, as if in battle, taking aim at her imaginary targets.

'*Mbeberu chini*—coloniser down!' She signalled as if she was commanding an army.

Other times I've seen her walk around, cradling a maize corn to her long-withered breasts, shushing it as if it were a baby.

Rumour has it that when she was heavily pregnant, she carried guns and food to the freedom fighters in the forest. She avoided detection by the occupying army due to her condition. One night she was arrested and taken back to the barracks where she was raped by coloniser soldiers and home guards so many times that she gave birth. Whispers are that they kicked her baby like a football until there was nothing but splodges of his remains scattered around. For many years, she wore nothing beneath her belly button in protest. Her nakedness, it was said, was to bring shame and misfortune to the soldiers who raped her, because that was the curse of an old woman.

She sticks her hand out to Kīmathi. He hands her an empty squash bottle, but she doesn't take it. I'm puzzled by their exchange. I force myself to look at her face. It is masked with broken dreams, her eyes faded like an old fabric in the sun. Whispers are that she was full of bitterness from watching traitors selling out the tribe to colonisers for large farms and big cars. That's when she went mad. When asked of the whereabouts of her child, she points to the big mansion on top of the hill saying her child was independence.

'I gave them that,' she thumps on her chest.

The woman looks at me. The anger in her eyes is frightening. Kĩmathi edges closer, he too seems frightened. Her mannerisms appear unstable and dangerous. He extends his hand and places a twenty-shilling note into her filthy palm. Her long witch-like nails stick out, layers of grime visible. With her other hand, she snatches the empty squash bottle Kĩmathi brought with him.

She steps further out of her hut into the light to look at the note then nods. She walks backwards, disappearing into the darkness of her hut, her jigger-ridden toes curled upwards. I'm on edge.

'Are you not worried about the curse?' I ask, not looking at Kĩmathi.

'What? What curse?' he laughs. 'Curses are not real Madonna, don't worry your pretty head with such nonsense.'

'My grandmother told me she curses everyone she encounters.'

Kĩmathi smiles. There are bashing sounds coming from inside the hut. The woman emerges handing Kĩmathi the bottle. Alcohol fumes hit my nose. A clear substance is overflowing from the top. My eyes gape with shock. My surprise end of mock celebration is to purchase *chang'aa*. A criminal offence, and the seller is the very woman mothers invoke to frighten their children.

Chapter Ten

⌒

Having left the *chang'aa* seller's hut, we walk to the edge of the coffee bushes which are still dripping with cloudy droplets of pesticide. Dark clouds weigh down the overbearing late afternoon heat. The distant roar of the tractor spraying the coffee drowns out the unease I feel from the encounter with the *chang'aa* seller. The disturbing way her lower lip hung, and her slow closing eye are vivid in my mind. I want to walk far away from her and the intoxicating fumes of the chemicals in the air. Kīmathi halts. Wambūgū and I stop. Did he hear something? I stand still listening out. The tractor fades making way for the thudding in my chest.

We three stand, our feet sprinkled with soil, like warriors after a war dance. I am irritated and disappointed that Kīmathi thought this an apt end-of-mocks celebration. Why couldn't we celebrate by eating bhajias at the edge of the assembly ground? Why did we have to sneak out of school to buy *chang'aa*? From our position, I can see the rooftops of the science labs. I think about the students in those labs working on their final exams and here I am in the coffee bushes after visiting a criminal. I shudder. From the thick vegetation sheltering us I make out the shapes of the windows. I pray no teacher can identify us from that far away. I think about the duties I'm neglecting as a prefect. I have had enough and want to head back to school before anyone sees us. I start to move but Kĩmathi steps in my way.

'Why such a surly expression Madonna?'

Kĩmathi wanted *chang'aa* and we have it. I can't understand the hold up. Hanging around thickets outside the school's perimeter fence isn't my idea of fun. Sensing my hesitation, Kĩmathi reaches into the thigh pocket of his combat trousers, pulls out a handkerchief and leaning forward dries sweat from my forehead, like a mother to a baby. His copper eyes gaze into mine. I try to suppress the anger I feel. His face stretches into a smile revealing a set of even teeth. He spins me round before encircling me, pressing my back against his lean chest. His muscular arms hug me close, and he pulls out the bottle of *chang'aa* from the bag in his pockets, using the handkerchief in his right hand to unscrew the bottle top. I can feel his seductive breath over my neck, easing my annoyance. He pours the substance into the bottle lid as if it were a measure of medicine. Wambũgũ watches us like a spectator in a peep show, his school shorts riding up his giraffe legs. Kĩmathi brings the lid to my lips. My nostrils spasm from the fumes.

'Madonna, you go first.'

'I don't drink alcohol.' I squirm.

Kĩmathi leans forward and distends his lips onto my neck.

'Try a little, don't be such a coward.'

He takes a little sip then brings the liquid back to my lips. The alcohol burns. I cough at the smell. I try to step away, but I am imprisoned by his arms.

'Pinch your nose and take a big swig.'

I part my lips.

'Open.'

I tilt my head back and open my mouth. He tips the contents

in. It feels like someone is holding a blowtorch to my throat. My body spasms. My gut is alight. I splutter. I need air in my insides. He pours more into the white bottle top, discoloured with age. He puts it to my lips. I don't want the foul liquid on my tongue. I gulp. A brisk wind shakes the coffee leaves in disapproval. A mother bird squawks from the row of trees lining the plantation. Kīmathi steps round to face me, tipping more *chang'aa* into the lid.

'Good girl. Take this and knock it straight down.'

I take the bottle cup, tip the contents into the back of my throat. It's like someone has thrown fuel to the flame in the back of my mouth. Kīmathi takes a swig from the bottle, passes it to Wambūgū then to me. He encourages me to take another swig with a broad smile. He hands Wambūgū the bottle. He takes both my hands into his and starts dancing. My head feels loose, and I start to sway.

'See I told you. It's amazing.'

Kīmathi reaches over to Wambūgū and gestures for the drink. He brings the bottle to me, and I gulp. A wave rushes to my head making me dizzy. He offers me some more and I shake my head still gasping from the previous mouthful.

We are distracted by a loud noise coming from the direction of the *chang'aa* seller's hut. We turn round to see the *chang'aa* seller running towards us, stark naked, slapping the rolls of her overhanging belly.

'It was them. They stole my baby before I cut the cord. They raped me and then stole my baby. Someone stop them.'

Kīmathi puts the bottle to my mouth pouring more alcohol in, spilling some on the sides of my mouth. I gag and swallow. He drinks some and Wambūgū empties the rest into his mouth before discarding the bottle in the bush.

'Come Madonna, let's hit the road.'

Grabbing my arm, we run, with the *chang'aa* woman in pursuit. The earth around me spins like a bottle on its side. We change course tearing through the coffee plantation. I'm struggling to remain on my feet. Kĩmathi holds onto me whilst Wambũgũ supports me on the other side. We stagger back to the barbed wire fence.

'Get all the way down Madonna, go under the wire.' Kĩmathi forces me down.

My knees dig into the soil as I try to crawl under the wire, tearing my shirt in the process. I slither forward believing I am a snake. I don't make progress.

'You've got to move Madonna, you can't just lie there.'

I spit out the soil in my mouth and try to crawl on my belly. Nothing happens. I raise my torso and begin to move. A sharp sting in my back stops me moving.

'Careful, she is caught on the barbed wire.' I can't think who said that.

'You can go now Madonna,' that must be Kĩmathi.

Once on the other side of the fence, I try to get to my feet but crumple like a felled tree. Kĩmathi and Wambũgũ help me to get up. My head feels like a boomerang spinning in flight. It is getting dark, and the school lights come on.

'Quick the junior dorm is empty. Let's take her there.' Kĩmathi says under his breath.

I struggle to keep my eyes open. Their arms are under my armpits, and I feel myself being dragged, my feet are making scratching noises as we move. I'm aware that we are at the science labs. I think we should go to the labs. I need to inspect the cleaning by science students. I try to tell them to get me to the labs but my words slur. I try raising my head to see through the windows, but my eyelids flop to a close.

My armpits hurt from the pressure. I drag my heels to stand

but my muscles are in disharmony with my brain. There's crunching sound and I think we are walking on gravel. We must be on the assembly ground. I force my eyes open and see the slope. We must be avoiding the glare of evening floodlights. My legs slog against soft padding. We must be on grass. I'm aware of laboured breathing on either side of me. Kīmathi and Wambūgū seem to be struggling with my weight. We emerge opposite the Form 1 dorm. We are on the tarmac and walk towards the dorm. A door is being shaken.

'Damn. It is locked. Put her down and come,' Kīmathi says.

Wambūgū hesitates before slumping me on the floor. Kīmathi shakes the door again but there's no give.

'Stand against the wall.'

That sounds like Kīmathi giving instructions. If he is talking to me, I can't make my legs stand. I'm paralysed yet feel like I'm falling. I'm spiralling through a worm hole. I hear movements and catch a glimpse of Kīmathi hopping onto Wambūgū's shoulders. They look like an acrobatic troupe. If only I could prop my eye lids open. With every fibre in my body, I force my eyes to stay open. Everything is blurry. Kīmathi is stretched up pulling panes from the louvre windows. He's handing them down to Wambūgū who throws them on to the grass. It's not clear what game they are playing or why.

Kīmathi heaves himself on the window ledge, one leg in through the window and he disappears. I hear noises coming from the other side of the door before it swings open.

'What are you doing?' asks Wambūgū in a low voice.

'We are bringing her in.'

Who are they talking about? There's no one else. They are speaking in low tones. I am struggling to hear everything they are saying. It's like I'm searching for a bandwidth and different frequencies keep hitting the airwaves.

My body slumps backwards and I catch sight of the sky. It's spinning. I'm retching. There's no air getting through to my nose. A force turns me sideways and someone is hitting hard on my back.

'She's choking.'

That could be Wambŭgŭ's voice, but it sounds distant. My face is doused with a cold liquid. I open my eyes and see outlines looking down at me, wiping my face. I'm being dragged and the pressure in my armpits is pinching. I try to stand but my feet give way. I end up sprawled like a ragdoll on the floor. They drag me to the dormitory. It's pitch black. The darkness in my head is whirling. My eyes are shut tight. I'm going to be sick. They let go of me. I fall. I'm being dragged again. Then I'm lying on a cushioned surface. I open my eyes. They acclimatise to the darkness. The floodlights outside illuminate the surroundings. I see silhouettes of two figures moving around, then closing the door behind them. There's the sound of a door bolting. It seems like I am alone in this hollowness. I want to get up and go to my dorm, but my limbs don't work.

My brain is half asleep and half dazed. The image of the *chang'aa* seller is in my mind. I see her towering over me, slapping on the rolls of her flesh, accusing me of taking her baby. She's yelling something. It's inaudible. Slowly the words become clear. *Next it will be you.* It's the curse. I feel panic rising. She pulled her flab to expose herself, guaranteeing that I see her nakedness, to catch the curse. I close my eyes even tighter, so I don't see her. But she is in my mind. I can't get rid of her. She begins to walk away with her maize comb on her breast and I drift into sleep.

Nausea and the bile bubbling at the back of my throat rouse me from my alcoholic coma. My skin feels cold. I try to reach for a blanket. There is a crushing heaviness on top of me that

53

I cannot shift. I try turning to my side, but my legs are pinned down by the weight on top of me. I'm suffocating. Drowning. There's a tugging on my pants and I can feel them sliding down my legs. I try to reach, to pull them up, but I am weighted down. There's something between my legs pushing them apart. There is thrusting inside of me. I am rocking and it's making me queasy. I retch.

Suddenly the weight is taken off my chest allowing me to gasp for air. My body is shivering. The window is open, an icy breeze blowing in. It's making me cold. I feel exposed. Maybe I should go close it. I can't move my legs. It's as if they are pinned, akimbo. I try to get up, but I am pinned back now by another weight on top of me. There's warm breath on my face, rank with the stench of *chang'aa*, making me heave again. The weight on top of me is crushing my chest and there's a burning sensation between my legs. I am being rocked again. My mind is playing tricks on me. I see a warthog on top of me, smiling. I freak out. I try to scream but there is something on my face. My hands knot into fists as I begin to fight the beast. My attempt is futile. Someone is controlling my arms, pinning them above my head. My strength is waning. My consciousness exhausted. I can't comprehend what's happening. I just want to fall asleep.

When I come to, the heaviness is gone. My eyelids don't feel like lead anymore and I open my eyes. It's total darkness and the room is still spinning. Low murmurs from the corner reach my ear. I call to them for help, but no words leave my mouth. I struggle to make out what they are saying.

'We can't just leave her here,' sounds like Wambũgũ.

Who is he talking about? Where am I? What happened to me? I don't grasp what is happening around me. I cough, trying to clear my throat. I vomit again before slumping back onto the spongy cushioning. Then the weight is back on top of me again.

'Come on, leave her alone,' says a faint voice.

I drift to sleep again.

My eyes flicker at a bright light burning my face. I squint to see beams of warm sunlight. It's comforting. I turn my head round to see where I am. I do not recognise anything. I sit up putting my hand in a wet substance on the floor. Wiping it off on the mattress, I get up. My legs are stronger. I look around. It looks familiar. I'm in a dorm but there is nothing or no one. I look down and to my astonishment, I'm half naked. What's happened to my skirt and my panties? There's a stickiness on my thighs, and a burning sensation deep inside of me.

I look down and see my skirt is rolled up to my waist. I roll it down. My underwear is discarded away from the mattress. How did it end up there? How did I end up here? I have no recollection. I bend down to reach it but my head throbs as the room spins. My body screams to lie down. Onto my knees, I force myself to crawl and fetch my underwear and struggle to put them back on. My skirt feels loose. The zip is broken, the waist strap of my skirt agape. I pull my shirt down to cover the skirt. My shirt is ripped in two places and covered in blood and soil. My back hurts. My knees hurt. The space between my legs hurt. I am a big ball of pain. I need to get out of here and go to my dorm. I need to go home. Confused, I look for an exit. I see the big wooden door.

Chapter Eleven

With the mocks long forgotten, Form 4 students are a boisterous lot. Sounds of laughter, chattering and banging desks
fill the classroom. A worn copy of James Hardley Chase's *No
Orchids for Miss Blandish* sits on my aged desk which is graffit-
ied with the insignia of past students. I sit in the front middle
row, close to the teacher's vacant desk. It's mid-morning and
the mood is one of laissez faire. The teacher is late. I turn the
pages of my novel. I can't concentrate. My eyes are jumbling
the content before it reaches my brain, and it makes no sense.
Not even the death of yet another female riles me out of this
stupor.

It's been seven days since the mocks' celebration incident.
An invisible line has been drawn, separating me from my
past and current selves. My current self needs to remain in a
shell and not leave my sepia world. All colour is gone from my
reality. I am numb. Unable to process the events of that day, my
brain has locked the memory away and I've been carrying on
as if nothing happened but, deep down, I know *everything* has
changed. In my free time, I lie on my bed reading incessantly,
preferring to be lost in the world of make believe, instead of
in my own stark new reality. I can't bring myself to think past
yesterday, any further feels like peering into a pit of darkness

and with it there's a growing sense of impending doom, that I can't put my finger on.

These days, I avoid classroom chatter preferring to keep my eyes glued to my book. My gloom is alienating. I am unable to turn backwards in case I catch sight of Kĩmathi or Wambũgũ. That feels like a forbidden space. I keep my face towards the blackboard and if I could, I would wear blinkers to prevent any side vision.

Kĩmathi leaves class at the heel of the teacher, and he is the last to walk in when class begins. He's never in the lunch hall. He is never anywhere during break times. Wambũgũ avoids me and turns back whenever he sees me. He walks around with a scowl for company.

The classroom door swings open and the wall of noise halts. The headteacher Wamakũbũ bounces in, in a cloud of rage. His body is stiff. His thin frame and his gait is that of a cat in a fight. He turns the lights on even though the class is well-lit from the tall louvre windows. The headteacher never comes to the classroom. His presence induces fear and anxiety. The History teacher is behind him as the lesson is about to begin. The door squeaks and the History teacher scurries into the corner.

Wamakũbũ's narrowed eyes swoop the room. His gaze rests on me. His chin is lifted in the air, nostrils open wide like a dragon about to breathe fire. Our eyes lock. Mine enlarge with fear.

'You,' he says.

My knees freeze.

'Get out.'

I can't move. His steel hand lands on my neck bringing me to my feet. I gulp. My windpipe closes and I can't breathe. I am dragged and flung out of the door. I land on my jelly legs and lean against the wall. My bladder is going to give way. He's yelling. What could I have done to warrant such anger? I can't hear my thoughts through the chatter of my teeth. I want to disappear into thin air.

The door opens with such force I fear it's been torn off its hinges. Kīmathi is flung out and lands in the corridor next to me. I do not look at him. From the corner of my eye, I see his knees trembling. He senses I'm looking and places his hand on the wall to steady himself. He is wheezing. He takes his inhaler from his pocket and makes gasping noises as if he can't get enough air. For a split second, I want to scoop him in my arms to stabilise his breathing.

An iron fist grabs me by the back of my neck and the other fist grabs Kīmathi. Wamakūbū's shoes clunk down the corridor and onto the pavement, dragging us along like a hunter with lifeless prey. I smell the rubber being scraped off the tip of my shoes. A sea of eyes peer from other classroom windows surrounding the courtyard. He takes us up the steps of the administration block. The secretary who has been watching us through the window runs to the door and flings it open. We are thrown in like sacks of potatoes. He takes a deep breath as if relieved to have offloaded us. The effort of dragging us all that way is manifested in tributaries of sweat running down his face. He straightens his limbs and walks in front of us down the hall, towards his private office.

'Follow me,' he says.

I jump at the ferociousness of his tone. We follow. The secretary runs ahead and opens the door.

He halts in the middle of his office, the bald patch of the back of his head glistening with sweat. He is seething.

With a slow purposeful rotation of his head our eyes lock. I know that look. It's the look of disappointed anger reserved for troublemakers. Why am I here? I am a good girl. A prefect. I am entrusted with responsibilities. The one overseeing student compliance to the school code of conduct. His judgemental look sears my conscience. I can't stand it so I look at the blemished leather of my shoes.

'Is there anything you want to tell me?' Wamakūbū asks.

My mind is blank, and I suspect Kīmathi's is too. My blood thuds in my ears. His eyes are boring into me like a soldering iron. There's a stillness in the room fuelled by his anger and our anxiety. My mouth is dry and I am unable to utter a word.

'I will ask again. Is there anything you want to tell me?'

Wamakūbū's voice ripples through my eardrum like a bomb blast. My knees give way and I crumple to the floor. He takes a stride to his desk. I'm going to die of fear.

'Get up.'

He doesn't even turn round to look at me and I jump to my feet. He reaches for the telephone and dials.

Oh no! God no. Who could he be ringing?

'Send in the carpenter,' Wamakūbū says.

Geremani? Why would he call him in? It dawns on me. It must be about the sambusas. That's it. Someone must have seen me buying sambusas from his workshop. But why is Kīmathi here? Did he buy Geremani's sambusas too? Is this anything to do with his secret hustle of selling to students? Is Wamakūbū gathering rule breakers? Wamakūbū is building a case against me. He knows I am a frequent customer of the carpenter's shed. That must be it. Someone saw me buying his sambusas.

It seems like eternity before the door opens and Geremani walks in, his navy overalls covered in sawdust. Wamakūbū beckons him in, and he walks to a chair in the corner, starts to sit then gets back on his feet.

'Mr Mbugua, do you know these two?' asks Wamakūbū.

'Yes, I do.'

'When was the last time you saw them?'

'Last Thursday.'

Oh, think quickly. Did I buy sambusas last Thursday? I can't even remember what I did yesterday let alone last Thursday.

'Where exactly did you see them?'

'Once a week, I visit a relative on the edge of the farming cooperative.'

I haven't been to any cooperative farm. I have no idea what he is getting at.

'Aha!'

'I thought I recognised the uniform; thought they were visiting the homes on the edge of the farm.'

'Were they not?'

It wasn't me. I have no business visiting the cooperative farm. It's clearly a case of mistaken identity. The noose round my lungs loosens a little at the thought.

'No, they were at the home of the mad *chang'aa* seller.'

My stomach constricts at the mention of the *chang'aa* seller. I want the earth to open and swallow me now. I am going to be sick.

'Sir I wasn't there,' says Kīmathi.

My mind loops. I thought I heard Kīmathi deny it, but I think my mind is playing tricks.

'What?' barks Wamakūbū.

'My parents were entertaining the UK ambassador,' Kīmathi says.

What? Did he just deny being at the *chang'aa* sellers hut? It was he who took me there and now he's going to wriggle out of it. Ever since meeting this rat I've had nothing but trouble. Now he is going to throw me into the fire. Even this is too cheap for Kīmathi. All the pain and anger I have felt since meeting him starts bubbling from deep within me. My body stiffens and my fingers curl into a fist. Before I can stop myself, I find myself leaping into the air and landing on Kīmathi. I'm about to land a blow, but instead my fist smacks right into Wamakūbū's palm. Squeezing my hand, he shoves me in the corner. I come to my senses and see what I have done. I don't believe it.

'I will ask again. Did you or did you not visit the mad *chang'aa* seller?' says Wamakūbū.

An unrecognisable sound escapes from my throat. He turns to Geremani.

'Are you certain it was them?'

'One hundred percent.'

I plummet into a black hole. There's nothing I can do to dig myself out of this mess. I can't deny my crime. Geremani is here to seal our fate. I'm shocked by the callousness of his voice. I'm angered by his betrayal. Consumed by hatred of the man who I'd seen as a jovial grandfather, telling us gripping stories of his time in the British army. That mask has been replaced by one of ugliness. He feels me looking at him and turns to look at me. He sneers with pity as if he knows this is the beginning of the end.

Wamakūbū paces up and down. The suspense is killing me. He walks to his desk and grabs the receiver from its handset.

That's it. He's calling the police on us. They must be on their way. I can't be held in remand with criminals and prostitutes. Mama can't afford to pay my bail. My face scrunches up and tears begin to roll down my face. His fist slams on the table. I choke, pushing down the contents of my stomach, seeking to escape. I will be on the news for buying *chang'aa*.

He yells down the telephone. 'Agnes, did you order the consignment of wood?'

Oh God he's going to crucify me. My mind veers. That is ridiculous.

'Why on earth would you visit the mad *chang'aa* seller? In your uniforms? Bringing my school into disrepute? Buying illicit beverage is illegal. Everyone knows this. Not even a baby can claim ignorance,' Wamakŭbŭ screams.

The questions drench me with fear. The words tear down my curtain of denial. I am exposed. There's nowhere to hide. I am mute, trembling. How on earth did I end up here?

With a wave of his hand, Wamakŭbŭ dismisses Geremani who hurries to the door.

'Sign for that consignment on your way out.'

Geremani shuts the door behind him. His departure leaves an uneasy quietness in the room. The tick tock of the clock is loud. The anticipation is killing me. Wamakŭbŭ strides to the corner. Each stride instilling more fear. What's he doing in the corner? I don't want to look.

'Get over there,' says Wamakŭbŭ.

Which one of us is he addressing? Neither of us move. No one wants to go first. With the speed of a panther, he pounces from the corner with a long cane. My heart stops. Kĩmathi's wheezing is back. Wamakŭbŭ ignores it.

'You. Get over there and pull your trousers down.'

Kĩmathi whimpers. He drags himself to the leather armchair. He unbuttons his trousers with reluctant fingers. They drop to his ankles revealing blue Y-fronts.

'Bend over.'

Kĩmathi gasps and stretches himself over one arm holding onto the opposite arm of the chair, his face smeared with panic. For the first time, I don't see the cheeky American with a swagger, rather a dark skinned pathetic boy with long hook nose and an egg shaped head. I blink. *Whack!* goes the cane and I jump with a scream. Kĩmathi screeches, a mixture of shock and pain.

Wamakũbũ's fingers are welded on the cane. Arm raised high he strikes with lightning speed. Crack. Another one lands on Kĩmathi's bottom. He howls even louder. My body is about to combust with fear. My chest will erupt any minute now. I fear for my heart as it thumps louder watching my fate unravel. There's no escape. I'm trapped.

'Two,' Wamakũbũ is concentrating on his counting as if an error would be a detriment.

Breathe. I tell myself. I am hypoxic. Whack. Goes the next strike.

'Three.'

I am clenching my jaws so tight, it hurts.

'Four, five...'

Kĩmathi sounds like a trapped animal. His wail is a continuous throttle from the back of his throat. The sound of the cane stops. I'm engulfed by terror. Wamakũbũ walks to his desk and opens a drawer. He pulls out a handkerchief and wipes the sweat dripping from his temples. Kĩmathi is still sprawled over the armchair.

'Get up.'

Kĩmathi stands and starts walking away from Wamakũbũ. He is struggling to walk, pulling his trousers up and trying to find his inhaler in his pocket.

Wamakũbũ looks at me. 'Your turn.'

I can't move. My legs are anaesthetised. He cracks his cane. Adrenalin sends my body flying onto the arm of the chair, adopting the same position as Kĩmathi. The swish sound alerts me of the cane making its way to my bottom. My whole body tremors like a mini earthquake. It feels like hot lava is oozing from my bottom ricocheting down my legs. I'm absorbing the first one when another one lands. I wail. Another one lands. I'm growling. And another until I can taste blood in my mouth from biting my tongue. I'm limp with pain. Bloody saliva is leaching from my mouth.

'Ten.'

I can't move. I have never been in so much pain. Every bit of my body stings. Incomprehensible noises are coming out of my mouth. I want someone to cool my burning body.

'Get up.' He screams like a demented devil.

I try, but my muscles have no strength. He grabs my collar and tosses me out of the door. The secretary eyes me like faeces on the roadside. I steady myself and rise. I am weak. I stand against the wall willing my legs to move.

'Go get your belongings. The carpenter will show you to the gate. You have been expelled!'

Chapter Twelve

The stillness of the dorm compounds the finality of my predicament. There's not much to pack: school shirt, socks, jumper,
and then I see it. My spare skirt, which sits on the bottom of
my locker. I stop and take a deep breath. My hand shaking as
I lift the skirt. It's crisp, caked with soil. I have a flashback of
crawling under barbed wire. It's jumbled up with images of
the *chang'aa* seller running after us, slapping the flabs of her
belly before lifting her floppy muscles to reveal her nakedness.
There's no clarity but my heart is racing. The shock of that
late afternoon manifesting in small doses, like a trailer from a
horror film. The word *Curse* is floating around my mind. Even
in the vagueness of it all, I know the implications of seeing the
nakedness of an old woman. Her final words ring in my ears.
Next it will be you. This is it. This is the curse she spoke of. I saw
her nakedness, and this is my punishment. I want to run so far
away but I am immobile. How long does a curse last? Does this
mean there's more to come? There's a loud bang on the door to
the dorm. I nearly jump out of my skin.

'I don't want to come in there.'

It's Geremani. His nickname is Geremani because of his
stories about how he killed a German for the British army.

'I haven't got all day.'

My mind is dark like that night. I lift the skirt, stare at the jagged tear on the back, the broken zip, and the missing button. I smell the odour of *chang'aa* from the mouth of a faceless body on top of me, pounding me between my thighs, rocking me back and forth. I don't know how long I'm standing by my locker. I want to move but I'm immobilised. It's as if my legs have turned to lead.

The banging on the door is loud, persistent.

'Don't make me come and get you.'

The hostility in his voice brings me back to the moment. I throw the skirt in my tin suitcase and, as if to confine a monster, shut the lid. Looking into my locker again, I see the chiffon dress there among a few home clothes which I wear during the weekends. That night seems like a million years ago, and I would do anything to bring it back. Start it over. Change the outcome. I feel like a broken rocket hurtling through outer space. I gather more clothes, flinging them into my case. I stand up and look at the bed on the top bunk. I lower myself to my bed and peel off the sheets, blankets, and pillow and stuff them into my suitcase. I look round the dorm, the louvre windows bringing in light sparingly, the bunk beds whose owners I may never see again. I don't even get a chance to say goodbye. I will never eat *kamixy* with Shi Shi by my locker again. At that thought, the musty smell of lunch I will never eat wafts in. There's a distant bell whose commands I will never get a chance to obey. There's another bang on the door. I bend, lift my suitcase and head out.

From my dorm to the gate is a mile. The longest mile I will ever walk. I'm shuffling because my buttocks are flaming raw from Wamakūbū's cane. The pain is like sitting on hot charcoal. I'm hunched forward carrying my suitcase and bag of books on my road to oblivion. A journey without a map. There's a short fuse in my brain refusing to connect with any logic of what just happened. Geremani, his eyes fixated ahead and clouded in hostility, is escorting me since I am now persona non grata. There is a palpable barrier of silence between us. Geremani's face is now a stranger's and not one glowing with warmth and kindness. All that has been replaced with petulance and treachery. He has no stories about the war to tell.

I should have something to say to him right now about his treachery, but nothing comes to mind. Maybe some time in the future I will have some questions for him but for now my mind is vacant. All I know is that he threw fuel onto the fire that burned me. He didn't have to be the tell-tale. To think that there was a place in my heart that was fond of Geremani, listening in admiration to his tales about the war. Buying sambusas was more educational on the second World War than history class. But this is who he really is. A traitor.

For all the years I have been at the school, I have never been in trouble. I wear my uniform in the way it was meant to be worn. The right shade of maroon skirt with matching jumper, with grey socks pulled up to display the maroon strips. My white shirts always clean. No shortened ties or rolled up skirt, always just perfect. I am studious and get good grades, and all it took was the words of a carpenter to bring me down. All my efforts, doused in fuel and thrown to the flames. I Mũkami, an ordained name by ancient Gĩkũyũ writs. The diligent maiden who milks, always punctual and studious. Now fallen from grace and expelled after being caned by the headmaster. My clean record dirtied by my weakness. When I was nominated to be prefect no one objected, and now here I am, being escorted out of the compound like some criminal. I am a criminal. I participated in purchasing of *chang'aa*.

I have watched countless news footage of haggard old

women, forgotten by society, being loaded into police wagons, with their brew confiscated for evidence in court. Commentators showing them in dark lurid rooms, with only giant rats for audience. I've watched those who purchase it, that have fallen off the treadmill of modernity. The people needing to dull the pain of their existence, who can afford little else and whose existence is hell on earth. The dead inside, burning the dregs of fuel before their bodies collapse in the gutter. This is how far I have fallen. Not even a purgatory to give me a chance for redemption.

Geremani stops and turns round to look at me.

'I haven't got all day.' He turns and carries on walking.

I look at him full of contempt. Anger bubbles from inside me. If my shoulders weren't aching from carrying my suitcase and my buttocks burning from pain, I would have punched this old man. I thought old men were endowed with wisdom. I drag my feet as the merciless sun beats me down. My mouth is dry. There is nowhere to quench my thirst. I look and see the gate at a distance. Then I think of Mama. I can't go to her, no I can't. I couldn't bear to be the one that crushes the final ounce of her strength. I would rather die than she be disappointed in me. My heart constricts, the anguish overshadowing the burning on my backside. My internal pain must be the kind that leads the many to become addicted to *chang'aa*. This is how the *chang'aa* woman lures the weak into her spell, those whose addicted bodies beg for stronger concoctions to dull the pain. This must now be my destiny.

A hum from the distance makes me look up. From the gate, a cloud of dust alerts us of an approaching car. It's driving at some speed reminding me of the Safari Rally. I barely get out of the way of the army green Volvo, throwing dust and gravel into my eyes as it passes me. Its tyres skid as it disappears round the bend. I place my suitcase down blinded by the dirt in my eyes. As if I wasn't already suffering. I need to rinse my eyes, but I have no water, and even with all this torment, as I flutter my eyelids trying to get the grit out, I can't summon tears to wash away the pain in my eyes.

'I really don't have all day to wait for you. Hurry up.'

The man has no sympathy. I lift my suitcase and begin again. I regret stopping because the blood caked on my bottom is stuck on my underpants, and they separate as I begin to walk. I summon my strength and persist. There's a roar of a car and I turn in time to see the same Volvo that blinded me. It's slower and I peer inside. At the steering wheel, is a woman with an afro and sunglasses. On the passenger's side, I see Kīmathi. He has a stern expression on his face and doesn't turn to look at me. Her window is open and she's yelling at him. They drive past. From the side mirror, I see his eyes staring ahead. I make a loud guttural noise as tears flood down my face. It's a mixture of pain, anger, sorrow, and frustration. I place my suitcase down and drop my head into my palms. Geremani keeps walking. A fuse is lit. I speed up absorbing the pain in my buttocks.

'How does it feel?'

'What?'

'Being a traitor?'

He says nothing and carries on. I walk furiously overtaking him as we approach the gate. I stand in front of him. His sun-bleached face turns to look at me.

'How does it feel destroying the life of a young girl.'

His eyes are cold, and they gaze at me. It sends a chill down my spine. He looks dangerous. He turns and walks to the gate. He waves to the watchman and the gate swings open. He steps aside as I walk through the gate into oblivion. I turn to watch him close the gate to my future and just then a seed is planted in my brain.

Chapter Thirteen

As I step through the gate the tarmac shimmers from the heat. My legs are frozen with indecision. The sun searing on my head urges me to decide whether to turn right or left. Where does one turn when their world has been blasted to smithereens. The events of the last few weeks overwhelm me. I can't go home and look at mama in the eyes and tell her I was expelled. That like a fool, I let myself be misguided to run away from school to visit the mad *chang'aa* seller. That at this stage of my life I don't understand what is right or wrong. My mind is too stunned to comprehend my predicament. I want some kind soul to hold my hand and show me the way. I never thought my educational aspirations would come crashing down before sitting the exams I prepared so long for. I want to sit under the shade but can't decide what hurts more, my buttocks, my head, or my heart. The metal handle of my tin suitcase is biting into my palm, as if I wasn't in enough pain. Placing my suitcase by the side of my shoes, I stand and think. I am surrounded by a vacuum. The map of my future evaporating before my eyes.

It was only a few weeks ago, when I was stood on the peaks of Mt. Longonot, inhaling the dry savannah winds that swept up the ridged sides of the mountain. That was the day I decided my calling was geology. Hiking up to the top, on the heel of my geography teacher, I asked endless questions.

'Why isn't Longonot one of the holy mountains that Ngai resides in?'

'Four holy mountains are more than enough for the Creator and Divider of the universe,' he said struggling with his rucksack.

'Is it because it belongs to the Maasai God?'

'Engross yourself with the chorus of nature. It's good for your soul,' he said.

The four and half-hour hike flew by. The mountaintop did not disappoint. It was a price worth paying if only to catch the views. Looking down at the pinhead shapes of herds of antelopes and giraffes grazing, was nothing short of awe-inspiring. I wondered if that was Ngai's view of us, the Gĩkũyũ people, his chosen tribe, from his bed of snow on the peaks Mt Kĩrĩnyaga. Peering down at the crater floor I gasped.

'Look there are animals at the bottom. How did they get there?' I implored the disappearing back of my teacher.

I stare at my shoes as if seeing them for the first time. What I would do to go back to that day on the mountaintop. Back to when my future was bright and clear. Now my head buzzes like a bee with broken wings. Unable to fly.

I'm in a deep trance wallowing in self-pity and don't see the matatũ approaching. It stops by my feet and the turnboy hops out and grabs my suitcase, loading it onto the roof rack.

'Get in,' he says.

I walk to the door. It's going in the opposite direction, but I have no destination, I guess it doesn't matter where I go. I step at the ledge of the matatũ door, and the turnboy heaves me in. I could scream in agony but the matatũ is too full.

There's nowhere to sit so I remain standing. Not that it matters my buttocks are flaming raw.

'Mũkami.'

I recognise that well-oiled voice, but I can't think who it might be. I am in no state for pleasantries and so refuse to turn round.

'Mũkami, Mũkami.'

There's a tap on my shoulder and I can't ignore it. It's the turnboy who points to the back. I turn to see Auntie Eunice waving. Her comforting smile warms my heart a little but then I remember everything that's happened to me. Oh no. She'll want to know where I am going and where I am coming from. I think of running out of the *matatũ* but its doors are closed and it's already speeding down the ragged road. I must compose myself and if she asks why I am not at school probably tell her I have no money for school fees. My body does otherwise. I turn away from her and bow my head and weep. I know she is coming over because I hear the commotion as she shuffles from the back.

'Wangari's daughter, what could be the matter?' she asks lifting my face with her fingers.

I want to blurt everything out, but no words leave my mouth.

'The next stop is my stop,' she says.

We step out of the *matatũ* and the turnboy climbs to the roof rack and holding onto the reinforced steel, heaves out my tin suitcase. He leans forward and hands it to me, but Auntie Eunice reaches over and takes it. I worry that the small hands sticking out of her chubby arms might not be able to bear the weight. She holds the case in the air, steps back, then places it down on the ground. The *matatũ* speeds away leaving a cloud of dust behind.

Auntie Eunice stops and gives me a sympathetic look. It feels like oil to a rusty machine. She scoops me into her arms in a deep embrace. Energy has been sapped from me and I'm limp in her arms. She pulls back and studies my face. My lips are dry with cracks like clay soil in the drought. My eyes must be puffy, and my face bears the hallmarks of being caned by Wamakŭbŭ. She can see the invisible load on my shoulders. She points to a kiosk by the roadside. We walk towards it, she, carrying my suitcase.

'What do you want to drink,' she asks.

'Fanta,' I say realising how hungry I am.

Auntie Eunice is part of the consortium of women who form financial support groups for each other throughout the country. She's in Mama's group. Of all the *kĩama* women, she is my favourite. During *kĩama* meetings, held to correspond with my school holidays, she's always first to arrive. Her happy flawless face can transform anyone's mood. Her laughter and mannerisms are like fresh drinking water. On meeting days, she unclips the buckle of her boxy maroon handbag, dips her hand in and brings out a packet of Wrigley's Juicy Fruit gum. She opens my fingers, squeezes the stick of gum into my palm and folds them closed, as if I was incapable of doing so unassisted. Her infectious laughter punctuates hilarious stories of how she composed songs with the poison of a scorpion, to mock the soldiers who guarded the women's camps during the emergency. She once halted the *kĩama* meeting recounting how she faked madness as we threw our heads back in laughter. When they locked her up in Kamĩtĩ women's prison for mocking British soldiers, she was revered as the master entertainer. She was the reason the District Commissioner outlawed singing because the words were hurting the morale of the soldiers who imprisoned them.

I press my eyelids together and drops of tears seep out. She thrusts her hand into her handbag and fetches a customary stick of Wrigley's gum, which she places in my palm. I peel the wrapping, put the gum onto my tongue and chew, letting the sugar sweeten the bitterness in me. We down our sodas, returning the empty bottles to the crates by the side of the kiosk. She lifts my suitcase, and we walk on a narrow dusty road where goats are grazing. A he-goat greets us with a plaintiff bleat as I walk past.

We arrive at the front of her smart wooden house built on concrete foundation with glass windows. To the side, there is a small hut with smoke rising from the apex which I assume to be the outside kitchen. An elderly woman emerges adjusting a rithũ around her waist.

'Mother, I have asked you not to be cooking. That's my job,' says Auntie Eunice.

'There's still fuel in this old body of mine,' laughs the elderly woman.

'This is my mother and she insists on doing all the house work as if she was a young woman,' says Auntie Eunice.

'Hello Cũcũ,' I say stretching my arm to shake her hand.

She disappears into the mud-built house and emerges with a calabash of mũkimo and a teapot filled with warm water to wash our hands. Auntie Eunice invites me to sit on one of the stools outside but my bottom is in no position to accept. I wash my hands and remain standing, scooping large handfuls of food and stuffing it into my mouth. She's staring at me but doesn't ask questions. She knows I will tell her when I am ready.

The sun sets on what is the worst day of my life. We walk indoors to the neat living room with sofas laid out against two walls and a small TV nestled in the unit. She offers me a seat but I remain standing. My legs ache from standing but sitting is not an option. Both Auntie Eunice and her mum can see I am in pain.

'Tell me what happened,' she says.

She takes my hand into her hand and listens squeezing my hand with encouragement as I begin.

'Now I have been expelled from school and I will never be a geologist,' I finish.

She gives me another embrace. I am so exhausted. I close my eyes. I could fall asleep standing. She lets go of me and walks out towards the little outside mud house.

'Mother has heated some water for me but you should have a bath. I will help you,' she says walking in carrying a basin of hot water.

'Come this way young one,' says Auntie Eunice.

I follow through a door in the corridor. She places the basin on the floor of a small room with unfinished plastered walls. On the window ledge, there's a bottle of Dettol. She opens it, pours some in the lid and tips it into the water.

'This will help with the wounds.

I take my clothes off. With a flannel, she scoops the water and massages it into my aching muscles. All I can do is accept the searing pain, that comes combined with such sweet kindness. When she's finished, I dry myself slowly and follow her to a room where she points at a nightdress on the bed and asks me to put it on.

'Go to sleep for now, things always look better in the morning.'

Chapter Fourteen

⌒

When hell was created it was modelled on the Ministry of Works compound. It's the small and wet version, and the perfect breeding ground for every undesirable virus, vermin, and people. The Ministry of Works compound was designed to hold entire communities living on top of each other, confined by a concrete wall. Created when the British pounced in these lands, it was an enclave meant to hide the black workers. The place where the indulgent whites living in extensive farms forcefully taken from the Gĩkũyũ people, needed their servants at moment's notice, but didn't want to see their existence. These days it's where residents fester in their disdain for black colonisers, the newer beneficiaries of the independence. Where conmen and prostitutes attempt to outdo each other in competition for non-existent wallets. It's also the place where the unfortunate people like my Mama and I found ourselves when we fled our home when Baba died.

Mama has not spoken to me since Auntie Eunice brought me home a few days ago and recounted the events to her. She sat stone-faced absorbing it all. Occasional outbursts of *Ngai Mwathani,* let me know that Mama was still breathing, and the reason her eyes were shut was not because she had died of shock, but from disbelief and shame. She walks around dragging her feet like her world has ended. Her glowing dark face is faded with despondence. I want to reassure her and explain the situation but I lack words. I want to tell her she holds some of the blame for telling me not to allow anyone to touch my special place without giving me an alternative. If I had known what to do, Kīmathi would not have been upset and maybe none of this would have happened.

I am angry with myself for not having the courage to say no to the end of mocks celebrations. I shut the door to those memories before I delve any deeper. I don't understand how I ended up here. I did everything I was supposed to do but this last term is like a derailed train. It's like I went to sleep one night and now I'm in a never-ending nightmare. Mama has no questions being as mystified as I am. We both find equilibrium in silence. Unified in the disgust we share about me. Our irritation is compounded by the claustrophobia of our communal room in our corrugated iron shack which serves as the kitchen, living room, and my bedroom. Our gloom is only interrupted in the evenings by Kaminde's mundane combing our cowhide drum coffee table, our pain dulled by his infantile mediocrity.

My diligence, intellect and striving were the light at the end of the tunnel. The attributes in me that kept Mama going, in the hope that I'd one day rescue her from this hellhole of a life. That I'd take her away from Kaminde, her useless boyfriend, and from the struggle of selling second-hand clothes in Gīkomba market. My failure is her condemnation and she's unable to accept what's happened to me. I can see deep down; she's weighted down by the same helplessness I feel.

Every time I walk into this compound is like entering a cave of doom. My shoulders stoop and my heart's rhythm alters to accomodate to the chaos. I am like the animals that hibernate until the conditions are right to rouse. I survive being here during the school holidays by crossing out how many days are left until I return to school. At school I had space, grounds, grass, books, and intelligence. Now I spend my days staring at the smoke-blackened walls because I can't stomach the sight of the residents. I would distract myself with books but being expelled disqualified me from borrowing books. I fear this mind-numbing place will drain my brain and leave me drooling like the residents of the Ministry of Works. My mind is frozen. Unable to see past this.

I dream of becoming a geologist, escaping from this place and going to the Rift Valley where I would buy a small house and live with Mama. Like her family once did. By the shores of Lake Naivasha, Mama's family found solace after escaping labour camps under the British District officers. In those days women and girls were drafted into forced labour digging trenches and terraces to combat soil erosion. Mama, her parents, and siblings left Kĩambu for the Rift Valley where the British colonisers still had an ounce of decency to pay their works a fee for their labour. Pittance but still a fee. They ducked in the shadows by night to avoid arrest by unscrupulous home guards. They sought freedom and did not want to be branded like sheep and forced to wear ID cards by Central province colonisers. They could grow their food. On arrival they were welcome in a Gĩkũyũ home, because a Gĩkũyũ home was always open to anyone for a bed and food.

Mama became an apprentice under a dressmaker learning how to use a sewing machine and mending garments. In no time, she was hired by Douglas Rose farm as a tailor mending uniforms for workers. This is where she met Baba who worked as a gardener. Mama and Baba fell in love and built the home

I was born in. My heart belongs there, and I crave the days we breathed the highland air and not the musty sewage air of this place. I crave the solitude and not the chaos of Wa Njŭgŭ scolding her children. Never to hear Firifo, his wife Jane and their emaciated daughter Ruth, wailing all night in the name of prayer. If I never hear that ill-mannered imbecile Gĭtonga with his antics with the dying woman again it will be too soon. Never to see old man Gathuki with his blanket and above all never to catch sight of the always exposed oversized genitals of that Rwandan Ndekezie. I want to be far away from here. Just Mama and me.

Baba would be distraught to see us now. How his hard work, his vow to do everything so I could get an education and live like the Whites, has all turned to ashes. The countless nights of revision under the covers will never come to fruition. I am condemned to the life Baba dreaded most. The life of a peasant, trapped in a well of hopelessness.

Every day, Baba hung the plastic pump on his back. His right-hand pumping, his left hand directing the fine mist spray onto the green leaves. Rumours said he had a hand for nurturing roses, for his were the finest. Every day, he inhaled into his lungs mists of poisonous pesticides, confined by the polythene domes that shielded roses from the highland frost. Never complaining, even as he was slowly dying, he watched the fragrant roses packed and sent to rich people abroad.

'The foremen and the *mzungu* knew what was coming. They could have protected him,' Mama cries into her hands when she's alone. She doesn't like Kaminde to know she still cares for Baba.

The memories are etched in my mind. There was a growing movement against farm owners enforcing unsafe work conditions. One night, there was a knock on our door and a young white man with a clipboard and a ginger beard accompanied by two women turned up. Mama rushed around to make them tea, but he refused. He was a lawyer with a humanitarian organisation. He had heard about Baba and wanted to take a testament before it was too late. Baba could barely speak, his body ravaged by cancer. But he knew what was at stake and spoke to them for forty minutes. Thanking him, they were gone.

I think about his eyes that seemed to shrink with every passing day. His body slowly ebbing away before his soul gave in. I stared into his eyes trying to hold onto his soul. I refused to leave his bedside after the hospital discharged him saying there was nothing else they could do. I feared that if I let go his soul would have nothing to hold onto. The day I left for school was the day he died of lung cancer. The night after the burial the white man with the clipboard and ginger beard returned with the two women. The sat in our living room chatting to Mama as I lay in my bed trying to make out what they were saying. When I woke up in the morning, they were gone.

Two nights later there was a knock on the door and a little breathless boy said his mother wanted us quickly. We rushed out and ran after him, but he disappeared into the night. It was only when we looked back that we saw our house was ablaze. Letting out a guttural wail, Mama sunk to her knees, all the energy sapped out of her body.

⌒⌒

My schooling issues have plunged her back into sadness. Her face is overcast with a curtain of gloom. What can I do to make things better? I never wanted to see her this sad again. That night still haunts me. Watching our home and belongings go up in flames. Just like my life. Everything we worked for to move on, is all gone. Our neighbours sat in their homes in silent collusion waiting for our lives to evaporate. Mama hugged me till I thought she'd break my bones. Then we heard a voice,

'Run. They were asked to finish you.'

We turned round to see a hooded man welding a machete. Grabbing hold of my hand Mama and I tore down the slope into the night.

And that was when I gave my mother my promise. That I Mŭkami, will excel in my education and I will look after her in her old age. The thought of that promise makes me cringe with shame. I have humiliated myself and Mama. People in this compound will begin to gossip.

The corrugated iron walls give no acoustics. No one has privacy in this compound. All our affairs are on show. We are the living metaphor of the pit latrine. Excreting over each other's heads. Every little misdemeanour no matter how small or large comes under scrutiny. Secrets are like elephants hiding in long grass. Nothing goes under the radar. I know I must find a solution but, unable to engage, my brain has turned to porridge.

They say that when the sun sets in the west it's so that it can take a bath in the tributaries. Today's sun must have got a great rinsing because it's beating down hard on the corrugated iron roof. Stifling heat, bleating stray goats and Wa Njŭgŭ's yelling at her kids is driving me insane. I am staring into nothingness when I hear footsteps coming towards our door.

I walk to the door and I see Auntie Eunice. Her freshness is a welcome change to the monotony of this place. I welcome her in and run to the tap to fetch Mama where she's collecting water. At the news, she sends me to Firifo's shop to get her a soda on credit.

'Everyone falls, and Mūkami tripped,' she says when we are all seated.

Mama and I stare at her curious as to why she's visiting without notice and speaking in parables.

'I spoke to my sister Nduta, who spoke to the headmistress of a school in Gīthunguri,' she says.

We gasp at the mention of a school. I can't breathe.

'I went to see her this morning and she has agreed to give Mūkami another chance.'

I don't think I am hearing right. She's mentioned another school and chance in the same statement. Mama jumps up and throws her plump arms around Auntie Eunice. She is sobbing into her blouse. I don't want to get excited in case I'm in a dream.

'She can begin as soon as possible,' she says.

Mama stops crying and is overcast. We both know there's no money for school fees.

'I have forgone my turn for the *kīama* visit so you can take the money for Mūkami's school fees.

Chapter Fifteen

Mama wrenches the top drawer of our utensils cupboard. Her eyes light up at the sight of the crotchet drapes folded flat as if they were treasure. Her hips sway, the pleats of her yellow skirt rippling to the tune she's whistling. She pushes the drum out of the way and drapes the cloths with pink flowers on the back of the tan leather sofas. The ones with blue flowers are tucked underneath her arm as she looks around as if unsure where to place them. She walks to the high bar stool in the corner and lifts the transistor radio and places a drape. Tugging the corners flat, she places the radio back. She turns it on and it's the midday broadcast. She drapes the rest of the cloths on the borrowed stools scattered around our living kitchen space.

I stand on the sofa and suspend one corner of my clean bedsheet on the nail above the window by the sofa. I step onto my bedframe which creaks as I walk across it and jump down, still holding the other end of the sheet. I tie a string on the corner of the bedsheet and climb on to a stool to tie it to the window above the cupboard. That separates my bed from the guest area.

'Look to see is the ageni are on their way,' says Mama.

'Ĩĩ,' I say.

I walk outside letting my bare feet bask in the warmth of

the concrete steps. The aroma of the chapatis Mama made earlier linger in the air. It's been several days since my expulsion and since Auntie Eunice's visit, Mama's and my mood have lifted. I turn my gaze to the gate in time to see the tips of the headscarves as the *kīama* begin to arrive. One by one the women, harmonised by colourful *kitenge* dresses, walk in through the gate. I run to the gate and give Auntie Eunice a hug. Her infectious laughter and hilarious stories begin on embrace. I chuckle with pleasure in anticipation of the sweet ritual we share. She reaches for the buckle of her boxy maroon handbag and unclips it. Her hand disappears into it and out it comes again. Clenching her fist, she opens my palm with her other hand, like a magician about to perform a trick, and places the Wrigley's Juicy Fruit chewing gum into my palm. She then folds my fingers and squeezes my fist as if it was top secret.

Sighing with contentment, I peel the yellow outer wrap to reveal the silver foil encasing the chewing gum. The sweet smell hits my nose and I salivate. I stuff it in my mouth and begin to walk back holding Auntie Eunice's hand.

'Where do you work now Auntie Eunice?' I ask.

She turns her head slowly with a broad smile.

'Mūthaiga Golf Club, I am a receptionist, 'she says reaching into her bag and proudly giving me her business card. 'You must come and visit me some day. I'll buy you lunch or anything you need.'

I skip with excitement at the thought of dining with Auntie Eunice. It's the first time anyone has ever given me their business card. I rush to my bed and tuck the thick white card underneath my pillow.

Laughter begins before the *kīama* women walk into our house. Embracing each one, Mama leans over to one side, then shifts onto the other. Then she stands back and follows up with the squeeze of a tight handshake. Their buttocks barely touch their seats before Mama pours the fatty milk tea, only reserved for *kĩama* women. The grease glistening on their top lips like moustaches.

The afternoon flies by and when the sun tilts to the west, each one of the women thrusts their hand underneath the flabs of their breasts, withdrawing sweaty one-hundred-shilling notes which they offer to Mama. She accepts the money by wrapping her hand around each giver's hand. When everyone has made their offerings, she draws open the neck of her dress and spits into her chest. Clutching the notes, while others hold their breath, she raises her hands and looks to the sky. Everyone bows their heads, and Mama leads in prayer.

'Ngai wa matuini nĩ ndacokia ngatho!'

With that, they hug and they are gone.

The *kĩama* visit is a special day for Mama. It's the only day she sheds the worry, as if their presence alleviates the weight on her shoulders. After they are gone, we close the shutters and crowd the lantern, our eyes gawking at wad of notes as if it were treasure. Mama brings her thumb to her mouth, sweeps it across her protruded tongue, leaving a trail of saliva and with a flick, she counts the notes one by one. Her eyes enlarge and the skin of her face peels back with a contented smile.

'I don't know how we would survive without the *kĩama*.'

Slapping the notes, she parts her cleavage and burrows them under her breasts. That is her bank, free from the interfering hands of bank staff.

'No maintenance fee just to have a bank account. Banks are for the *mdosis* and not *maskini* like us. We go to the *kĩamas*; the poor woman's bank. Helping uproot each woman's financial worries in some ways,' she says with a glint in her eyes.

Chapter Sixteen

⌒⌒

The matron taps on my shoulder as I stand in the breakfast queue. The dining hall is scattered with a few early risers. It is filled with smoke and the smell of burnt oats. There are few of us at this hour. It's gone 5 am and the silhouettes of night are melting into colour. Distant birds greet the daybreak with cheerful melody.

'Don't go to class this morning. Meet me at the assembly ground at 7:30 am.'

She smiles, her toothless gums shiny with saliva. Her mouth is ugly without teeth. She is waiting for her dentures but seems unperturbed by her present appearance.

I walk to the stainless-steel counter and the cook is standing on the other side with a ladle filled with a grey stodgy mess. She dips the ladle into the huge *sufuria* and stirs breaking the skin on top. She scoops a large helping and pours into my tin plate. I thank her, and she nods her dark sweaty face as I make my way to a vacant table. I can't think why the matron would be in the dining hall at this hour when she has the option of staying in bed and making herself breakfast. Even more curious, why she would want to see me.

The matron introduced herself to me when I joined the

school. Auntie Eunice arranged for me to resume my studies in late November after my expulsion. I missed the final exams which was crushing but the headmistress allowed me to repeat the year. I was grateful for being given a second chance. I was home in December for the school holidays and returned at the start of term six weeks ago. The matron explained that I should visit her if I need medicine for menstruation. For some reason, I haven't needed any. She then explained the reason she was toothless was because she had her teeth pulled out so she could wear dentures.

I scoop a spoonful of the porridge and raise the spoon to my lips, but the smell makes me gag. I'm nauseous all the time. It must be the vile sludge they call food. I fear I will vomit in the dining hall, so push the bench I am sitting on back and run to the door. I catch sight of the matron who gives me a curious look.

Unable to eat breakfast, I walk back to my dorm which is still dark with many fourth formers still sleeping. I lie on my bed. My nipples are stinging and breasts are tender. I turn on my side and rest my eyes. I am woken by the chatter of everyone getting ready for class and remember my conversation with the matron. I check my watch and its 7:30 on the dot. I run to the assembly ground to find the matron and the headmistress who glowers at me. I met her several weeks ago when the kĩama women brought Mama and I to meet her. She seemed hostile then as she processed my admittance to the fourth form, but today, she's angry. I am confused. Maybe she is not a morning person. I shrug.

A few more girls of various sizes have joined us. I estimate we're about 10 in number. I am wondering what the gathering is about when the driver of the school bus outside the gate begins to rev the engine.

'Njoro is here. You can take them now,' the headmistress says facing the matron.

'Let's go,' says the matron, turning round to lead the way, her wide behind rocking from side to side.

I look at the other girls and none of us register what is going on but follow. I am the last to get into the bus. I stand at the entrance and look round. The matron is sitting on the other side of the driver. The girls have each claimed a seat. The matron's eyes and the bus driver's scowl both suggest I cannot stand there. I hesitate, walk halfway and slide onto a vacant worn leather seat and press against the window. The driver turns the ignition and starts chatting to the matron. They seem well acquainted. The bus reverses from the school entrance and turns into the dusty road. I look at the rusty tin houses outside the school compound and wonder if we are going on a school trip. I don't recognise any of the girls and there's no one I can ask so I continue staring out of the window.

Half an hour later and the bus veers off the main road and stops at the gate of the general hospital. The watchman salutes and releases the sisal rope forcing the barrier to pivot upwards making way for our school bus.

At the parking lot, the matron gathers her bag, stands up and beckons us. Confused, I stand up and follow her out of the bus. She doesn't say anything as we head to the casualty department of the hospital. I am not ill, and haven't told her I am ill, so why has she brought me to the casualty department? My heart begins to pound, and I wonder if something has happened to my mother. That must be it otherwise why would they bring me here? She hasn't been to visit me this term. I pray she hasn't been in a road accident.

A waft of iodine, steriliser and general hospital smells hit my nose as we enter the foyer. The floor is covered with patients overflowing from the waiting room. I scrutinise every face as we enter the waiting area expecting to see Mama's face. My eyes land on the bandaged head of a young man whose one eye is swollen closed. He stares with his other bloodshot eye. Next to him is a woman rocking back and forth holding in her arms a boy of about twelve years old, his bulging eyes half shut, his body wracked with fever. My ears ring with a variety of human sounds. The boy's groans and the sharp cry of a baby. A weak voice calling for a nurse for help. An impatient nurse yelling for him to keep it down. Mama is nowhere.

We stand behind the matron. I am aware of the other students standing close to me, but I don't engage with them. We are silent, unified by our discomfort and school attire.

The matron is talking to a nurse in crisp white uniform, with a matching cap at the apex of her head. She turns round and summons us. We walk behind the nurse and matron as they enter into a side room. She points to a bench, and we sit. The nurse sits behind a desk.

'You, come here,' she says pointing at me.

Her tone is hostile. I jump to my feet and walk to her. She asks me to extend my arm. From the tray on the table, she takes a strap and ties it around my arm above my elbow. She slaps on my arm before wiping with a cotton ball dabbed with spirit. She takes a syringe and pierces my skin, drawing my blood into a vial and I squirm.

'Go wait outside,' she says.

I am irritated and confused but do as she says. I fold my stinging arm and walk back to the waiting area. One by one the other girls join me, each pressing onto the cotton ball on their arms. Moments later, the side room door swings open and the nurse and matron step out and march to us.

'I sure do hope you enjoyed spreading your legs because

you are all pregnant,' says the nurse. Those words slither from the wide gap between her teeth to the full waiting room. She finishes with a sarcastic laughter.

I don't understand what the nurse is saying. I didn't spread my legs. Surely there's got to be a mistake. I raise my hand and say so. She laughs even louder.

'Come see this. It's the Virgin Mary with the divine conception.'

The room erupts into laughter. I thought this room is full of patients but from their laughter they can't be that ill. My skin burns with shame and I bow down and sink lower, wanting to disappear.

'Instead of being in class now, you're planning the births of your unwanted children,' another nurse says her face devoid of emotion.

Those words land in my ears like a ton of rocks. I try to process what she is saying but none of it make sense. I am not pregnant. I can't be pregnant. I thought I was bloated from the porridge and that was why I could no longer do up the button of my skirt. My mind throws out an image of me lying in the dark, and the silhouette of a figure gyrating on top of me. The smell of *chang'aa* fills my nose and I feel nauseous again. I get a sinking feeling that incident is related but I cannot figure out how.

The nurse hands the matron the envelopes containing the results that seal our fate. She leads us out of the waiting room, our heads bowed down like village thieves on parade. We go to the waiting bus. I am consumed by self-loathing. I think about the nurses sniggering as we left the clinic. We sit in our seats on the bus in silence contemplating our bleak futures, as the bus snakes its way back to school.

From the bus, we are led through the gates. We think we are going back to lessons and begin to scatter in different directions towards the classes.

'Follow me.'

The matron's voice is harsh and sarcastic. We regroup and walk in a file like inmates. We are silent, our heads drooping in shame. For the second time in my life, I feel the judgemental eyes of students peering at me from behind the glass of classrooms. The classroom already seems a world away from me. The one place I truly love has once more, become illusive. The surety that once lit my path into a bright future slipping away.

The headmistress's secretary is stood by the door, poised with scorn. She signals us to wait. They've been forewarned of our prognosis. One by one, the headmistress screams our names. My body is tense with the memory of Wamakūbū's beating. I want a sinkhole to swallow me now. I cannot comprehend anymore pain. I am deep in thought when I hear my name.

'Mūkami! Your Auntie Eunice begged me to give you a second chance. Those don't come often.'

My heart shrinks in anguish and shame. I open my mouth to say something but have no words.

'She told me your mother is a poor widow on the brink of a nervous breakdown.'

I want to cry but my eyes avail no tears. I let my mother, Auntie Eunice, and myself down. But can't think how. I am unable to explain it to myself, let alone others.

'You will never amount to anything. Ten years from now, you will be selling *chang'aa* with six children to feed.'

Those words leave me cold. Will I become like the bitter old *chang'aa* seller? Her curse is catching up with me. I am numb.

The headmistress continues with her tirade. I can't make head or tail of what she's saying. All I see is the movement of her angry mouth. I shut my eyes and force myself to pay attention.

'Take this note to your mother and tell her you couldn't keep your legs closed.'

The note slips out of my hand landing softly on her polished ebony desk.

'You are expelled.'

The headmistress shoves me out of her office and slams the door in my face.

Chapter Seventeen

⌒

I alight the *matatũ*, unable to comprehend what just happened. Pregnant. I can't be pregnant. Maybe with ideas from too much revision, but I can't be baby pregnant. It's got to be a mistake. My face burns with stunned humiliation. I'm ravaged by anger at the way that wicked nurse mocked me in front of those ridiculous patients. The way she threw her ogre head, *come see this. It's Mary with the divine conception.* I didn't spread my legs. What a vulgar person. I clench my fists and wish I was still close to her. I would knock those teeth off her saucer face.

My palms are throbbing from the clenching. I look down. The headmistress's note to my mother is crumpled in my sweaty palm, my tin suitcase is in my other hand. That headmistress didn't give me a chance to explain before slamming the door in my face. I knew she hated me from the first time she saw me. If it weren't for Auntie Eunice and her sister, I would never have got a place in the school. Pregnant. I have never done what Mama told me not to do. There must be a mistake.

'Where do I go from here?' I'm thinking aloud. I seem to do a lot of that these days.

Walking without purpose or destination, the headmistress's voice is in my head yelling, you are expelled. I need to wake up from this nightmare. There's no way I am breaking the news of my expulsion to Mama. What would I say? Three months ago when Wamakūbū expelled me, I had Auntie Eunice to cushion me. Now I am alone in this fog, unable to see anything, weighted down by the curse that's following me like dog shit on my shoe. It's out to get me and it doesn't matter how far I go; I am still within its grasp.

The mid-afternoon sun beats down on me and I need to sit down. I step away from the busy road and find a shaded grassy patch underneath the mango tree. I sit, weighing my predicament. I contemplate not going home at all but where will I sleep? I am wracking my chaotic brain when I spot a phone booth and it then it hits me. Kīmathi! He is the root of my problems, and he must be my solution. I know deep down he has a heart. He must do. He cared enough for me once. There's a pang of pain in my core at the thought of how he made me happy. I could reason with him. I'm sure he'll help me.

I open my tin suitcase and bury my hands under my crumpled clothes. I didn't get a chance to pack before the matron manhandled me out of the gate. I'm frantic, sweeping the bottom with my hands. There's nothing. I am convinced there was a shilling in my suitcase. Hot and sweaty, I chuck everything out, tossing it to the side. My heart skips at a silver coin flashing in the sunlight. I stuff everything back in and, leaving my suitcase by the tree, walk quickly to the phone booth.

The stench of stale urine hits me as I open the grubby door of the phone booth. I lift the receiver and place it back at the sound of the dialling tone. I am about to walk out when someone bangs on the door and yells that I should hurry up. I bring the receiver to my ear and my fingers, pre-programmed with his number, tap on the buttons. I hold my breath as the bleeping updates me on the status of the call. I am on edge with anticipation. Waiting. Listening. My eyes drift above the handset and land on the dirty walls of the telephone booth. It's inscribed with a biro pen *mamako ni matako*. I think it's addressed to me.

'Your mother is an arse too.' I whisper under my breath as the phone clicks and a woman's says hello. Her accent tells me it's the maid and not his mum. I ask for Kĭmathi. She hesitates then shouts his name. My intestines contort. I'm scared but before I can think any longer there's a rustling on the other end as he picks up.

'Yo,' he says.

The sound of his voice sends my emotions into chaos. It's the first time I am hearing his voice since that day at Wamakŭbŭ's office. I think of the way he used to put a big slice of bhajia in my mouth and nibble the other end until our lips touched. My body aches for the tenderness he showed me. I am perplexed by what happened to our love. It seemed so real and alive. It was magical and organic. In those days I laughed at his jokes and my heart was light, filled with cotton candy. Now my heart is packed with rocks and smothered with a blanket. There's no joy but gloom.

'Hi, it's me. I don't have much change please can you ring me back?' I say.

There is a pause.

'The phone's locked, what's the problem?'

How I crave to thaw his dry voice. Moistness seeps in between my palm and the black warm plastic of the handset making it slippery.

'I must talk to you, please ring me back. I don't have change.'

'Tell me what it's about.'

There's a beep and the phone goes dead.

My heart twists in anguish. The urgency of the situation ignites my desire to get him to understand the trouble I am in. I step outside and the man who was banging on the door prepares to step in.

'Please give me a shilling. My brother is very ill, and I am looking for a car to take him to hospital,' I say.

His furrowed face softens as he digs into his grubby trousers and hands me a shilling. I am back in the booth and dial.

One ring and the maid picks up again. This time her voice is cold. 'Kĩmathi *hayuko anatomba musichana mwingine.*'

What? Fucking another girl! The maid's undeniable malice is like a sword slicing through my heart. The receiver drops out of my limp hand. I drag myself out of the booth too numb to cry. I'm overcome by jealousy and confusion. *He's fucking another girl.* Why would the maid say that to me?

The man outside the booth puts his hand on my shoulder full of concern. I roll his hand off as I walk to the tree to collect my tin suitcase. Is there someone else? Did he just tell her to say it so I could stop calling him? Maybe she's her. The maid. Was that why she sounded so menacing? How could he do this to me?

I shudder at her coldness as the line buzzes me off the phone.

I sit by the mango tree as the world around me crumbles. My life is like a runaway train, and I can't find the brakes. It seems to be gaining momentum and there's nothing I can do to stop it. The thought of approaching Auntie Eunice again leaves me cold. My head aches. It feels like a gourd rattling with beads. I can't think. So many things flying around. Kĩmathi fucking another girl. My heart constricts. That wicked nurse. It's as if she was there. My mind reveals snippets of the events of that night like a macabre striptease. If only I could get a clear picture, but everything is hazy.

The Mango tree shadow grows longer as dusk draws closer. I cannot face Mama. The humiliation I feel now is nothing compared to the shame of facing Mama. Her poor heart cannot face it. She will drop dead. If I am going to end up an orphan, I might as well die now. I look up at the tree and think of the girls who hang themselves rather than face their families. I never thought that would be my destiny, but there's no way out. I have nowhere to go and no one to turn to. A goat tied to a nearby tree wanders close. I look at the rope. This might be a sign. Why would the goat with a rope round its neck come to me at this precise moment? I'm entertaining that thought when someone, a woman, grabs my suitcase and begins walking away with it.

'No. Oh no. You don't get to steal from me today.' I say out loud. I jump to my feet and run after the thief. 'Give it back to me now.'

'I always knew you were not as innocent as you pretend to be,' says the thief.

'What?' I ask.

Thieves these days try any trick to confuse victims and I am in too foul a mood to fall for this. I yank, but the iron hand grips my suitcase tight with one hand and a shopping bag with the other. She has a baby strapped on her back.

'Hurry up, unless you want to get murdered in the dark,' she says.

I look up and in the dying light I see the unmistakable bleached face of Wa Njũgũ, the gossip courier of the Ministry of Works compound. I am horrified. I didn't think my day could get worse. Her presence just complicated my predicament. She's sure to tell Mama she saw me but facing Mama is not an option. I grab my suitcase and begin wrestling it out of Wa Njũgũ's hands. She grips tighter.

'Your mother would want to know I helped you, and maybe she won't steal my place in the water queue.'

How dare she, Mama is a decent woman.

'Your mother is not as helpless as she seems. She can entice a man to sleep in her bed more than once and I can't.'

This is too much for me. I can't stand any of this woman's vulgarity. I must separate myself from her. I need to think. Quick. I'm about to make another attempt at snatching my suitcase when she hoists it high on her head. She takes bigger strides. Wa Njūgū's mannerism is guarded. I can't figure out if she's stealing from me or helping. She's picking up pace. The sun wastes no time in setting, it's hurried like the rest of us. Light is fading fast, and the mood feels different. Her demeanour tells me she's scared. I thought she was fearless. She keeps looking back. Shadowy figures are following us. It's the night robbers. They emerge at dusk, like shift workers. She walks faster. I follow quickening my step. The figures behind appear to be gaining on us. We break into a run. We reach the maize stocks and burst through the gates of Ministry of Works. She walks straight to Mama's house, knocks with urgency.

Mama steps outside accompanied by Kaminde. My world caves in.

Chapter Eighteen

'Which one of you shat the bed?'

Wa Njũgũ yells from her house which is positioned at the back of our house. She is loud and her voice sounds like metal grinding. She might as well be in the same room. God, I hate this hell hole. I burrow my head under my pillow wishing I could stay here for ever. I don't want to get out of bed and face the reality.

'I am your father now,' says the deep voice of a man from Wa Njũgũ's.

Those poor children. It seems like they have a new father every day. My body flashes with panic as I remember the nurse in the clinic, *I sure do hope you enjoyed spreading your legs because you are all pregnant.*'

There's a smacking sound and then crying. Stray dogs howl from a distance. Mating frogs create a backdrop to my misery. Chattering from the neighbouring houses, pipe through the stifling warm air. The sun is still radiating its overbearing heat, stored in the corrugated iron roof and tin walls long after it's gone.

'Supper is nearly ready,' says Mama.

I get up from my bed which is tucked behind the armchair, next to the kitchen cupboard and adjacent to the cooking space.

The stifling heat, aroma of the food cooking, and Kaminde's stale sweat, is making me queasy. I need to get away from here. I don't know how or where I'll go. I get out of bed and sit on the armchair.

The confined space of our kitchen and living room gives little wiggle room and its playing havoc with my clogged head. From across the cowhide drum coffee table, I can see Kaminde's golf ball knees protruding through the fabric of his polyester trousers acquired from Mama's kiosk. He pushes the drum with his knees as if trying to squeeze me out of the space. I push back and glare at his bald head which reflects light from the kerosene lamp. I clench my jaws and thrust the drum into his knees. His angled chin juts forward, resembling a turtle. Coarse spikes of a grey beard on his cheeks makes him look like a turkey. The cowhide drum coffee table keeps us apart. Placed at the centre of the drum, is the kerosene lamp at which we both glare. Our lungs are competing for air, as the hypnotic orange flame tiptoes on the wick, in order to diffuse the tension.

Kaminde makes a snoring noise deep in his nose, drawing in mucus, then makes chewing noises, as if he was a cow chewing the cud. I gag. This man is repulsive. He sucks the patience out of me. What evil spirit can be haunting me that I must share the space with Kaminde. He must know I'm irritated because he continues making that noise. I stare at him with venom eyes. If looks could kill, he'd be dead by now. As if reading my mind, he reaches into the top pocket of his sleeveless shirt, he pulls out his purposeless comb. Starting from the edge of the drum, he glides the comb across the stretched hide as if it were a pet. My eyes are spectacled with scorn at the erect hairs. He repeats the motion only stopping to look up at me, his jaundice eyes full of menace. He must feel my resentment. Then he resumes combing the drum hairs until they are all upright. My teeth grind. It's as if this is therapy. Since his head is bald the need to comb something must provide some sort of catharsis. The scratching of the drum hide continues. Again and again. It's grinding on Mama too. I see her twitch.

I feel his warm breath on my face from across the room. He's stretching and pushes the drum with his golf ball knees. I ground my heels and push back. My thighs shake from the effort it takes. I have enough problems without his pettiness consuming my energy. I wish I had my own space where I could escape from him. My situation is unbearable. But sharing the space with him is like chili in my eyes. His presence pollutes the air with stale sweat and irritation.

I am on edge, unable to think straight. I'm consumed by the secrets in my heart like maggots in a dead body. I must find a solution before Mama finds out. I need to get away from here. Every day I spend here in this compound gnaws a bit of my soul. Day times are bad, but the nights are worse.

I stare at the sharp blade of the knife Mama is holding. It's positioned at a forty-five-degree angle, her fleshy arm poised ready. She is standing by the cooking table; her curvaceous back is tilted so as not to obscure light from the lantern. She lowers the blade, slicing through yellowy cabbage separated into quarters. She throws the shreds into the oil and onions and steps away as the pan spits back. The aroma of the frying food overwhelms Kaminde's permanent stench of stale man-sweat. On the other burner, water boils. She tips the bag of maize flour into the water which bubbles as it thickens as if to reflect the mood. With her other hand she stirs the contents.

The wick flickers, reminding us to top up the kerosene. Mama, still in her *kitenge*, leans over the cooking table determined to finish cooking before the flame dies. Both her hands encircle the flattened wooden spoon like a fisherman's oar. She's watching the mass of *ugali,* driven to the top of the *sufuria* by the steam, trapped between the stainless-steel hot pan and the volcano of maize meal. She wrestles the stodge, pats it, then suppresses it, hot steam bubbling underneath it as if it were a monster from the deep. This is a metaphor of my life. I am wrestling with forces I cannot control. I am defeated. I have no option but to own up to Mama. She thinks it's half term and that's why Wa Njũgũ brought me home last night. All day I've been gathering courage to tell her.

Our ears are tuned into the funeral announcements on Gĩkũyũ service on the transistor radio, which sits on a crochet mat in the corner. I am about to open my mouth when the announcement comes in.

'*The death has occurred of Mũthoni of Gĩkambura.*'

Mama stands upright, puts her hand up in the air warning us not to utter a word. The warm glow of the lamp is reflected onto minuscule globules of sweat on her shiny face, like a thousand lights. The mesh of our old transistor radio vibrates as the announcer continues.

'*The cortege will leave Nairobi mortuary at 12 noon. The service will be held at the Church of The Torch in Thogoto soon after. The funeral will take place at Lang'ata cemetery.*'

'That's her. Mũthoni is no more. Hit by a minister's motorcade whilst crossing the road.'

I hold my breath absorbing the words. It's hard to make sense of it. Mũthoni, a member of Mama's *kĩama*, always kind to me. Her flawless face beaming with a smile during the *kĩama* meetings is fresh on my mind. I press my eyelids together and tears seep out.

Mama tosses the wooden spoon on the cooking table. Her

face transforms like a melting candle and tears glide down her face. Involuntary sounds escape her mouth as she covers her face with her plump fingers and sobs. I ease the pressure on the drum and stand up. Kaminde slides his comb back into his shirt pocket and I catch a glimpse of victory on his face. What is wrong with this man? Even a time like now he still claims his childish victory of defeating me in reclaiming leg room. I wonder why Mama tolerates him. He adds no value to our lives, but Mama is convinced it's good for me to have a father figure.

I walk to her and throw my skinny arms around the spread of her chest. She breathes heavily and holds me tight. For a moment the room stands still, my chest inflating and deflating in rhythm with Mama's. Our embrace erases everything in the dark room. We both sob unified in sorrow. She, from the loss of her friend, and I, from a world that's crumbling around me. Forlorn, face downcast, Mama walks from me and the cooking table as the rising *ugali* blows angry steam on the edges of the *sufuria*. She walks to the door then turns round and walks to the utensils cupboard. Her cheeks blow out like a puffer fish before deflating with a large breath as if competing with the *ugali*. Her cheeks become hollow with anguish. The flesh beneath her chin drape with a sagginess I've not seen before. I hate to see her like this. Mama's only comfort is my welfare and I can't bear the self-loathing that consumes me. I want to make her sadness go away. Make everything okay but I don't know how.

'We didn't raise enough for Mūthoni's funeral. Why must these *mzungu* funerals cost so much money?'

Her shoulders drop.

The simmering *ugali* blows jets of steam as if to answer her question. I have no words for her grief, all I can do is stare at the cooking pot.

'Where are the days when hyenas did the undertaking, and we mourned silently at the release of the spirits to our ancestors.'

'Aaah! We don't have time to sneak around basting the dead with goat fat for the benefit of the hyena. Funerals are now civilised. You can't take the white man's education and reject his ways,' Kaminde says.

I scowl. The man has no heart. A real man would do something and not spew out empty ideologies.

'Only coffin makers and grave robbers benefit from funerals these days.' Mama turns to the cooking, pressing back the *ugali* that has been pushed to the top by the steam.

'I'm going to the funeral on 19th February. Next Friday.' She turns to look at me. 'When do you get back to school?'

My heart races. Shame casts a veil over my face. My grandmother opined my light skin is a blessing and a curse. That my beauty is unsurpassed, but I wear my feelings on my cheeks. My gaze fixated on the flame of the lantern; I tilt my head away from Mama hoping the weak light disguises my discomfort. I feel my blood drain. Saliva spirals into the sinkhole of my throat making it feel like caked earth. I pause too long. Her stare X-rays my thoughts. I'm exposed. She must know of my disgrace. Images of a creature on top of me writhing up and down, salty sweat dropping into my mouth, reappear in my mind. I can't breathe. I want to stretch and open the tin shutters to let in more air. My limbs refuse to cooperate as if reluctant to draw attention. There's a disconnect between my body and my mouth.

'Next Thursday,' I hear myself say.

My skin burns at Mama's stare. I wonder if she suspects anything. A rumble from Kaminde's rotund belly interrupts. She turns back to the *ugali*. I return to my seat, my chest visibly rising and falling. The *ugali* whistles back as if in a secret code. Mama's actions quicken. Her face looks drawn, large bags under her eyes. I am filled with dread. What I would do to take all that pain away but instead, I am piling onto her misery. The death of her friend Mũthoni came as a big shock, as she was just recovering from the shock of my expulsion. Her shoulders droop with worry. She turns off the gas and reaches for a plate, covering the *sufuria* with the *ugali*. With a food-stained cloth, she turns the pan upside down and the hot stodge slumps onto the plate. She lifts the pan and brings it close to the lamp revealing a crusted base which she lifts with her spare hand. It lifts in one piece. She breaks it into small pieces like a holy man conducting a communion. She hands me a piece and watches as I put it in my mouth. Kaminde's hand is stretched, breaking off the largest piece from her hand. She puts the remainder in her mouth.

'Where is the bone?' He salivates staring at the baked crackle.

It's like living with a cave man. I can't understand why anyone would willingly spend any time with this imbecile. I blame him for taking away my privacy and taking Mama's attention from me. She hurries back to the cooking table. She scoops the watery cabbage into a bowl and places it in front of him as if he were a dog. He dunks the crackle into the broth and squeezes it all into his mouth, before throwing his head back to chew and swallow.

Mama says nothing. I'm pained by her eagerness to please. The man has no redeeming qualities, if only I could shake some sense into her. Kaminde fishes his short fingers inside the reddish broth pushing the white stripes of cabbage out of the way as he swashes around in the bowl. With a glint in his eyes, he pulls out the core of the cabbage, holding it up as if it were a

105

trophy. He brings the tip to his mouth, bites it off and begins to chew. Bits of spit flee from his mouth. He submerges the stump in the broth again, then brings it to his mouth, sucking the liquid from his bone. He gnaws the end crunching it between his stained teeth like a hyena.

'You know how much I love the bone. This is where all the goodness is.' He belches with a mouth full. He rolls big balls of *ugali* and dunks it into the broth, licking the grease and bits of cabbage that run down his fingers and his hairy arms. I try not to look at him but he's like a caged animal. He sticks his long reptile tongue into the crevice between his upper lip and teeth, slurping bits of masticated starch stuck in there into his cavernous already crammed mouth.

I gag. Bitter bile rises from the back of my throat.

Mama hands me my bowl of cabbage. I grab a piece of *ugali* from the plate in the middle of the drum before his short fat fingers now covered with bits of cabbage claim another share. I can't bring myself to eat.

'The mechanic is coming tomorrow to look at the *matatū*, maybe I can drive you to the funeral.' Kaminde glances at Mama then tips the bowl to his mouth emptying its contents.

Our silence at the offer is louder than any words we could utter. The mention of the *matatū* plunges me deeper into my anguish. The promise of owning a *matatū* once gave me hope. It's all evaporated. I dared dream of a future away from the pathetic people of this place whose nosy gossips drags one into the sludge they are stuck in. I saw myself away from here but like water thrown on to embers, the sight of the *matatū* put out that shimmer of hope. Every time his lips utter those words, he slowly smothers any sprouting optimism. I wish I could burn that worthless old pile of metal, held together with delusion.

It was in the early days of their courting, before I realised that Kaminde would be encroaching into our space. He'd knocked on the door with a half kilo of meat. In the days of Moi's Nyayo everyone learned to tighten their belts. With all the money looted from the country, there were no luxuries. Mothers thinned meals by adding water, and meat was a treat only afforded by those with a salary or when there was a new man in the household. Like a dog marking his territory, Kaminde marked his with a kilo of meat wrapped with old newspaper. He shook my hand, his little hands feeling more like a child's. He handed me a ten-shilling note and sent me to Firifo's shop to buy bread and sodas. I sprang to the shop and returned moments later with a Sprite for him, Coke for Mama and Fanta for me and a large loaf for the morning.

'Run back and bring Blue Band margarine,' he tipped more coins in my hand.

Mama fried the meat alone not wanting other ingredients to tarnish the full flavour. The aroma of fried meat alerted the neighbourhood that a man had claimed his stake in our household.

After supper we sat back sipping our sodas. This was before Kaminde realised he could spend the whole evening combing the drum. We sat with the glow of satisfied bellies when Kaminde cleared his throat.

'I didn't want to say anything until I'd done it, but I purchased a *matatũ*.'

Mama put her soda down and looked at him in disbelief. I thought I was drunk from my Fanta, and I misheard him.

'Ati atia? *Matatũ* ya ma?

'Yes! A real one. A *matatũ* is the modern cow. We will milk her generous udders until the cows come home.' Kaminde burst out laughing. 'Like the cow, passengers have no options, and we will milk them to our heart's contentment. A *matatū* is a route to success,' he said.

My heart pumped with delight.

'Ngai works in mysterious ways; I have prayed for a piece of land to call our own but he knows better. He has extended us a bridge to cross to the promised land,' said Mama.

A *matatū* would elevate us from the underclass to the fortunate, the ones lucky to have a roof over their head, but still hovering on the jaws of poverty. We could rent a self-contained flat in a stone building that would keep us cool even when the sun beat down with intensity. We could have our own toilet and bathroom with no queues for the pit latrine and tap. We would have our own space where we could wash the dishes without the neighbours prying to see what we had for dinner last night. We would be in a place far from the gossip, away from Wa Njūgū's crying children and the unforgiving tin walls which deny us privacy. We would no longer compete for space with the stray animals that prowl the compound like rival gangs. This was our ticket out of the filth and dysfunction of the Ministry of Works.

I felt something rise from the pit of my stomach and make its way through my chest to my heart. The feeling was pride. I would no longer endure my name being called out in assembly with other poor students for school fees deficit. The slow walk to the front of the assembly hall, standing in a line paraded like a criminal, judged by richer people's children for not having enough money to pay fees upfront. A *matatū* would clear my school fee arrears and maybe help me move to a better school.

A *matatū* would buy me a pair of shoes. I thought of the beaten leather school shoes under my bed misshapen with age.

My growing feet had pushed the back of the shoe to overhang the heel. Thinking about the heel of my shoes made me wince at how the worn heel had been patched up with bits of tyre by the shoemaker by the crossroads to resemble strata. Each layer marked another school year. The heel that an aloof boy pointed at laughing his head off.

'What kind of shoes are those? They look like the shoes of a cripple.'

My arm ached to slap him across the face. Mama did everything she could to provide for me. She and I shared those shoes when I was home because her regular shoes were worn out. Did he not understand that not everyone worked for the council and could live off bribe money?

A *matatũ* would mean I had school pocket money and on Tuesdays when the bakery lorry delivered loafs of bread in the canteen, I would treat myself to a half loaf to be devoured with a wad of margarine.

Mama pinched me out of my reverie, unable to conceal her delight. She raised her hands and, with her eyes shut, she began to pray.

'Ngai, King of Kings, who stood on Mt Kĩrĩnyaga and gifted Gĩkũyũ and his descendants with these red soils. We appreciate your gift. This is the ladder we needed to step up to a plot in this landscape you protected with four holy mountains. In accordance with your wishes, we will work the soil again because farming is in our blood. I'll grow *njahĩ* and *njũgũ* like we once did, before the emergence of the white men who herded our mothers into reserves like lost goats. I will own a piece of land on which to grow vegetables and graze a cow so I can raise my daughter.'

'It's doing its maiden journey so meet me tomorrow at the crossroads.' Kaminde beamed with pride.

109

For the briefest moment, I was converted to his creed. If Kaminde came with a *matatū*, it would go some way to sweetening his personality. I could overlook his shortcomings. His burping and drum combing may even cease to annoy me as I would have my own bedroom where I would spend most of my time. I could not believe the change in our fortunes.

It's ironic that in his bid to prove himself, he chose the very place where, like old cooking pots in a curse, aspirations were smashed. It was nicknamed the crossroads of despair because that was where people, fleeing the mud huts of tradition in pursuit of modernity, came to their senses. It is situated at the junction where the fare increased because the road was tarmacked, sinking in the cold reality that Nairobi was unattainable. Unable to afford the fare to veer left onto the tarmac towards the bright lights of the city, these hopefuls alighted, their backs hunched in disappointment, and settled for the only viable option, Kīrigiti. Their mouths curved downwards with disdain; they slowly accepted their status in this purgatory.

That day is seared in my memory. Mama and I squinted at the distant object, drawing ever closer, whipping up dirt around it like a dust devil. A whistling sound whetted our curiosity as the object rattled towards us, standing by the crossroads of despair. At first, we thought it was a contraption put together by idle village boys. We stared at it making its way, wondering what on earth that could be. The clanging of metal and wobbly tyres begging to be let loose, engine coughing up like an old man with eroded lungs. The screeching fan belt warned us to dive out of the way as the 'new' *matatū* ground to a halt. Kaminde jumped out of the driver's side door with the demeanour of a conqueror.

Too stunned to speak we gaped, expecting him to burst out laughing for managing to fool us. And then it dawned on us that he was serious and that this ramshackle object was what we'd pinned all our hopes on. Realising this was it, I inspected the wreckage with growing unimaginable anger to have expected more from a man who combs a drum. There would be no moving house, there would be no school shoes, no reprieve from school humiliation.

Mama could not hide her bitter disappointment either. 'Even a baby is born and dies,' she shrugged.

What could have persuaded the passengers to get into this death trap? The answer landed promptly.

'There's a minibus strike in town. It's all about taking calculated risks,' Kaminde said.

How could I have been so stupid as to let this clown deceive me? Only an imbecile would turn up anywhere and offer anyone money for this.

'A bargain, just two thousand shillings,' said Kaminde.

Even in my optimistic adolescent mind, I should have known it was too good to be true. Having no hope is one thing, but building those castles in the air only to fall from the sky, completely deflated, was incomprehensible.

Unable to hide my disappointment, I stormed off, kicking the pebbles on the marram. A brand-new Jeep flew past blowing clouds of dust as if to make a statement. It's only when I reached the maize stalks by the curved marram road that I saw the Jeep had stopped. A white man sat behind the steering wheel, beeping the horn outside big brown gates on the opposite side of the road.

By the gates was a gleaming sign I'd never noticed before. It read *Kitch Sarajevo*. For a moment, I was distracted as the gates glided open revealing a pristine compound with beautiful multi-coloured flowers and thick green carpets of trimmed lawns. It was like looking into a parallel universe inhabited by white men dressed in sand-coloured boots, matching combat trousers and white vests. A few white dogs roamed the compound as if to maintain the theme. For a while, I was lost in this world I hadn't been aware of before.

The compound stands out in Kĩrigiti like a bride in a funeral. No one knows what it is or why it is there. But standing there on that day after Kaminde's display at the crossroads was like a slap in my face. As if the god of jealousy had deviously intervened to show me a different world. A neat, clean, orderly world of tidy chalet cabins draped with colourful roses.

As the smooth gate slid close, Kaminde's *matatũ* rattled as if to remind me where we belonged. Angry customers quarrelled with him, demanding the return of their fares. I felt like diving into the white people world before the gates shut. Instead, I turned round and walked back to the Ministry of Works.

Mama, leaving Kaminde to resolve the issue with his customers, followed me. She got home to find me a sobbing mess. If only I could convince Mama to leave him. We could find somewhere else, far from the chaos. A place where we could finally have peace to mourn the loss of my father. Kaminde had a strange effect on me, like a snail recoiling into my shell. Never finding space to tell Mama how I feel.

'We can't live here anymore! Please can we leave,' I said.

'It's either here or the streets.'

'Of all the places we could have ended up, why here?'

'If it weren't for my friend in the municipal offices, and a little chai, we would be out there with the rats.'

Was she that foolish to pay a bribe to live in this objectionable hell? 'Why don't you get a job at the Ministry of Works? Maybe they will pay you good money.'

She laughed with a back snort. 'There is no Ministry of Works. The colonisers created it before independence. I guess their dreams too faded into thin air.' She sounded defeated.

I roll my eyes and bite my tongue keeping my head down. I do not wish to cause Mama anymore distress than she is in by fighting with him. I have done enough damage. I hang my head in shame. Mama wants to sit down. I get up and the drum surges forward from the pressure from Kaminde's knees. Mama squeezes through and sits in her place in the centre of the three-piece sofa. She stretches her arm and pinches a handful of *ugali* placing it on the side of her bowl and starts eating. I bow my head to erase the image of Kaminde eating. I stare at the flame of the kerosene lamp for something to busy my eyes.

I get back to the rest of the cabbage. We synchronise our chewing to the sombre music on the radio at the end of the funeral announcements. When I'm done, I rinse my hands in the *sufuria* that contained *ugali,* now topped with water to soak stuck-on flour. I rinse my plate in the same water, dry my hands, and sit back in my armchair.

It seems like eternity since the sun sunk into its cavernous bed but it's only nine o'clock. We sit in silence, each one of us wrestling beasts within. Despite the crowding in this room, I feel alone in the fog of uncertainty. I am trapped in a room with no doors or windows. A room full of judgemental eyes staring at me. I can't breathe, choked by everything in this room. As if the air has been sucked up by some invisible force. In this compound. I am consumed by lack of space. I want to escape but I am trapped. At school, there was always someone I can borrow books from and lose myself in the world of story. In this space, there are no books. Just gossip and the radio. The radio is depressing. It's dedicated to the life of the president with intermissions for funeral announcements. Death seems to be what everyone wants to listen to in their leisure.

I feign a few yawns prompting Mama to heat some water for

me on the gas burner. She fills the bucket for me. I think about the long stare she gave me earlier during supper. I wonder if it's suspicion about my situation or worry about her friend's funeral.

'Sleep in peace,' Mama says as she and Kaminde stand to leave for their bedroom in the adjacent room.

Stripping, I stand in the middle of the bucket like a giant baby in its bath. It's the only way I can clean myself. Mama recommended I wash this way as the pit latrine is grotesque. She doesn't like the neighbourhood men queuing outside whilst I'm in. I place my bucket by the door where there's a slope for the water to flow out. I let the warmth soak the freeze in my heart as I contemplate what lies ahead of me. I scoop water with my palms slapping my skin with it, hoping to wake up from this nightmare. I am careful not to soak the drum. The bucket is almost empty, so I step out leaving some water to dilute my urine in the middle of the night. I dry myself then climb into bed. My body feels less tense and it's good to stretch my limbs. I blow out the kerosene lamp and stare into the black hollowness of my existence.

Chapter Nineteen

My bladder throbs urging me to rouse. My eyelids glide open. Daylight brings no reprieve. Dust particles pirouette in the beam of sunlight sneaking in from the nail holes reminding me the night is over. My gaze rests on the ridges of the corrugated iron ceiling. Like a decrepit machine my mind still chugs. I throw off the rugged blankets resting on me and sit up rubbing tiredness from my eyes. I reach the two ends of the grubby curtain that separates my bed with the living space and tie them together. I swing my legs over the worn tan leather armchair wedged against my bed banging my toes on the cupboard in the process.

My skin tenses at the feel of the cold leather as I slide down the arm of the chair. My hands land on the erect hairs of the cowhide reminding me of the drum combing. Like a dog, this is Kaminde's way of marking the territory. Anger wells up inside me. I resent his intrusion into our lives.

'He's a good man and the sooner you learn to accept him the better,' Mama always says.

She thinks that I, Mũkami, should accept the repugnant way he soaks bread smothered with Blue Band margarine into his tea in a saucer before tipping the wet bread into his wide mouth. That I shouldn't walk behind him analysing his stout short neckless tortoise body. That I should resist the urge to smack a ripe mango on the apex of his small bald head. That I should resist the urge to swing my leg between his legs, set apart even when he doesn't intend them to be, and kick his balls. To turn that shrill of his laughter to one of agony. That I shouldn't wish he was made of clay so I can rip his head and limbs apart like a toddler during art class. How can a beautiful woman like Mama allow him to have that body close to her?

I free myself from the confines of the drum and sofas and walk over to the small table wedged up against the window. I slide the bolt freeing the tin shutters which swing outside. My eyes settle on the floral wipeable plastic tablecloth on which the two ring gas cooker rests. It's crusted with reddish broth and powdery flour from last night's cooking. I peel it off and put it on the side. Underneath is a stiff newspaper marked with water stains.

Hurry. Take your child to boarding school, a clean slate to absorb the new way of being, a civilised education. Those who don't send their children to boarding will cry till their death bed. Not sending your child to boarding school risks them being dragged down by old traditions riddled with suspicion and witchcraft. Your child will only speak English for we punish those who speak their mother tongue. They will learn manners, etiquette and to carry themselves with grace and dignity. Your child will be so civilised, white people will be shocked. Declares the advert. I remember the day Kaminde brought it home.

'Boarding schools help cut the cord of ancient ways of the tribe, of rituals that have no place in the modern world.' He slammed the paper on the drum.

'We can't afford boarding school.' Mama said.

Not to taint me with outdated traditions Mama and Kaminde trekked the breath of the country looking for a boarding school to suit our budget. We saw rich schools set in opulent grounds staffed by foreign teachers. Our eyes popped out in astonishment at way rich children boarded and learned in luxury. We saw average schools whose finance only afforded East African teachers. The children there lived and learned in mediocre boarding houses. And then there were poor schools where children boarded in hovels of tin and learned in windowless classes. We saw all manner of boarding schools catering for every budget. My school is somewhere in between the hovel and average.

It is his idea that I should move from home to boarding school, then he can have Mama to himself. But Mama is always gone, working even harder to cover my school fees arrears which was like feeding a beast with a bottomless stomach. Sometimes I am grateful that I can escape this compound and him to be away at school. Maybe it was for the best because I would have lost my mind having to look at him every day.

I sink back into the chair my body refusing to accept my situation. I want to go back to school, an escape from this place. I want to immerse myself in learning. Reading tales of foreigners and foreign places. Learning of Napoleon Bonaparte, Benito Mussolini, and other white people achievements. Here in the compound is all about idle gossip. Everyone is always pouncing about fertilising hearsay. Peaking behind bedsheets draped on windows, they sneer, pointing, cursing. They talk of the scorned spirits and how they are out to get us. I love losing myself in irrelevant stories in books. The Famous Five adventures, immersing myself in solving crimes in England. I hate the cold reality of being here, there's no escape. There are no books or libraries. Just tumble weed and gossip.

I force myself out of my reverie. There's no water. I pick up the jerrycans from under the table, slide the bolts and open the door. I look left to the adjoining room, to see Mama's room is padlocked, so conclude she must be at her kiosk. She never has breakfast when I am home from boarding school as I sleep in our cooking room. I walk to the edge of our shack and head to the ablutions area.

The warm sunshine attempts to lift the fog that clouds my soul but like storm clouds its unflinching. The hoods of my eye lids flop heavily on my eyes from crying and the insomnia that fanned the fires of my grief. I stand in the queue of yellow plastics and humans alike. Elephantiasis is lunging his humongous leg on his way to the ablutions. His walk is a two-step process. He puts his good leg forward and with all his might, hauls the leathery mass of his elephant leg, panting, sweat running down the sides of his face, leaving a gully behind.

Children run after him singing 'Look out it's the one-legged giant.'

Everyone calls him Elephantiasis, but his real name is Njaũ meaning calf. Given his size, that's ironic; he is more of a bull. An Elephant bull. According to rumour, some village folk in Nyeri gave him the evil eye, maliciously complementing his looks before she disappeared. But majority say his leg is a blessing. It is said that he once stood in the middle of a river anchored by his heavy leg against the fast tide, saving drowning children. It was also his heavy leg that stamped on a snake that was about to kill a child.

A few people not wanting to be held up by his slowness rush ahead to beat him to the ablutions. They place their jerrycans in the line before disappearing into the dark holes of the tin walls, from which they peer. Others watch their place whilst queuing for the toilet.

'I had pointed breasts like yours!' I look up to see Wa Njũgũ who has emerged from house number five. I frown, not sure that she is speaking to me.

'My body was all straight and beautiful like yours once, but these children ruined me,' she says.

I scowl.

The small eyes of the baby strapped with a threadbare *kanga* on her back swivels round at the helter skelter. Its head bobs up and down as Wa Njūgū rushes back and forth with more jerrycans from her house. Its small round bottom is perched on its mother's generous buttocks, anchored on her long dark legs; a contrast from her pale, chemically bleached face. She scolds her children to place their jerrycans in the line. She is breastfeeding her baby on her back by passing her long breast underneath her armpit. A small toddler tries to mount her to finish with her feed on the other breast which is hanging out, a drop of white milk clinging on.

I can't keep track of her many children who loiter the compound with their rounded kwashiorkor bellies clothed in dirty rags. In between gossip and childrearing, she serves rowdy men warm tuskers at Kīhoto bar, whose wily penises result in yet another baby.

She's going between her house and the tap where I am queueing.

'It wasn't me,' cries one child after some accusation, followed by a smacking sound. The resulting loud wailing shatters my peace.

'Now I am haggard and ugly. I am your future,' she says.

Those words horrify me. The nurse's words at the clinic ring in my ears. *You are all pregnant.* Wa Njūgū cannot be my future. Watching her is like watching a horror film. She's always giving birth, feeding a baby or cleaning their shit. I stare at her cracked feet and shudder. The thought of ending up like her is throttling me. She pushes her jerrycans in front of mine. I pick up my jerrycans and place them in front of hers. She's trying to overtake me and I won't let her.

She stares. 'Only a fool can't tell what you are hiding underneath that shirt.'

Her words send a shiver down my spine.

'I hope you got something out of it.'

I collect my empty jerrycans and run back to the house, closing the door behind me. I bury my hands in my face in panic. I am now wailing.

She knows. The compound's gossip knows my secret.

Chapter Twenty

I've heard the washerwomen at the communal tap say one must never peer into the pit latrine because it's littered with aborted foetuses. In their cutting ways, they snigger at girls who have had an abortion, those thinking of it or ones who died from it. They speculate about the current trend, it is drinking Omo detergent for the ones with money, but for the penniless, they opt for the coat hanger, preferring to bleed alone in their beds, opting for potential death over the wrath of their parents. There are stories of girls beaten by their families and thrown into the streets before taking their own lives. They whisper of the abattoir which sends chills through my body and talk of the dark alleyway in the south side of Kīrigiti where girls pregnant with shame disappear, carried in the dead of night wrapped in sisal sacks.

To my adolescent mind, these are ghost stories, like those told by my grandmother. Things that happen to fictional people. They were. Now everything has changed. I try to sift truth from fiction, force myself to think harder. Yet the more I think about it, the bleaker my future looks. In my mind there's a distinct difference between me and those girls who carelessly, maybe even wilfully, get pregnant. I am not like those girls. I am a good girl. Obedient. Who has unfathomably, ended up here. But Mama will know the difference. She must. Even if I cannot have been good since I am in this predicament. I am a disgrace and deep down, I know my body is changing. None of my clothes fit around the waist. I want to be swallowed up like Jonah was swallowed up the whale and taken to a new land. I want to go to a land so far away from this mess.

I think of Mama and her heartaches. A dead husband, an oaf for a boyfriend, a dead friend, the threat to her kiosk from the municipal council, the never-ending quest for money. Now this. Mama must never find out I was expelled, and wallowing is self-pity isn't going to help me. I must resolve this situation before the half term is over. It suddenly hits me, it's actually half term. When I said it to Mama, it was the only thing that came to mind, but I thought I was telling her a lie to protect myself. I wasn't going to tell Mama I was pregnant in front of Wa Njũgũ and Kaminde. I was in a fit of panic. A small feeling of relief, that I have bought myself some time, courses through my body. I will find a way of getting this thing out of me. Oh God. This is the first time I'm admitting to myself the truth. I have been hiding from the truth but others like Wa Njũgũ saw right through me. The thought of Wa Njũgũ brings terror into me. She's like a hawk, never missing anything. She broadcasts gossip faster than radio. It's just a matter of time before the washerwomen ravage me; before Mama finds out and before everyone will make commentary on my every move. I feel exposed with nowhere to hide. I must resolve this situation without a moment to waste.

My mental inventory of names of those I can trust and who can help is small. In fact, there's only one name on the list. Bũi! She is my only option. She will know what I should do. I can confess to her the whole sorry story, safe with the knowledge she lives too far for the nosy residents of the Ministry of Works to find out. I must see her. Although she'd never said anything to me, I know from rumours she has been in my predicament before. But I am desperate for the toilet, and I must wait. Thinking fast, a sudden rush of adrenaline induces composure. I peer at the sun through the window to check the time. I can still make it to Eastleigh to speak to Būi! And be back before Mama gets home.

I dry my tears. With a mask of indifference, I pick up the jerrycans and walk back to the ablutions. I place my jerry cans in the water queue but my need for the toilet beckons so I abandon them. Wa Njūgū's nowhere to be seen and I sigh with relief. I cannot stand the sight of that uncouth woman. I evaluate the five people ahead of me. Elephantiasis is in front of me. No. He will take forever.

Ahead of him is the Dying Woman. Her face is forlorn, her head drooping. I hear her singing funerals songs all day, but at night, the tune changes to 'Hallelujah' when she gets a visit from Gītonga, resident of house number twelve. I know she is menstruating because I can see a roll of cotton wool under her arm. That means she won't be long.

In front of her is Gītonga. Gītonga means wealthy, which is ironic as all residents here are living on the poverty line. He turns round and sees me leaning forward and spots the desperation on my face. He pouts his lips as if blowing me an air kiss then circles the ring of his mouth with his wet tongue. The fingers on his left-hand curl to make an o. He then inserts his index finger into the hole, then withdraws it. And does it again. He is giving me some signal, but Mama says I should not engage in conversations with him, so I look away. When I look up, he is still staring at me and flashes a smile, his big yellow teeth and dimples giving the impression of friendliness, but I know his morals are rotten. He has the sort of face that lets you know he will con you, rob you or screw you at his earliest convenience. I know for sure that he can read and will be a long time because he has a newspaper underneath his armpit. We all know how long he takes in the toilet and the stink bomb he leaves behind. Not even the evil vines that embrace the toilet can absorb those fumes. Flies buzz in anticipation.

The thought of using the bucket under my bed is tempting. But I would have to find some way of getting rid of the waste. At least with urine, one just dilutes it with water and chucks it outside; the sun's rays take care of the rest and by midday all evidence is gone. I clench my butt cheeks even tighter praying that everyone is quick. The line is moving when I feel a tap on my shoulder.

'*Tafadhali* let my daughter go before you she is very desperate.' I turn round and see Jane, Firifo's malnourished wife, with her very thin daughter Ruth perched on her thin hips. The scrunched up look I give her tells her there is little chance, but she doesn't give up.

'She is a little girl.'

Eyes still fixated ahead. Not even Firifo, Ruth's father, who is in the queue flinches. Jane's dark face is full of sweat beads as she changes tactic. Jane's huge over-sized dress concealing her thin body gathers red dust as she moves from behind me.

'I am fasting for Jesus,' she says as if to justify her thinness.

She taps on everyone's shoulder, but everyone ignores her. Now she is begging Elephantiasis, but by the time he replies she has changed her mind. She walks over to the pile of rubbish where the goats are scavenging. She lifts Ruth's dress and lowers her pants and tells her it's okay to do her business there. Ruth is relieved. The dogs move in quickly grabbing her thin faeces before it lands on the ground. She doesn't need toilet paper because they lick her clean. Seeing Ruth defecate triggers an involuntary muscle in my bowels to flex, moving things down. I am envious of Ruth and on the verge of opening up, so I clench even tighter.

My eyes wander to distract myself and I see goats stretching their necks to reach the toilet vines.

'People say the vines are so lush because evil spirits dwell in them plotting our demise,' says the dying woman taking a break from singing a funeral song.

My bladder throbs.

I look to the left and I am distracted by Ndekezie who sits eating his breakfast outside his house close to the tap. I watch his powerful iron fingers clutch a large sweet potato, breaking chunks of it and stuffing it in his mouth. He reminds me of a mechanical digger. His big jaws and the way he rolls his food around his mouth. I've never heard him speak and wonder whether he is arrogant or just shy. His eyes are fixated on the hand action as if controlling it with his gaze. His long ebony arm is reminiscent of finely chiselled stone artwork and I wonder what he does for a living. I never see him going to work. The valleys of his tightly packed muscles are served by a strong network of veins that flex as he raises a plastic cup to his pouted lips. He's sipping *turungi* as if time is infinite.

A thin grey cat sits between Ndekezie's legs looking up at him. Its delicate paws mop the showers of sweat dripping on its fur from Ndekezie's forehead. Undeterred, it stretches its paws and tries tapping on his hand. Ndekezie's right foot is in a pink slipper. His other foot is in a yellow slipper. With his right leg, he flings the cat into the muddy water by the tap as he rushes back into his house. The cat flounces off shaking the water off its limbs. To add to its misery a boy chasing a bicycle tyre driving it with a stick pauses to kick it into the rubbish pile. I feel sorry for the kitten, but I too have problems.

One person gets into the toilet but it's no consolation for

my bowels as I am getting close to soiling myself. Ndekezie steps out of his shack, his wide once-beige shorts, now a dirty brown, flapping around. He is back on his stool with a fresh mug in his hand. He is still holding his transistor radio which he places close to his ear after playing with the dials. He is listening to a Gor Mahia vs Leopard's football game. It's all I've ever seen him do. Some people assume he is Luo due to his love for Gor Mahia since Gĩkũyũ always support Leopards. He spreads his legs out guiding those in the queue to look lower. One is forced to hold their breath by what's visible. His wide shorts act like a theatrical curtain partially concealing his large luggage which lies like an actor waiting for his cue. I've noticed the washerwomen seem to prefer doing their laundry at this time of the day, giving side stares at Ndekezie. Wa Njũgũ's children are playing nearby pointing and diving into their house and I wonder whether she's going to tell them off.

Ndekezie is oblivious to the merriments he awards the residents of the Ministry of Works. He continues to sip his beverage. He doesn't look up nor does he give eye contact preferring to stare at his feet. He rarely speaks, is abrupt with a low attention span. It's as if he is about to solve a puzzle and doesn't want to be interrupted. He has a vulnerability that contradicts his masculine physique. I think his breakfast has gone right through him as soon as he finishes eating, he jumps into the toilet queue.

'If you don't need the toilet then get off the line,' a voice bellows from the crowd behind, startling me. I edge forward.

Gathuki fronts the queue and eagerly darts into the toilet when it becomes vacant. Moments later the door flings open. Gathuki is met with Firifo's wide nostrils breathing down on him. He seems startled to see Firifo standing so close outside the toilet door.

'Step away so I can get out,' says Gathuki.

From this encounter I detect a venomous undertone beneath Gathuki's quiet demeanour.

'What does it say?' asks Firifo ignoring Gathuki's protestation, his eyes fixed on the space behind Gathuki's head. Gathuki now looks up at the tall man, his face full of disdain.

'We will find out in a little while if you allow me to step outside.'

Just then Firifo farts like a motorcycle with a broken exhaust, making it clear he is in desperate need to relieve himself. I fear the same fate. Gathuki shoves him to the side in disgust.

'Why is it that men of God are always the most discourteous?'

A gust of wind slams the toilet door. And that's when we see the notice.

Dear esteemed toilet user,

Sorry to catch you at such a time, and in such a manner and I am well aware you have urgent business to attend, so I will not keep you long. I chose to place this notice on the toilet, not to symbolise your status, but for practical reasons really. Everyone must attend the call of nature, therefore a guarantee that no one will plead ignorance. I placed it on the way in so that you can digest it whilst doing your...., you know, your business. I will not take any more of your time so let me keep it short. It has come to my notice that lowlife unsavoury characters live in the compound and as a result, at the first cock's crow on 28th February 1989, the bulldozers will be moving in to clear the ground for building a mansion for a new owner, a God fearing, law-abiding citizen from a decent family born in wedlock, brought up by his God-fearing mother and God-fearing father. Make sure you have vacated all your belongings by then. It shouldn't take long; I expect you don't have much.

Enjoy your shit!

Chapter Twenty-One

Arm stretched out; I curl my thumb upwards. A Datsun Sunny veers off the strip of asphalt on to the gravel stopping at my feet. Beady eyes behind sunglasses scan me from the waist up. I crouch to see the driver's mature face. He stretches over the passenger's seat and rolls down the window revealing a neat afro. Droplets of hair oil balance on miniature coils of coarse hair glistening in the sun. There are maps of stains on his sky-blue suit on which the oil drips. The corners of his mouth glide into a smile.

'Where are you going.'

'Eastleigh.'

The enormity of my destination makes me pause.

'I have urgent business in Industrial area, will that do?'

'I can jump off at Pangani.'

He nods. I open the door and step into a jungle lair of faux leopard skin upholstered seats imbued with Old Spice. I shuffle my bottom creating static. He starts the engine and clutches either side of the steering wheel which is wrapped with furry zebra. Attached to the rear-view mirror, a monkey tail air freshener dangles as the car skids back onto the road. On the dashboard, a box of tissues slides with the motion of the car.

I look that the clock it's ten minutes to twelve. With any luck Bŭi will be in before her shift at the salon.

The driver pushes a cassette into its dock and music blasts out of the speakers.

'It's James Last in concert,' he says.

I smile. The song starts to drag followed by a sound of the mechanical winder chewing the tape. He presses eject, cursing under his breath. I wonder if the jungle theme is to distract the uncomfortable silence that sets in with a hitched ride. Drivers may strike a conversation, but I prefer the quiet ones. These days everyone is wary of being loose tongued with strangers in case they criticise the government accidentally. I've heard Mama and Kaminde discuss cases of people getting a knock on their door only to turn up dead in Karura forest. I don't want to die in Karura forest. I get comfortable and we sit in silence.

Our bodies wobble as the Datsun navigates the valleys of worn asphalt. I like humming whilst riding in a bumpy car just to hear my voice wobble but not today. My world is a plateau of misery. My sense of fun has disappeared. I stare out of the window as we veer to the left on the fresh tarmac to Nairobi. Formidable mansions that line Kĩambu Road fly past. Delicate bougainvillea hedges stand guard, their petals wave to me like cancan dancers revealing underskirts of vibrant orange, lilac, white and yellow. Miles of coffee bushes in various stages of ripening huddle round the mansions as if the owners have something to hide.

The road is littered with women veiled by clouds of smoke, bending over cooking pots sat on open fires of their makeshift eateries. Men in overalls hurry out of the manicured gardens converging with uniformed maids guided by the trail of the smoke. A group of young men lounging by the roadside are laughing. A lone boy clothed in tattered shorts sits on a rock reading a newspaper. My concentration is jarred out of the sight and back to the car by the driver's deep voice which reminds me of grinding metal.

'Which is it?' he asks as if to remind me I am still sharing his space.

'Sorry I didn't hear what you said.'

My thoughts are on pause and I am tuned in. He says nothing and I slip back into my head space. From the corner of my eye, I catch a movement that makes me look at his lower torso. My lungs halt mid breath forcing my eyes to jolt from their sockets. The driver's white shirt is untucked, and lower buttons undone. Dangling by his hips are the ends of his tan leather belt which rests on either side of his unzipped trousers. From a nest of course hair, his erect penis protrudes. My pupils dilate and anatomical functions abort as I stare ahead. An internal alarm urges me to jump out of the car.

'This year is going to be very hot. Do you prefer hot or cooler weather?' he says.

I sit still. Has he read my mind?

'Yes, I think this January is going to be very hot.'

Unable to remember whether he locked the doors or not I decide to check if the stubs are down. Still facing forwards, I force my eyeballs to swivel round imitating a chameleon. That hurts my eyes, and I can't see. Somehow, I must turn my head without attracting attention. For my plan of jumping out of the car to work, it must be a complete surprise. Maybe I should sneeze and quickly turn. I do and slant my head to look. The quick glimpse of the stubs by the window reveals nothing. I couldn't tell if the car is locked or not. A light sensation down the side of my face makes me nearly jump. It's a drop of sweat.

His long tongue is out and it's circling his mouth like a slug, leaving a slimy trail. We breathe heavily for different reasons.

\'Personally, I prefer hot weather,' he says, dragging out the word hot in a way that makes me queasy.

'Yes, everyone is different.'

If I jump, I don't want to land on the gravel. I scan the road ahead for soft verges. I look at the sideview mirror. There are no other cars behind us. I'm very aware of my movements. The speedometer is too far to the right requiring a ninety-degree head rotation. I try to calculate the speed. Like those mathematical scenarios in tests, I have no formulae. I do a simple risk calculation of either breaking my bones or remaining in his claustrophobic lair. On probability broken bones seem more appealing. I estimate we are doing about fifty kilometres per hour. It seems fast but I can't be sure.

'Hot and then a shower of rain,' he says.

'Yes, must be quite refreshing.'

I'm trying to think of the road layout ahead. Nothing comes to mind. It's then I feel something deep inside my lower abdomen. I've never felt it before. It's like delicate butterflies dancing. I feel panic rising from deep within. That must be the baby. God. I am pregnant. Why does this thing inside me make its presence known now? Does it know my thoughts? If I jump from a moving car, I'll jolt it out of me and escape from this creep, killing two birds with one stone. My heart throbs. That thought is very frightening. Tears are welling but I don't want to draw attention to myself. I think about Būi. If I keep my mind focused on Būi, I can remain calm, and this creep won't know I know what's going on. I will be fine. I must see her. Please be there when I get to Eastleigh.

'Are you still in school or college?'

His voice jolts me back to the car.

'I said are you still in school or college?'

'It's neither.'

It's an inaudible grunt. My racing heart is overcome by sadness. The current situation is more salient, so I force myself to look at the dashboard. Cradled on the dashboard is a small jar of Vaseline which he is scooping out with one hand that keeps disappearing from my peripheral sight. His gaze is still focused on the road. The dial points at forty kilometres per hour. I can't jump out without sustaining significant injuries. I'm immobile. His movements are becoming erratic. All the hairs on my body are on edge. Ahead I see soft verges. It's clear what I have to do. My ribcage expands as I take a deep breath. One, two...

'You look like a bright student,' he says.

I freeze. I've lost my nerve.

The grunting noises coming from the driver are a running commentary in my brain. My handbag is on my lap and I have a nail cutter with a folding nail file. That could be my weapon. So far, he hasn't deviated from the road which I take to be a good sign. If he starts to veer off the main road, I will aim to pull it out and stab him in the neck. I sneeze again to coincide with the unzipping of my bag. My fingers creep in and are fumbling around. I feel nothing. It's not there. Then I remember Kaminde borrowed it to cut his toenails and never returned it. That swine!

My mind is processing what fighting and retaliation I could use on this creep. My key could be used to stab his eye. Getting my shoes off will be impossible before he attacks me. My skin quivers as the reptile skin of his fingers touch my thigh, fear bubbling in the cauldron of my stomach. Maybe I should attack now. I could jump on him, catch him unawares, and bite his face. That will blind him and with any luck the car will veer off and I can jump out and run. My gaze is still fixated on the road. I am working out how exactly I will jump on him. He's getting more Vaseline from the jar and his moans are getting louder and more intense. We are going round the bend and at a high speed. The breaks screech. The car jolts to a stop. Traffic. Out of nowhere a street hawker appears selling peanuts wrapped in newspaper. I try the door, it doesn't yield. He doesn't see me, as the hawker interrupts.

'Peanuts for madam?'

The driver waves his hand, and the seller disappears only to be replaced by another. More surround the car selling newspapers, oranges, flip-flops. If an audience is what titillates him, he is in for a treat. One hawker sticks his head into the car only to be met by a big throbbing penis. Without pulling his head out, he swivels and looks at the driver in the eye.

'Bananas for you sir?'

The driver reaches for the handle and begins to roll up the window. It's stuck. He is scrambling around knocking the Vaseline off the dashboard. Every window is full of eyes peering into the car their hands displaying their goods. The driver tugs his shirt to cover his shrunken nakedness. We are in Pangani and the traffic is back-to-back.

'This is my stop.'

He sighs and unlocks the door. Hooting cars and *matatũ* turn boys touting for customers greet me as I step out of the Datsun. Something compels me to thank him for my ride. I slam the door, cross the busy road to catch a *matatũ* to Eastleigh.

Chapter Twenty-Two

I'm rigid with tension. Nails sunken deep into my palms. Every blood vessel in my body throbs. I will explode. The fear I felt in that car has turned into panicked anger. Little gasps escape from my mouth. I need someone or something to steady me. I feel faint and need something to lean on. I was convinced he would attack me. I am shaken by his hideousness. I stagger to the bus stop. There's a bench and I sit down. I am gasping for water and air. I feel as if my life is booby trapped. Every day is an obstacle course, and I am jumping through hoops. Today it seems I tripped and fell into a bottomless pond. I'm walking on the quicksand of life, and I keep sinking. I want to scream but I have no strength. Instead, my mouth is chanting, *I must see Būi*. As if rousing myself from a nightmare, I wipe the tears and mucus pooling in my palms onto my skirt and cry out, 'Which ancestor have I wronged to unleash this on me?'

From my fog of despair, my gaze is fixated on display boards for the *matatū* heading to Eastleigh. She is not expecting me. What more could I lose, time? Time is irrelevant to one who's lost everything. Kīmathi's memories are sprouting all over my head like fireworks. Taunting me. Tightening the noose on my future. My heart is impaled by thorns of rawness at what's happened to me. Kīmathi's betrayal, Geremani's treachery,

Wamakũbũ's caning and that hideous man in his jungle lair. The urge to rip my nails out causes me to nibble them until they bleed. There's a relief as the blood oozes out of me. I think if I drain my heart, it will hurt less. How could I be so naïve as to let Kĩmathi hijack my future; being privy to his pulling up the drawbridge, confining me to this nightmare. Before he came along, things were settled, there was a certainty that existed. I was sure of myself, my goals, and my future. Now my life is scattered like a bag of mangoes with a hole at the bottom. I curl forward, head sinking lower, and I weep.

My situation is like a causeway littered with landmines. Each more explosive than the last one. No one can soothe Mama's anger when she finds out. Within a period of three and a half months I am expelled from two schools. One for buying illicit alcohol I didn't want and the other for being pregnant and not even be aware of it. I got pregnant against my will but like a grasshopper I will leap from this predicament. He will not get away with it, none of these men will get away with this. He will pay. He must pay. They all must pay. My mind drifts into the ways I could carry out my revenge. I begin to plan but a movement from deep within me halts my thoughts. It's the same butterfly movements I felt in the Datsun. Maybe it's sending me a message. I have been invaded. Like a zombie snail, there is a parasite living off me. I did not choose this situation or want it. I take a deep breath. The tightness of my skirt digs into my waist. There's only one skirt that fits me now and I wear it all the time. Mama hasn't said anything about me wearing my school skirt. I pull it up and roll the waist under my ribcage. That helps.

A melodious horn alerts me the *matatũ* to Eastleigh is approaching. As the driver slows down, the turnboy hangs out, his hands clinging to the handlebars, his legs twisting and turning as if he was a circus acrobat. I begin to walk towards the door, but he jumps out and runs towards me. I am confused because he seems to recognise me. He's a stranger.

'*Sema sister, bona una lia, charlie amekuacha?*'

He scoops me into his arms and lifts me like a new bride on her wedding night, carrying me into the *matatū*. A burst of burning anger hits the pit of my stomach, reverberating to my feet before making its way up through my spine to my head. With my folded fist, I punch his arms, but he doesn't put me down. He takes me to the belly of the vehicle and starts dancing. My head is close to his unwashed chest, choking me with the stench of stale perfume and accumulated sweat. I'm trying to get down, but his iron arms are no match. I open my mouth and dig my teeth into his chest filling my mouth with a salty taste. He puts me down.

'Are you trying to tune that chick?' the driver says honking.

'She is playing hard to get, on a different wavelength,' the turnboy says.

This feels like the definition of hell. I walk away looking for a seat further away from the massive speakers suspended from the ceiling from which The Whispers blare out.

And we began to rock, steady,

Steady rocking all night long.

The turnboy follows me and stands close to me and starts gyrating rubbing his crotch on me, trying to impress a group of rowdy men sitting at the back jeering and causing mayhem. I move further in. He walks over to me not bothering to pull up his acid wash jeans that hang under his angular buttocks. A long gold chain dazzles against his dark skin. The hostility on my face is palpable as I hand him three shillings for the fare. Someone taps on my shoulder and offers me a seat. I am relieved and think he'll leave me alone. He is still standing there. I sink into the coarse leather seat and keep my eyes away from him. He keeps winking at me every time I catch his glance. He sits next to me, and I look the other way. He whispers something into my face, a wall of rotting breath hitting me. Defiantly, I turn to look at him. Strata on his teeth is like a diary of everything he's eaten in the previous week. I gag. My face scrunches in fury. I look away.

'So, tell me darling did your boyfriend leave you?'

I am in no mood to discuss anything with this buffoon. Clenching my fists, I suppress the anger welling up inside of me. I want to fling my hands around his throat and throttle him until not a drop of oxygen can get into his body.

As if transposed by an external force, the face of the turnboy changes and I see Kĩmathi, then Oily Man with his jungle lair. It seems like men and boys are like midges springing up from every angle. Persistent and harassing. Mama says our forefathers must be stiff with shame at the men of today, unable to earn respect from society. She bemoans the era when men were defenders of women, serving as the backbone of society.

Grinding my teeth in irritation, I sense the turnboy is no longer sitting next to me. I realise the space next to me is vacant and see he's in the corridor by the door. Rick Astley's 'Never Gonna Give You Up' booms out of the speakers and he begins break dancing. The hooligans at the back are whooping. He gets daring and spins for his audience. The *matatũ* jolts to a halt and he's thrown forward banging his head against the back of the seat. He's out cold. Someone pours milk on his face and he rouses. He gets up, unstable, holding onto the metal pillars. Blood trickles down the side of his head. His lips are no longer stretched into a smile but instead now pouting with a bruise. He stands beneath the *matatũ's* insignia which reads *Pride comes before a fall.*

I move from my seat, leaning forward to see if we are close to Eastleigh. The windows are misted over with human breath. I walk towards the front for a better look. I see a familiar sight and realise we are in Eastleigh as the driver is driving off.

'Stop, please driver stop. That's my stop.'

I hurry to the exit as the bus draws to a halt.

Chapter Twenty-Three

Storm clouds glide over the sun like giant eyelids. The wind swirls dirty leaves into impromptu dance. Walking down the narrow pavements awarded to the pedestrians of Eastleigh is like an obstacle course. I'm trying to catch up with Būi but barely making progress as I tiptoe around withered vegetables on sisal mats, their vendors haggling them away like old maidens. It's mid-afternoon and cooking smells are beginning to diffuse the odour of the open drain which the residents seem accustomed to. I think I've lost Būi and quicken my pace stretching my neck trying to spot her powder soft afro. She turns round beckoning like a honey bird alerting me to a beehive. Būi's stout flat feet pounce around puddles turning occasionally to check that I am still behind her, her infantile frame swerving with confidence. She ducks and dives, weaving her way round Ethiopian men outside injera restaurants gesticulating over waning Soviet Union support for Mengistu Haile Mariam. I snake around Somali women draped in *buibuis*, perfuming the air with henna. My call out to Būi is masked by the Somali Swahili dialect of the women conversing. Shoeshines beckon me, pointing at my scruffy shoes, inviting me to sit on their strategically placed metal stools.

A tugging on my cardigan spins me around. It's Būi. We are

standing outside an obtrusive black gate. She smiles revealing a row of jagged teeth.

'We are here. How do you feel?' asks Bũi.

I shrug. I don't know how I feel. I suppose I feel derailed and ambushed. Like a turtle in the open seas for the first time dodging sharks and sea snakes, uncertain of the world I find myself in. Seeing my hesitation, Bũi pushes open a small door, cut out of the large gate, and we step into a compound. A woman throws ashy water onto the gravel courtyard from a *sufuria*. We duck out of the way but are too late. We are now decorated with white splashes. She continues holding it on the side of her hips, leftover maize meal still stuck to the bottom and sides. She stares at Bũi from head to toe, her lazy eye wobbling. She turns to me tucking her buibui behind her ear as if it would affect her hearing. Her eyes glint with suspicion.

'Are you here for the clinic?'

'Yes,' Bũi says.

'Come this way,' she says, before walking to the gate, sticking her head out to the streets, looking around and pushing it shut again with a satisfied grunt.

We walk at her heel. The courtyard has many doors. She stops outside the one with 'Clinic' written on it. She knocks and pushes the door in, triggering a bell. A whiff of rotting blood escapes. It reminds me of southern Kĩrigiti by the abattoir. A man opens and scrutinises us with cold eyes above the gold rim of his glasses. He's holding a clipboard pinned to his chest by claw-like fingers. A name tag with the name Dr Njaũ is pinned to the pocket of his blood-stained lab coat. He steps aside, his butter-coloured wellies making a sloshing noise.

We hesitate and the woman waves her hand as if she is dealing with pests. We walk in and stand on a dry island of the floor which a cleaner in dirty uniform has missed.

'Is it both of them or just one?' His endless forehead floods with wrinkles against a hedge of cotton tufts of hair.

'Just one,' Būi interjects pointing at me.

'Do you want surgery or pill?' he asks.

The stark manner those options are presented to me feels like a concrete wall. I cannot see through it. They are words without context. Words without meaning. Everyone looks at me. I blink. I feel interrogated, the three of them judging me. Thinking I am one of those girls. I never considered myself to be one of them. Those girls, spoken of by sneering people full of bitter contempt for the era we live in. I am the example of what is wrong with society today. I am who old women cry about.

'I don't have all day. Do you want surgery or pill?' Dr Njaū's knobbly fingers waves his clipboard.

His coldness is chilling. I'm not privy to this information and don't know the difference. How can I know? That's only for the ears of gossipers like Wa Njūgū and the washerwomen. Never for girls like me. I force myself to speak but nothing comes out of my mouth.

'How much?' Būi asks.

We are interrupted by wailing. We turn to see what looks like a makeshift ward with hospital beds separated by shabby curtains on wheels. Three girls lie in each of the beds. To the left, a lifeless girl lies on a filthy mattress, her eyes opening and closing, her limbs twitching. Her face is gaunt and skin is rippled like a sun-dried prune. The second girl stares into a void aware of our presence, salivary bubbles escaping her mouth. The wail comes from the third girl who's trying to get out of bed by holding on to the bedframe and dragging her body sideways. She manages to swing her legs to the ground. A blob of blood smacks the floor, pooling. Dr Njaū rushes and yells, 'I told you not to get out of bed. You want the blood to stay inside you.'

She collapses and Dr Njaŭ lifts her and puts her back on the bed. He pushes his glasses up the bridge of his nose daubing them with blood in the process. He then pulls the curtain, smearing it too. My instinct tells me to run but I am immobile. Behind the curtain, Dr Njaŭ is calling out for a nurse who rushes over carrying a mop and bucket and a tray of surgical instruments.

'Hold still.' They say in unison.

'Let me die. Just let me die,' the girl wails.

'Are you going out tonight?' The woman who brought us in pretends not to hear what's going on.

'What?' Bŭi asks.

'*Mnaenda* club?'

We shake our heads and turn our attention back to the drama behind the curtain as the girl continues to whine. There appears to be a struggle then the moaning fades into a murmur. Then silence. I hold my breath hoping for her sound to return. It doesn't. My palms are sweating. I am staring at the curtain trying to visualise what he might be doing to her. Me. That will be me. A bolt of fear strikes through me. I feel the woman's eyes scrutinising me. Bŭi's eyes are on me too. I see the door through which we came is still open. Outside, the sun is shining but this room is bleak. I long to be out in the sunshine. Perhaps Mama will forgive me if she knows the whole story. She will know what to do and help me. But I can't tell her. She just forgave me for my expulsion by Wamakŭbŭ. That's too much strain on her. Besides, she's distraught about Mŭthoni's death. There's no way I could pile this onto her. I look towards the door. This place creeps me out. I need to leave, but Dr. Njaũ emerges skimming off the blood on his hands. He dries his palms on his lab coat and walks over to us.

'Surgery or pill.'

I swallow.

'Surgery or pill,' he says again.

He's irritated.

I don't want to be like those girls. Nor do I want Mama to ever see me like that. It would bring bad memories of Baba in his last days. I will die first than let her see me looking like them. I am fearful but I also accept this is my destiny. I must be strong and must face up to it.

'Surgery.' The coldness of those words makes me shiver.

'Give her a gown.' He instructs the nurse who hands me a blood-stained threadbare gown inscribed with Pumbewani Maternity Ward.

Bũi's smiles grimly at me. 'I'll come check on you tomorrow morning.'

I thought she'd stay with me. The thought of staying here by myself fills me with torment. I want to get out of this place as soon as possible.

'Pill! I meant pill,' I blurt out.

'I don't have time to play games,' Dr Njaũ growls.

'I am sorry. How much is the pill?'

'It's twenty-five bob,' he says.

I have not thought of the money situation. When I set out to go see Bũi, I hoped she would give me advice on my options and prices and then I would think about it. I never anticipated that she would walk me straight here. I only have enough fare to get me back home and that must be before Mama returns. Dr Njaũ stretches his hand out. We look at him confused.

'I said it's twenty-five bob for the pill.'

I turn to Bũi. Always perceptive, she senses I have no money and thrusts her hand into her bra pulling out a twenty shilling note.

'*Tusamehe tafadhali tuna twenty bob tu.*'

Dr Njaũ grabs the note and walks behind a desk. A black telephone sits beneath a pile of manila files. The tower of files tilt with vibrations as the phone begins to ring. Dr Njaũ ignores it. His fingers hover over the clutter on the desk. The phone is persistent. His fingers shuffle through medical cards, miscellaneous papers, gauzes, rubber gloves, used and unused syringes. Against the wall is a wooden bookshelf creaking under the weight of books and medical paraphernalia. He searches there too. He picks up a packet then squints to read it. The phone stops then rings again. He flings that packet on to the bookshelf then pulls out another packet which he struggles to open with his still bloody fingers. The phone is still ringing. Finally, he pulls out a silver packet and with scissors, he cuts out two pills and hands them to me.

'Take them before you go to sleep, and you should give birth by morning.'

These words are like a shower of light masking the disgust and fear I feel.

By morning I will be rid of this thing inside of me.

Chapter Twenty-Four

Blinded by darkness, my hands fumble around utensils, parcels of grain and flour and the few tin plates that populate our storage cupboard. At the back, I feel the packet I am looking for. With my palm contorted into a human bowl, I scoop the beans which *ching* into the steel *sufuria* I'm holding with my other hand. My fingers caress the paper like a blind man with Braille. They settle on a bigger packet, feeling the maize kernels reformulate inside. I add a few handfuls into the pan. These will take for ever to boil. At least there is water in the jerrycan which I tip over and fill the pot to the top. Placing it on the gas burner, I pat around the table for matches. With the room plunged into darkness, with the iron shutters still closed from when I left for Eastleigh, the only light coming in is from the door and I can barely see. I have no time to waste on that so this will have to do. I flick the cooker dial on its side and strike a match feeding the flame to the hissing gas.

In great haste, I grab the hem of my blouse, glide it up to my armpits then heave it over my shoulders. The zip of my skirt is undone as it's become too tight. I pull it down my legs. Diving on my bed, I bury it under the blankets. I reach for my pillow, lift it, and feel for the rough cotton of my going-nowhere dress. I wrestle into it and jump off the bed just as Mama walks in.

'Why are you cooking in the dark?'

Words hover in my throat and by the time they leave my mouth they are just jumbled up sounds. My eyes nearly erupt from their sockets when I spot the pills from Dr Njaū lying on the cooking table like an art exhibit. She doesn't spot them. Maybe her eyes haven't acclimatised to the darkness. With the speed of a hawk stealing a chick, I grab them and stuff them into my dress pocket.

'I thought it was getting dark, but it's too early to close the shutters,' I half laugh.

I try to appear calm. Pretending I haven't run from the bus stop and that I am not haunted by the images of those girls on the brink of death at Dr Njaū's clinic in Eastleigh. It was all I could think about on the journey. Lost in thought I looked out of the window to see Kaminde heave Mama into the bus before passing her the laden *kiondo*. They must have been to the city market seeing they were carrying vegetables. I could have fainted as they took their seats two rows in front of mine. I slid into the well of the seat distracted by how I would explain this journey to them. I kept my gaze low in case our eyes met if they turned round. When the bus stopped at the bottom of the curved marram road, I waited for them to alight then ducked the incoming traffic, springing across the road, through the maize crops only halting at our door.

Mama places the bag she's carrying on the unpolished concrete floor and unloads. She hands me *matoke* bananas, tomatoes and stem onions.

'These are to fry with the *gītheri*.'

I accept the vegetables and begin placing them in the cupboard.

'I know Kenya Power and Lighting are having problems with supply, but why are we rationing on daylight?' says Kaminde walking in.

He hands me a half kilo of sugar wrapped in thin paper covered with greasy handprints. Why can't he place it in the cupboard himself? He's done nothing all day and still expects to be waited on. I take it and place it by the cooker. From the corner of my eye, I see him pushing the drum out of the way, his sweet potato buttocks in the air, then turn, sinking into his worn leather seat with a grunt. His hand begins tapping on the drum. I know he's looking for something to keep him occupied. I grind my teeth with irritation. From the same pocket he stores his purposeless comb, he pulls out a toothpick. Lifting his upper lip like a Doberman about to attack, he drives it into the gap between his two front teeth and scrapes downwards. He brings the stick close to his face and begins studying the yellowy substance at the tip with light from the open door as if he were a scientist. Satisfied, he scrapes it on the back of his hand. With the stick clear, he goes for the next tooth piling the contents on his hand like miniature trophies. There's no end to this man's vileness. Today of all days I have no patience for his vulgarity. I'm debating whether I should reach over to open the shutters and see the full horrors of the contents of his mouth when the *gĩtheri* in the *sufuria* on the stove starts bubbling.

Mama reaches to the window and rotates the bent nail which secures the iron shutters when they are closed. Light floods in revealing the deepening lines on her once flawless mahogany face. Her oiled hair glistens, curls drooping on her forehead. Even after all that's happened, she still looks pretty. She peers into the rattling pot. I feel sorry for her. She's stuck with this good-for-nothing sorry excuse of a man and a daughter who is an utter disgrace.

'When did you begin cooking this?'

'An hour ago,' I say.

I haven't had a moment to digest the events of the day. I am on autopilot and not in control of my words. What's another lie to Mama? That's who I have become. A lying *chang'aa* buying delinquent, pregnant with an illegitimate child in search of illegal abortions. One more lie is nothing compared to the magnitude of the things I have done.

'It's still raw,' says Mama.

I grunt. She decants some water from a jerrycan into a smaller *sufuria* and places it on the other ring burner. From the cupboard, she pulls out tea leaves, scoops, and throws some into the water. Adding sugar and milk, she watches the mixture for a minute before turning round and exiting the room. I hear her unlocking the padlock of her room and clattering. Moments later, she walks back into the room clad in her evening *kitenge*.

I busy myself avoiding a conversation with Mama. Anything I say will give me away, so I go to the cupboard and pulling out three mugs place them next to the cooker. She leans over the cooker to check the tea, the flowers on her *kitenge* drawing the eyes to her voluptuous curves. The milky tea in the saucepan is rising to the top and she blows it into submission before it spills over. She turns off the gas and pours the tea into the three mugs I put out.

Mama hands Kaminde his mug, his short stubby fingers encircling the handle like an alien baby. Kaminde sips his tea, a film of milky grease coating his upper lip. Heat emanating from the cup warns my pouting lips to stay back. I am blowing the vapours, about to take a sip, when we hear a knock.

'*Hūdi?*'

I choke and spit out my tea. Blood is drumming in my ears. Gossip in this compound spreads like wildfire and I'm certain Wa Njũgũ or another rumour mongerer is here to tell Mama about my situation. I am not ready for this. I have not had a moment to compose a response. I can't face it. My brain is in overdrive thinking of what to say to Mama. I'll bolt through the door and run. Or deny everything. But how will I explain my expanding bump.

'Good evening, Mama Mũkami, we are here to speak to you about an important issue,' says the voice through the open door, always ajar to let in more light.

My heart ceases to pump. Mama places her tea on the drum and hurries over to the door. I peep through the crack by the hinges. I see the unmistakable curved back of Gathuki, with his bare ashy skinned shoulder exposed from the blanket he wears. Standing next to him hunched forward like an upright bat, I see Firifo. My nerves jump to attention. I scan around the room to see if I can flee. Oh no. My secret will be revealed. Why else would these people who have never once entered our house be here? It's obvious. They asked the holy man Firifo and the elder Gathuki to bring me in for judgement of my immorality.

'These greedy politicians are like maggots gnawing the bones of a poor man. I am certain they are behind that notice,' says Gathuki.

My ears must be translating the words about me to maintain my blood flow. Why else would I be hearing things about politicians being maggots?

'What notice?' says Mama stepping further out of the door in alarm.

Mama must be hearing what I am hearing too because she is enquiring about a notice. As if drawn by an external force I poke my ear out to listen.

'Lord Jesus, there was a notice posted on the toilet door this morning,' says Firifo.

Phew. They are here to talk about the notice and not about me. Oh, the notice. With the events of today, I forgot the notice. Poor Mama will not take the news well. Placing my mug on the drum, I step closer to the door by Mama's feet. Kaminde jumps to his feet too and stands next to Mama, his pancake face peering at Gathuki and Firifo.

'Mr Firifo and Bwana Gathuki, we have not placed any notice anywhere. I was out buying spare parts for my *matatū*,' says Kaminde.

I wish I could shut him with a smack across his nose. As if anyone is interested hearing anything about his scrap metal. Kaminde waits for their reaction. They don't seem shocked or impressed so he carries on.

'Yes, I have a nice minibus which will be operating between Nairobi and Kīrigiti. It's having a few problems.'

A few problems? That car is practically rusted metal. Kaminde's words grind me like carrots to a grater. Nobody takes note and his bragging dissipates like dust in the wind. Firifo and Gathuki don't respond instead they turn to Mama.

'Mama Mūkami, glory be to the almighty, what we are here to say is in response to the eviction notice—,' says Firifo blowing his large nose into a handkerchief.

Mama's jaw drops.

'Eviction? Oh no! What eviction notice? I didn't see it.'

'It says that on the morning of twenty eighth of February we have to vacate the compound,' says Gathuki.

Mama goes pale. I think she'll faint. I rush to her and hold her. Firifo, Gathuki, Kaminde do the same all bashing heads. It's almost comical but no one laughs. They step back.

'That's the date they are coming to demolish the kiosks,' says Mama.

I look at her face in the fading light and see the wrinkles around her eyes. Worry has eroded her youth. I must protect Mama. I am all she has left. The finality of the date highlights the urgency of my situation. My hand slides down to the pocket and feel Dr Njaũ's tablets. *By morning you'll have given birth.* Those words ring in my head. I need to take them urgently.

'That's just over a week away. We can't leave, where will we go? We have nowhere to go,' Mama says.

She buries her face in her hands and begins to cry. I want to embrace her, but Wa Njũgũ's comments this morning made me self-conscious. If she can tell my condition, why wouldn't Mama? I am overcome with self-loathing knowing how distraught she'll will be when she finds out about me. Doesn't she already have enough problems? How can I be the one adding salt to Mama's wounds? Why can't I be the one she can rely on?

I step closer to the door feeling I should comfort Mama, but Gathuki extends his wrinkled hand to Mama's shoulder, his eyes laden with sympathy. I don't get closer, conscious of unwanted scrutiny.

'We all live in limbo, drifting around the soils of our ancestors without an anchor. Like lost nomads on unfamiliar grounds. None of us have anywhere to go,' says Gathuki.

Why does he speak in parables? Why can't he speak like everyone else?

'We have to pray to our Lord Jesus Christ to illuminate this path,' says Firifo.

He pats the top pocket of his shirt in which he keeps his grubby bible.

'Only we can help ourselves. We are inviting everyone to join us for a meeting tomorrow night to discuss an action plan,' says Gathuki.

By tomorrow night, I will have given birth. That thought is comforting. The world will be a different place. Once I get rid of it, I can be there to cushion Mama's distress. I must find the earliest opportunity to swallow the pills that will release me from this muddy wilderness I am stuck in.

'I guess we have nothing to lose,' says Mama.

She stops sobbing and lifts her face. She looks pathetic and sad. If only she had a real man to protect her, instead she's lumbered with a useless oaf. I want to be the one to dry her tears away. I want to return to school, and study even harder. I want to be a top geologist and she and I will live together in a beautiful home. Tears are rolling down my eyes.

'Don't cry *mwana wakua,* all will be well,' Mama says reaching out to touch my hand.

I didn't mean to draw attention to myself, so I smile.

'Some of the residents are hesitating, maybe you could join us in going round to convince the doubters that we can fight for our homes,' says Gathuki.

Firifo pulls out his black book of credit and opens a new page. 'I think we should make a list of residents to contact.'

Our eyes focus on his twig fingers and blunt pencil pointed on the paper. Nothing happens.

'I am suffering from a case of stiff fingers. Bwana Kaminde, you do the writing,' says Firifo.

He avoids my gaze. I've long suspected he can't read or write. He records credit in his book by drawing sticks. This man is a fraud hiding behind God. But then again so am I. A big fat fraud. Standing here pretending that all is well.

Kaminde takes the notebook and steps away from the door into the gravel outside our house. Everyone crowds him and I move closer. He thumps his chest, burps, then begins the list.

Bwana Firifo

Bwana Gathuki

Bwana Kaminde

Madam Mama Mũkami

'It might be quicker if we assume everyone is a bwana or a madam,' says Gathuki. 'Who else should we include?'

'Wa Njũgũ, women with many children always evoke sympathy,' says Kaminde.

At the mention of her name, I freeze remembering our encounter at the ablutions area.

'What do you think of that chap by the tap? Very odd fellow.' Gathuki paces up and down in deep thought his tyre sandals grating the gravel path.

Firifo looks up to the darkening sky as if reading a name from up there.

'I suppose he is a strong man but definitely very strange. The way he displays his muscular arms and well-formed manhood for all to see is ungodly. He drops his eyes and says, 'I could wrestle him.'

We turn to look at Firifo in confusion. He must sense our gaze because he shifts uncomfortably.

'God forbid if he were ever to attack me or my wife. I guess we need strong men like him. His name is... aw it escapes me... it's... Ndekezie.'

Gathuki nods, his grey eyebrows congregating above his nose in thoughtful agreement.

'Oh, wait a minute. Our case might be strengthened by the dying woman,' says Gathuki.

Kaminde scribbles at the same time releasing a fart. He doesn't even look up. Just like him to spoil the air and not even apologise. It smells vile and I stand back.

Firifo's face lights up.

'Oh yes, we will include her. If she speaks about her dying that will definitely strengthen our battle,' says Firifo.

How is a dying woman going to help the fight for the living? These village dwellers have zero common sense. She spends all the time singing funeral songs. She's already living in purgatory. I dare not make my reservations known for fear of attracting attention.

'How about the chap in the corner with an elephant leg?' asks Gathuki. But before anyone can speak, he continues. 'Yes, we could argue homelessness and hardship will worsen his ever-growing leg, demonstrating the harshness of such an eviction.'

Great. This is going to be a carnival for the sick and the dying.

Minds blank, we stare on the names on the list.

Bwana Firifo

Bwana Gathuki

Bwana Kaminde

Madam Mama Mũkami

Wa Njũgũ

Dying woman

Elephantiasis

'How about the fellow that strolls around the compound like he owns it?' asks Gathuki.

'Gĩtonga, his name is Gĩtonga,' says Firifo almost too quickly.

With all the names jotted in Firifo's black book of credit, everyone is absorbed with searching for names to add to the list. Mama looks as if her world has ended. She instructs me to step inside the kitchen and turn off the stove. Still preoccupied with Dr. Njaũ's comment, I step into our house. I need to swallow the pills now whilst everyone is outside.

Guided by the flame from the hob, I reach underneath the table and lift the jerrycan. It's empty. Mama used up the remaining water to make tea. I could swallow the pills with the tea we were drinking before the interruption by Gathuki and

Firifo. I reach for the cup but it's too hot to swallow the pills. I am fumbling around the dark looking for another jerrycan. Damn they are all empty. Mama calls my name.

'Mūkami, get a cardigan and join us.'

I place the jerrycans back, grab my cardigan and run out to join the group. I will find another opportunity, I'm sure.

Gathuki's tyre sandals step over the open sewer as we follow behind like ill-prepared soldiers. I am at the back of the queue. I should have brought a jerrycan with me to fetch water at the earliest convenience, but I forgot. Maybe I will get a chance later to fetch water for my pills. Sizzles emanating from open windows, greet our ears as we walk round the back row of houses. People are preparing their evening meals filling the night air with competing aromas.

Shadows begin to merge into the last of the daylight, and the dying woman is just rolling up the mattress on which she spends most of her days. Her sombre gaze is downcast accentuating her long, once elegant neck. The baubles of her plaited hair are erect. She is humming and picking out dried grass and twigs stuck to the sponge, to the rousing chirrups of crickets. She is startled to see Firifo and Gathuki standing in front of her, and me with Mama watching from behind them.

'May the Lord almighty give you his glory,' says Firifo.

'Please excuse us mama—,' Gathuki says.

Nobody appears to know if she is a mother to attach to her name in accordance with Gīkūyū traditions, so Firifo intervenes.

'May you receive untold blessings,' he says.

'I take it you have seen that notice on the door,' says Gathuki.

Firifo is gesticulating and pointing to the toilet clearly visible from her position.

'I will be dead by then,' the dying woman says.

She turns and begins singing a funeral song. *This world is not my home, I am just passing by.*

The two men hesitate unsure how to proceed with sensitivity.

'Please allow us to explain. We want to call for a *kĩama* to fight for our homes. May the Grace of God give you a long life and if that is the case, we would hate to see you homeless in your final days. If you join us, we can argue about the inhumanity and in the face of the corrupt efforts to evict us,' says Firifo.

'We would be humbled by your attendance to the meeting tomorrow night at the shop at seven pm,' says Gathuki.

They stand back awaiting her response. Still humming, she lifts her mattress, turning it round so that the bottom is now at the top. Maybe I could sneak to the tap and fetch some water. I can see the ablution area is clear. I'm about to walk away when the dying woman responds.

'I guess it's something to do,' she says arranging and rearranging her mattress.

'We would like to return your gratitude by nominating you to take a lead role in the matter,' says Gathuki.

She says nothing.

'We will leave you in peace for now as we have others to visit.'

We turn round and walk towards the next row of houses. I trail at the back of the queue. I don't want to encourage any loose-tongued residents to give me away by making myself prominent. I'm glad the fading light is giving me some obscurity.

Darkness is broken by speckles of light from lanterns and fires as families settle down for the night. A beam from the torch illuminates the door which is ajar as Gathuki knocks.

His window is open, and I stand by the ledge to watch from there as everyone crowds at his door. I don't engage with the residents but want to be here in case Mama becomes upset. I will be there for her.

I stretch my neck and stare at the resident of plot number one. He is blowing into an iron tube, coaxing the fire of his *thagiri* like a snake charmer. Ndekezie's ashen face is startled as he jumps to his feet. Unfocused eyes stare in fright. He is shirtless and his wide shorts cling on to his hips.

'What is it?' he asks.

Firifo steps forward extending his giant hand to him and clears his throat. 'Glory be to God on this blessed day for I have accepted the Lord as my—'

This is going to take all night.

'We are here about the notice on the toilet door,' says Gathuki.

The dim light of the lantern is enough to pick out Gathuki's wrinkles that appear to be entrenching deeper into his face.

'I did not put it there. You can't blame me,' says Ndekezie.

His mannerisms make me feel sorry for him. He recoils like a cornered leopard every time someone talks to him. He looks like he could run any minute.

'We know it's not you, why would you do it?' Firifo says letting his hand drop to his side.

'I didn't do it.'

'We've never spoken, let me introduce myself properly. I am Gathuki the one leading this mission.' Gathuki unfurls his back like an army general. 'This is Firifo. We are forming a committee to fight for our right to remain here at the Ministry of Works. We would like you to join the committee so that we can keep our homes.'

'What committing? I am not committing. Don't think you can just accuse me of committing anything,' he shrinks and cowers even further into the corner.

'We have a meeting tomorrow night. Please be at the shop at seven o'clock sharp. We intend on fighting to keep our homes,' says Gathuki his face tense as if trying to read the young man's reaction.

'Fighting, I am not fighting.'

'It's not a physical fight. Come if you can.' Gathuki signals that we should leave him alone.

I watch Ndekezie from the window, sensing the fear on his face. It's as if he is fighting an invisible enemy. I freeze. There go the flutters in my belly again. A constant reminder highlighting my invisible enemy. My life is headed into a precarious future. If only I can sneak away and take these pills poking me from my pocket.

Everyone congregates outside Ndekezie's house.

'Where to next, the evening is running away with us,' says Kaminde. His tummy rumbles corresponding with a burp.

'Let's visit that fellow at number eight,' says Gathuki.

We hear footsteps and Gathuki shines his torch to illuminate the large forehead of little Ruth who is anchored onto her mother Jane, Firifo's wife's, skinny hip. Not more people. Women with children make me feel uncomfortable. They are suspicious. They seem to take an interest in me in a way that makes me nervous.

'Approach him with caution. Gītonga is a very sly man. Can convince a mother to give him her baby for sure, but we may need his skills,' says Kaminde.

I look at Jane who chokes at the mention of the name Gītonga. Her thin face is uncomfortable. Gathuki and Firifo nod in agreement, their noses illuminated by the torchlight.

I follow the others' footsteps hopping around debris on the mud path leading to Gĩtonga's house. Maybe I should detour via the tap and take my pills. Mama turns and extends her hand for me as is sensing my intention. Gĩtonga's door is ajar. Gathuki and Firifo walk in first and everyone else stands to attention. I peep from behind everyone. It's the first time I've had a chance to study him and he's as grotesque as I made him out to be. His presence makes my skin crawl. The lurid gestures and his hungry eyes always make me want to hide. Looking at his large behind overflowing on a tiny stool is nauseating. He is in a duel with the smoke and waves his hand to shift it from his face. The stubble on his chin protrudes as he blows into the fire, which spits sparks. He doesn't look up instead stealing a side gaze at the legs in front of him. I see a machete glinting on the bare concrete and wonder what his intention is as he uses his foot to push it closer to him.

'Bwana Gĩtonga have you heard about the notice? We would like to speak to you about it,' says Gathuki.

Gĩtonga is silent but casts a gaze at us.

'Don't you think I have things to do. I am not an idler like people of this compound?'

'Oh no, as Jesus is my witness, that thought hasn't crossed my mind. We are forming a committee to fight the eviction,' says Firifo.

'And you want my permission?'

'Quite a few residents have agreed to come and discuss the eviction,' says Gathuki.

Gĩtonga looks at our faces and flashes a smile.

'Sure, see you there.'

I am glad he can't see me. I remember his lurid actions at the tap this morning whilst waiting for the toilet, and shiver. What's wrong with these men? It doesn't matter how old, how poor, rich or young they are. They are all horrible. I step away, feeling the anger from this morning's car journey.

Aided by the torchlight Kaminde consults the book, ticking off Gĩtonga's name and points to the next one.

'We will visit her next. Having other people to see, will help with our haste,' says Gathuki.

Everyone stares at Wa Njũgũ's name. From their reaction, it's clear I am not the only one that views her with apprehension. Most people must know the consequences of being trapped by her gossip. There are butterflies in my stomach. I don't want her to out me. She is unpredictable and I don't know what she'll say to Mama. I can hear Mama breathing heavily, weighted by the news of the eviction notice.

A crying infant alerts us we are nearing Wa Njũgũ's. My heart rate increases with every step I take towards her. Her unpredictability makes me anxious, and I don't want her letting off her mouth bombs tonight. I stand back waiting for everyone to enter her house, whose door is always open. I am hovering at the back and I can see her face, softened by the dim lighting of the lantern. Why does this woman cause me so much dread. Looking at her from my position she looks harmless, but I know her mouth is poison. She looks comfortable with the intrusion as if she was a queen in council. She is sitting on a stool her dress sagging between her legs which are spread far apart. The baby on her lap whose mouth is suctioned on her nipple turns to look at me without breaking the seal. I hold my breath but realise it's too dark for her to see me. On the other side, her stretched out toddler releases the darkened nipple which points at us. This woman repulses me. She's not my future, I mutter underneath my breath making the others turn to look in my direction. I'm now impatient to take my pills. Her elder daughter is hunched over the stove holding a wooden spoon which she thrusts in the pan swirling the *terere* in it.

'Come in. I saw you going to Gĭtonga's house and wondered if you knew about his escapade,' she says.

'Rumour is like pollen. It doesn't land everywhere,' says Gathuki.

'The night watchman knows the foreman of The Approved School and he was saying that he used to drive for a *mzungu* and fled after an accident.'

'May the blood of Jesus wash his sins away,' says Firifo.

Once speaking, no one knows where Wa Njŭgŭ's conversation will go so I remain tucked well away in the comfort of darkness.

'He run someone over on the way to Kilimanjaro. That *mzungu* was nearly killed in the slum. No one knows exactly what happened but apparently a woman was involved. Women are always involved with him.'

As if to mask the denigration of Gĭtonga's character, Jane, Firifo's wife, coughs making me jump.

'Mama Wa Njŭgŭ, we come in great haste to invite you to the meeting tomorrow evening to discuss the eviction. Seven pm at the shop,' says Gathuki turning round. 'It must be your children's bedtime. We won't keep you any longer.'

Everyone turns round and walks in the direction of Elephantiasis's house before she can say another word. He is out. After making our final call to a few others, we walk in a single file in silence guided by torchlight, saluted by rats on their nightly exploits. I think I should slip away. Doubting anyone will notice with the hullabaloo of the night, I am about to step away to take my pills when Mama holds onto my hand.

'My daughter deserves a stable home. What is the value

of this independence if we will never see the fruits of it? We were homeless because the *wazungu* stole our land and now the *mzungu* is gone we are still vagrants.'

Gathuki stops, turns round, and shines the torch on his wrinkled thigh. I look down to see knots of adhesion and dents on his thigh. I gasp.

'This is when I was caught by a snare in Burma fighting for the coloniser.' He rolls the sleeve of the coat he wears over his blanket to reveal another scar along his biceps.

'Oh Lord have mercy,' says Firifo.

'This is from a warthog, from when I served under General Mathenge in the Aberdares. I fought for the British and I fought against the British and what do I have to show for it? Just scars. I don't even have a home to call my own, our own leaders shunned their freedom fighters,' says Gathuki.

I see the same pained look of bitter disappointment I saw in the eyes of the *chang'aa* woman. Gathuki's old eyes appear to weep with the burden of history.

'When we returned from Burma, they didn't even tell us the mission was finished, they just dropped us in the middle of a street in Eastleigh with no money or food.' He draws a phlegmy breath and rubs his face. 'That's how they told us the mission was over. Being dumped in the streets,' says Gathuki.

'We should not hold grudges and we should forgive and forget, following in Jesus's footsteps,' says Firifo.

Gathuki is struck by those words and his face tenses with anger, his beady eyes full of scorn.

'Who does the white man ever forgive? He did not forgive us when they grabbed Gĩkũyũ land. If it weren't for the white man, we would not be destitute.' He slaps his hollow chest in anger.

'Aha. If it wasn't for the white man we wouldn't have roads,' says Kaminde.

'Our lack of roads wasn't because we couldn't create them, it was for safety. You don't give enemies access to your home, we ensnared and booby-trapped paths to keep slave traders and raiders at bay,' says Gathuki.

'But we have civilisation, education and—,' Kaminde scratches his egg head in animation.

I am cold, hungry, and have an abortion to conduct. I don't have time, nor do I want to be here listening to this debate. I let Mama's hand go as I intend on sneaking away from them. They are distracting me from my mission.

'Destitution. We had civilisation before the white man. What we have now is chaos and backwardness. Every Gĩkũyũ was equal. Living in similar houses, eating, and wearing the same thing. No one was allowed to be poor,' says Gathuki full of bitterness.

'Too much belief in superstition,' says Kaminde.

'Why does the white man greet magpies if not for superstition?' Gathuki is silent. 'He fears the strength of our power thus destroying our people and our habitat. Our lands once ripened with lablab now rots with useless coffee.'

I take a few steps back careful not to attract attention. I am about to take another step when Mama reaches out to Gathuki.

'Bwana Gathuki, our tummies are rumbling, and they say a Gĩkũyũ house is open to all. Come let's have some ũcũrũ.'

Gathuki's face softens in the harsh lighting of the torch. He turns illuminating the way as everyone heads towards our house. I thrust my hand into my pocket. The pills. *By morning you will have given birth.* It replays in my mind, and I am still clutching the pills when we walk past the pit latrine, then the tap. Turning away from the group, I bend towards the tap, twist the faucet, shove the pills in my mouth, and in one big gulp, I swallow.

Chapter Twenty-Five

The tin walls of our ramshackle house are closing in. It's claustrophobic. Our impromptu guests compete for the stale air with our rusty kerosene lamp which flickers in protest. I wish I could escape but there's nowhere to go, if only to sift through my thoughts. I am not allowed to go to the ablutions area by myself at night in case there are creepy men lurking in the dark. So, I am confined to this space crowded with ambivalence.

Crouched on my narrow bed wedged behind the sofas, my internal feelers are on high alert for signs that Dr Njaũ's tablets are working. The glow of the kerosene lamp illuminates the sombre faces of Gathuki, Firifo, Kaminde and Mama. From my position the group appears ghoulish and long like a bunch of robbers in a den. Gathuki's bottom is squeezed in one corner. He looks ill at ease as if his bony buttocks are unaccustomed to padded seating instead of the usual old men preference of *njungwa*. His traditional blanket is misplaced against the aged tan leather like a clash of eras. Firifo's long limps protrude from his hips like a praying mantis. If I wasn't in such torment, I would laugh because they look like caricatures from *The Tales of Abunuwazi*.

My mind is cluttered with this morning's events at that wretched 'doctor' Njaũ's clinic. My fingers are curled around the empty foil casing that held the pills, the edges biting into my palm, but I am too afraid to unfurl. The presence of the pill casing provides tangible hope for my salvation, my future. I long for the days when my holidays from boarding school were a blur of boredom. My escape was reading and re-reading the formation of the Rift Valley in the geography textbook I found discarded by the classroom. That was a lifetime ago. Dr Njaŭ's words, *by morning you will have given birth* resound in my ears. That hope creates an impatience for the morning, a new dawn without the baggage in my abdomen.

I can begin again days of innocence with a clean slate: wearing my uniform without the shame of an unwanted bulge, playing hockey without my nipples stinging, eating in the dining hall without running to the toilet to vomit. In my redemption, maybe I will recapture the innocence and trust that existed. Reclaim my decency as a top student. That place seems so close, yet so far away.

My thoughts are interrupted by the heavy sound of sorghum porridge crushing against the gourd walls in sync with my hunger. For a moment, I'm drawn to the drama, a reprieve from my woes. Mama invited them for sorghum porridge, but I suspect she wants comfort about the eviction. I should have objected. But my throat was clogged with the pills from Dr Njaŭ. By the time I turned round the figures were turning the corner heading to our house.

I sweep my eyes round the room, and something strange happens. The earth is spinning, and I am still. Gathuki's mottled skin seems to shimmer like stagnant water in the moonlight. My insides are being pulled by an invisible force towards an imaginary sinkhole. I keep my gaze at Gathuki to ground myself. His furrowed face is motionless, his arched back still like a startled iguana.

The lamp is creating long shadows, their hunched backs crowding round the slender corner stool on which our transistor radio usually sits but now is replaced by the lamp. I remember our drum coffee table was moved in the adjacent room to create leg space for the guests. Now I imagine it sprawled with its legs in the air like a drunkard on Mama's bed.

I look at their faces hooded with a worry distinctly different from mine and yet intertwined. I am excluded from their world by the gulley between adulthood and adolescence, with a bridge riddled with obstacles and I am expected to navigate without tools to help me. I am lost like a small boat in ferocious seas. I need guidance and I can't ask. In this crowded room I am engulfed by loneliness. The call of a distant dog is greeted with an eruption of enthusiastic howls as if to mock me.

I haven't thought of what to expect but all I know is I will have given birth by the morning according to Dr Njaŭ. I'm clueless as to how the baby will come out, but the reel of his reassurances keeps replaying in my mind. Maybe it will wriggle out like a worm but from which end? The washerwomen said there are aborted babies in the pit latrine. That's possibly how they end up there. When Mama gave me worm medicine, I defecated on a newspaper so she could see if the worms had come out. We peered at the miniature albino snake-like worms milling around the faeces. I wonder if that's how the baby will come out. Is there a newspaper close by that I can defecate on to check if the baby has come out? Then I remember someone saying that babies come out of the urine hole. I shudder at the thought. It's disturbing. I think of a wet worm-like baby on my pants. Maybe I will fling it out of the window. I am horrified by the thought of it landing on someone's head on their way to the ablutions.

Mama shakes the gourd. Kaminde's longing stray cat eyes

follow her hand movement. Firifo licks his cracked lips with a silvery tongue. The rumbling *gĩtheri* on the stove and the shaking gourd provide the background to the drama. Mama shakes it again making sure the flour and liquid harmonise. She tilts the gourd's mouth to the cups she just rinsed. The porridge splodges as it lands in the bottom of the tin cups. Gathuki's hand is extended like a chameleon in motion. Mama looks like the high priest offering me redemption. I stretch out to reach for the *ũcũrũ* she is handing me.

From the pit of my bowels, a steel hand clenches me. I freeze. Mama's and my eyes meet. It's not the high priest, it's my mother. She is staring at me a bit too long as if trying to read something inscribed on my face. I think of the baby inside me, and my face is overcast with the shame I brought onto her. Her look of perceptive tenderness slices through my heart. I take my porridge and bow my head. I don't want her to unearth my secret, but I can't mask the sharpening pain in my abdomen. She is still staring at me. I summon all the courage I can muster and bring the porridge to my lips to sip it, but the tensing is too intense. Gathuki slurps his porridge like a mating frog and Mama turns in his direction.

'They don't make *ũgĩmbĩ* like they did in the olden days,' says Mama.

The noise they are making is amplified by an invisible megaphone. I want them to shut up and let me concentrate on what is happening inside of me. I think the baby is having a dual with the medicine I took. I'm having visions of the baby dressed like a Gĩkũyũ warrior, slicing through the pills which have miniature faces of Dr Njaũ.

Gathuki's slurping makes me turn in his direction too. His mug remains close to his mouth. He sips the thick mass of the *ũcũrũ* through his pouted lips. He then turns to the side and sprays the contents of his mouth to the floor, nodding to the ancestors. He slurps again.

'*Mwathani nia agathuo. Thaai thathai Ngai Thaai.*'

'You blaspheme the true God with your idol God,' says Firifo to Gathuki gulping down the porridge and springing to his feet ready to leave. 'Our merciful God will purify you if you repent.'

Repent? Maybe I should repent. Is this why I am in this predicament? Because I turned away from the true God? How can I tell the difference between the two Gods? I prayed every night. I asked to be a top student and what does God do? He throws me into this pit of desolation and expulsion from school. Should I repent to an unresponsive God? At least Ngai the God of my grandmother always responded to their pleas of rain. But I guess that's all everyone always asked for.

I sense the presence of my ancestors. They are watching me flinching in regret and pity. They must be wondering how I, we, rejected their influence that once guided the tribe. Their sadness permeates the invisible barrier between immortality and mortality.

'The white man's God has no redemption for the black man. That's why the black man is always the white man's slave.' Gathuki is irritated. His tummy rumbles rattling his ashy legs protruding from underneath his blanket. The corners of his wet eyes are plugged by white gunk as he stares at Firifo. I hold my breath hoping they'll all leave.

Kaminde burps. He is sitting in his armchair; his fat fingers twitching with excitement. His small potato head swivels between Gathuki and Firifo, who are sharing the two-seater, revelling in their quarrel. The dense sisal-like aroma of boiling beans, mixed with the odour of unwashed bodies, is overshadowed by their animosity. The two are separated by their very differing views of modernity. I shift to get comfortable.

'*Tafadhali wazee*, please calm down. Can't you see we worship a new god that doesn't see colour nor background,' Kaminde says belching and thumping on his chest. Again.

His words wobble to my ears as if they have been processed by a mythical medium. It reminds me of an eerie sound made by a steel sheet being shaken.

'Money is a more powerful god, one that makes a woman poison her husband. A god so powerful that a man will kill another to service this god,' says Kaminde.

Dr Njaũ has given me poison. This is why I feel so queasy, and my abdominal muscles are spasming. This is what he did to those girls in his clinic. I push those memories into my chamber of unsorted issues. *By morning you'll have given birth.* I need to suppress the rising panic. I chant the words with my inaudible voice. Everything is crammed into my head and compounded by the crowding in our living-kitchen-bedroom.

The sagging skin underneath Mama's arms sways, as she shakes the gourd even harder, as if to disrupt the argument. The motion roils the contents of my stomach, so I look away covering my eyes with my hands.

'Bwana Gathuki, you rise at dawn as if you are still in the clasp of the coloniser. Bwana Firifo you are never without your two bibles. You are both governed by a new god. The Maasai say the evil red god *Enkai Nanyuoki* is always seething with anger causing evil but when it rains, the low growl of thunder is a rebuke of *Enkai Narok* the kind black god,' says Kaminde.

Maybe my problems are the rebuke of a red god. I want to know more about the kind black god. I need him to show his prominence because I'm in search of redemption.

For a moment, everyone is silent. Each of us wrestling with our inner beasts. There's a rhythm to the bubbling *gītheri* on the cooking table. Mama reaches over lifts a steel lid and places it on the pan. Firifo is immobilised by the promise of a second helping of *ŭcŭrŭ* as Mama pours out more.

'Judgement day will be upon us soon, come to church and listen to the word of a just God,' says Firifo.

This is judgement day. The day of my reckoning. I am being judged for the weakness of allowing Kĩmathi to lead me astray.

'Thou shalt not worship fake gods,' says Firifo.

He sounds Godly. I think he's rebuking me, but I am in too much pain to say anything.

'I worship Ngai Mwene Nyaga, like your father and his fore-fathers,' says Gathuki.

I am puzzled because I think I uttered those words but I'm certain they came from Gathuki's mouth.

I shift on my bed trying to ease the discomfort I feel.

'Jesus Christ died on the cross for you Bwana Gathuki.' Firifo is now standing up, a growl on his face.

I need to cover my ears. I can't listen to their arguments anymore. Of all days, this had to be the one. The one day I needed head space is when the ideological war of gods is in full swing. A bolt of sharp pain passes through me and is ricocheting to every tissue of my body. I'm going to die.

The pain passes and I open my eyes. From my position, and the dull lighting of the room Firifo looks like a middle-aged tortoise. I watch the movement of his jaw and the slit that is his mouth open and close. His words are fading, and I can't make out what he is saying. It reminds me of the scrambled paper underneath my pillow with the list of my enemies and my revenge. They are flashing in my mind like neon lights.

My enemies

*Kīmathi * —physical punishment and prayers for bad things to happen*

*Wambūgū * —physical punishment and prayers for bad things to happen*

Geremani —physical punishment and prayers for bad things to happen*

Oily Man in jungle lair —physical punishment and prayers for bad things to happen

Eastleigh turnboy —prayers for bad things to happen

*Kaminde *—physical punishment and prayers for mangoes to fall on his pointed head or his matatū to get stuck in the mud*

Gathuki wipes his nose and looks at Kaminde who's taken over the debate with a deep interest, his eyes squinting.

My abdomen cramps and I think I am going to scream.

'What's all this got to do with religion?' Firifo's keen ears, enlarging like satellite dishes, tune in to hear Kaminde's response.

Their voices flow in and out as if transmitted on distant radiowaves.

Mama tips more *ūcūrū* into Firifo's mug.

'You see in those days the white man did all the work for himself, just him and his ox.'

My body weighs heavy as if I am dragging an ox. Hot and

sweaty, I need air. Gathuki and Mama are silent. I am gasping but trying not to make a sound and there are multiple tug-of-wars taking place in my belly. I take a deep breath and that helps a little.

'Like the Maasai, we have two gods. That's Want and Money. Both are evil. Both feed on greed and need. We are addicts, always wanting. How many suits do you own bwana Firifo? How many dresses does your wife Jane own?'

'I had a dream last night.' Gathuki turns away from everyone's glare.

My reality is warped. I'm having a dream too. I don't know whether these people are arguing in my head or in real life. If they are in my dream, I want to wake up.

'Everyone has those,' Firifo bows his head.

'No, you don't understand. It was a premonition.' Gathuki looks disturbed. 'I dreamt that we were having a meeting in Firifo's shop, and I was addressing everyone. Firifo's wife Jane was standing behind me with her daughter Ruth close to her feet.

Gathuki's narration, his solemn intonation, is drawing me in.

'I began speaking and noticed the menace in the attendees' eyes. I turned round to Jane, who stood close to me, and her eyes turned blood red with stark black pupils. On her head were long sharp horns like the devil. It was the look she gave me,' Gathuki shudders. 'She gave me the most wicked look, and when my eyes shifted to little Ruth, she too, had the same red eyes and horns.'

I look round the room, now everyone here has horns like Jane and Ruth in Gathuki's dream.

'She was staring at me with the same contempt of her mother. I was petrified. When I turned round, the attendees too had configured to look like Jane and Ruth. It was hot, as if I was in hell surrounded by demons. It's a warning!'

The eyes in the room glare like leopards in the night. I blink desperate to confirm it's a dream.

'The whole place smelt of death. I began to scream but everyone began laughing at me,' continues Gathuki. 'When I looked out of the window, the plants were all black and vultures and crows circled in the air and began swooping towards me. The bird's sharp claws began tearing my flesh away. Everyone laughed even louder.'

The flesh in my abdomen is being torn away!

'When I bled, they licked my blood. The only person that looked normal was you Mũkami.'

All eyes turn round to look at me. An owl hooting from close by seems to signal a shift from the stuffiness of the night to a sudden chill.

'It was as if you had magical powers to heal. Everyone was a demon but you. You tried to help me, but the birds got in the way. They drained all the blood away from me and that's when I woke up.'

Firifo is shaking with worry. 'What could it all mean?'

This revelation deepens my fear. Gathuki's words are real and tangible. As if they are coming to life, blending with my thoughts. I can see the vultures circling me. They are hungry for my baby. MY baby. I thought of it as my baby. It's not my baby, it's THE baby and I want it out. Give it to the vultures to feed on. This plunges me back to events of the morning, the girls in the clinic on the cusp of death, bleeding out, the vultures' sharp beaks piercing their fragile skin. There's a whirling in my abdomen. I fear there's going to be an eruption.

'That *dudu* is too close for comfort,' says Gathuki. 'I fear it's an omen!'

'These are days of Sodom and Gomorrah, we must repent,' says Firifo.

My abdomen is clenched by the claws of a thousand crows and images of the girl bleeding everywhere flashes in my mind. The wrath of the pills is now evident. Fear rises from the well of my stomach. With my hands wrapped tightly round my abdomen, I resign myself to my destiny. It's the price girls pay for bearing a womb. When our great ancestor Gĩkũyũ was commanded by Ngai to descend from the peaks of the mountain of brightness to find his bride Mũmbi, this is not the destiny he had in mind. Mũmbi's womb was sacred. She would bear the sacred fruit sustaining the Gĩkũyũ, but those girls in the clinic do not possess the sacred womb. Theirs is cursed like mine.

I let out an involuntary moan that fills the room. My arms are crossed against my belly, and I am doubled over in pain. Everyone turns round to look at me. Mama looks at me with confusion, then clarity, then looks at them. She heads to the cupboard and pulls a packet of Panadol. She pushes two out and hands them to me with a mug of water.

'It's woman trouble,' she says, 'the full moon.'

The men nod in ghoulish embarrassment.

She rushes to her room and brings back a big ball of cotton wool wrapped discreetly in newspaper. The headline reads Modern Girls, No Barrier to Success. Those girls in the clinic found being on the cliff edge of life and death is a big barrier to success. I have never known any girl that has made it smoothly through into adulthood, without having to fight the piranhas and sharks first. Not many are unscathed. It's the modern initiation of girls, no longer the circumciser's razor, but this reality of back street abortions, men with no scruples and AIDS.

I swallow the Panadol and tears are streaming down my face.

'Those will make you feel better,' says Mama returning to the gourd. To distract from the sombreness of the room, she shakes the last of the porridge. Gathuki now staring at the gourd says, 'Give that to me.'

'You can have the last bit,' Mama laughs, but notices that he is looking at the markings on the side of the gourd. 'It's just decoration.'

'*Gicaadĩ*, it's ancient Gĩkũyũ writing. Where did this come from? Rinse the porridge out and please hand me the gourd.' Gathuki hands the gourd back to Mama.

'Wariara, a new woman who joined our *kĩama*. She brought it today.' Mama tips water from the jerrycans, shakes the gourd, rinsing the last morsels of the porridge, then throws the water out through the window. A cat meows from the unexpected soaking. She does it again. When the water is clear, she hands the gourd to Gathuki. Gathuki swings his worn leather pouch to the front, digs his hand in and brings out several stones.

'What on earth are you doing? Are you a *murogi*? asks Firifo.

'I am a medicine man,' says Gathuki with determination.

Firifo moves away from Gathuki as if he was suffering from a contagious disease.

Gathuki puts the first stone in the hollow gourd, then drops the other two. Everything is still.

Drawing long breaths in and out, I appear to gain some reprieve from the pain, and I lean forward to have a better look.

Gathuki shakes the gourd with vigour. Ripples of thin skin from the underside of his arms stretch like elastic with the hand movement.

'If the first pebble is red, we are in trouble. If it's black, we are in less trouble. We need the white one to come first.' He sighs. 'For too long I have ignored my calling. I thought the world has no role for me. I can't ignore any of this any longer.'

'Do the stones!' says Mama who can no longer hold the suspense.

Gathuki rattles the gourd. We are captivated. Even the pain offers me an intermission. They are all squeezed around the mica stool, and I am peering from my bed. We are holding our breath. He removes his thumb from its mouth and the pebbles fall out. We gasp. The first one out is red. The second one is black and the third one is white. Our gazes oscillate between each other's faces in alarm. It's as if the ground underneath our feet is opened and we are falling.

Chapter Twenty-Six

Mama, Kaminde and the guests leave. Not a moment too soon. I barely notice engulfed by pain. The monster in me is taking revenge. We are in a duel. I'm on my knees, the only position I tolerate, writhing my hips trying to sooth my abdomen. I'm in the throngs of hell and I'm delirious, drifting in and out of sleep. Everything around me is spinning. I don't know how to stop the pain. The pain from the pills and pain from my heart are merging into one sea of anguish, tormenting me from all angles.

I see Kīmathi standing next to me like he did when he named me Madonna. He stretches his hand out to me, his gentle fingers stroking my face, soothing my bruised heart. I feel his arms around me. He is holding me close, and we start to dance, our hips swaying in sync. At first a slow dance. There are spectators. They are envious of us. He's holding me so close I can feel his breath on my skin. His heart is beating next to mine. He is singing, 'the lady in red.' And then the beat quickens, he is spinning me round and round until I lose control. The floor is turning crimson and rising like the evening tide. It's whirring and I'm being swept into it. When I look around, Kīmathi's gone. I'm alone in the tide of pain. I'm shipwrecked. Out of nowhere Kīmathi reappears. He has changed again. He is the nice and chivalrous Kīmathi he was when we first met, smiling, and holding his hand out, calling for me.

'Come Madonna, come and be mine.'

I swim, reaching for his hand, but every time I nearly touch his fingers, he kicks me in my face. Covered in bruises, I'm begging his forgiveness. It was my fault for denying him during the school disco. He's holding something in his hand, feeding me. Bhajias. I begin chewing, but I'm choking. He's growing more vicious, like a trained Doberman at the scent of a burglar. I fight back. None of my punches land. He moves further away, and we are now on two separate islands drifting apart. I'm peddling in the water, trying to reach him. He starts laughing at me. His laughter gets louder and louder. He is joined by Dr Njaũ, and the headmistress, who wave their fingers at me in disapproval. Then everyone at the Ministry of Works join and begin laughing at me too. I'm humiliated. I'm crying crimson tears adding to the volume. There's fire in my abdomen. Then I'm rolling around and writhing on my bed. I don't know how I got there. I'm getting tangled with my blankets drowning in sweat. Every time the pain subsides a new wave emerges stronger than the one before.

I'm tired. Tired of the pain, my heartache, watching Mama cry. I want to sleep and never wake up. I doze off. Then I'm roused by another punch in my belly. I open my eyes. I'm puzzled by the headmistress towering over me yelling *you should have kept your legs shut.* You are a *malaya, malaya, malaya.* Then it is Dr Njaũ with his bloody lab coat standing over me like he did with the girls at his clinic. I'm consumed by anger and yelling at him. But he's retaliating, yelling that I shouldn't get up from the bed. I tell him he is the agent of death. His menfolk did this to me, us, and he's here to finish us off like a vulture, destroying any ounce of dignity we have left. I see the anger in his eyes as he punches my abdomen, his face full of venom. He's yelling die, die, die. I'm dying. He splashes my face with cold water. Gasps for breath leaves my mouth agape. I wake up drenched in sweat.

Wa Njũgũ's loud voice drags me out of my insentience. The room is suffocating. Everything is still. Like the calm after a hurricane. There's a burning sensation in my throat from the growling. It was the only way I could breathe through the pain. My head is clogged with the cement of my heavy thoughts. I am relieved the intensity of the pain has tapered. I am still hunched in the position I must have fallen asleep in. Most of the night was a haze of blinding pain.

I lift my hand and bring it to my forehead. My temperature is raging. I need cold water on my face. My lips are scorched with thirst.

I force myself to get out of bed. All energy has been supped out of me and my legs wobble as I try to stand. I jaywalk to the door, open it and step outside. Another punch to my abdomen sends me to the floor. Buildings are topsy turvy and I'm reeling. My legs can't take my weight, so I remain on the concrete paving steps to my room. Mama is out because her room is locked. I want someone to bring me water. I feel faint. I remember that I didn't eat the githeri saying to Mama I was full on the porridge. But I was incapacitated by pain, something I couldn't explain to her.

I need a drink of water but can't get up. I am now on all fours. A stray dog comes over and starts smelling me. I try to shoo it away, but I have no energy. The dog begins to walk away, and I copy its movements which don't require me getting up. Crawling, I make my way to the tap. There are a few people in the queue. Water trickling down beckons me. I overtake everyone, my knees sloshing in the filthy water. No one says anything. I suspect for them it's entertainment whilst they wait. I reach the faucet and begin to scoop water with my cupped hand, drinking it and splashing my face. A few people tut but I continue.

'If you want a proper abortion, spread your legs for money.'

I look up and Wa Njũgũ is towering over me.

'Those rich pigs can never get enough, and they will pay to have a dip in your well.'

My soaked eyelashes' part and I expect to see her still standing there but she's gone. That woman is disgusting. That's the crudest thing I have ever heard a woman say. I feel like I should permanently block my ears, so I never hear her speak. Her words are searing, and I am burning with anger. Some strength returns and I stand up, streaks of dirty water running down my legs. I catch sight of people in the queue. Elephantiasis offers me his arm and walks me back to the house. His laboured walk matches mine. We get to my door and it's still ajar. The dog that was smelling me is inside my room and it's licking something on the floor. Clenching it in its jaw's it runs past me, and I don't see what it's stolen. Elephantiasis is still at the door staring at me. Perhaps I should thank him but I'm too weak, so I walk into the room and close the door. Then I remember the pills.

By morning you should have given birth.

It's now morning and I don't know If I have given birth. I pull down my pants and stare down. I get a numb feeling as I look at the white lining of my pants. There is no baby. I am shocked. I expected there to be a baby sprawled there. That Dr Njaũ lied to me. We paid him twenty shillings for the pills but there is no baby like he said there would be. I lay back in my bed and close my eyes. If only I could drift into sleep again. The dog. It must have just eaten my baby. I want to run to the door to find it, but my body is too weak. Then the answer comes instantly with a movement inside me. Despair sets in as I am simply not ready to face *this* reality. I want to scream or weep. Either will do just fine but neither comes. That doctor promised me the baby would be out of me. Well, it's still in me. Perhaps I should have opted for surgery. I am now wailing when a thought so nasty that I shudder, flashes in my mind.

Chapter Twenty-Seven

The effect of the pills has tapered, and I'm riddled with anxiety. All that agony and nothing has changed. It's still inside of me because I feel the fluttering. I am gripped by a force I cannot escape. It is an evil spirit that won't leave my body. I am deflated and unable to see a future through the fog of my life. I hate daytime and would rather hide in the comfort of night. But nights are when I confront the beast within, searching for answers. I lay back in bed, staring into the tin roof.

Mama walks in.

'Aren't you ready for the meeting?'

I've lost track of time. I must have left the door open earlier when I went to the tap and drifted off. I didn't hear her return. My belly rumbles and I'm faint with hunger. She opens the shutters, fills a pan with water from the jerrycan and begins to make tea. She warms the leftover *gĩtheri*. I get out of bed to eat and drink my tea in silence.

'Get dressed,' Mama says. We don't want to be late for the meeting. This is your destiny too,' she says.

What does she know about my destiny? My fate is worse than death. I am gutted and confused by my tormentous night. Like the farmer that labours, planting with vigour, only to have his crops fail, all that agony was futile. I'm haunted by the images of the girls in the clinic. That is my destiny. I have no choice but to return to Dr Njaū's clinic. As if that's not bad enough, the fluttering in my belly is driving me insane. I've been invaded by an alien, and I am taunted by Wa Njūgū at every turn.

By now everyone must know about my situation, and someone's sure to blurt it out in the meeting. School is where I want to be and not attending residents' meetings. The people at the tap must have been gossiping about me all day. The only good that can come out of my presence in the meeting is to deter gossipers.

The silhouette of the distant trees fade as the sun blinks into night, inducing evil *ngoma* to slide into deep sleep. I step out following Mama's footsteps. Doors slam from every corner of the Ministry of Works compound quietening the chorus of insects, alerting all that the meeting at Firifo's shop is about to convene. As I step out of our house 'No Secrets in the Name of Jesus' by gospel singer Wanja, blares out of Firifo's shop, as if to shame me. The strumming of the guitar bears prominence, overpowering the vocalist. This could be mistaken for one of Jane's church gatherings, with droning emanating from the shop late into Sunday nights. Firifo and his wife Jane are Christians and want everyone else to be especially on Sundays.

Jane greets me as I walk into the shop, now transformed with benches arranged in a rectangular manner so that everyone can face one another. She zig-zags the wooden benches, placing crochet tablecloths as if soften the hard seats, her maxi dress sweeping the floor. I step over the benches and stand in front of Mama and Kaminde, who are already sitting down. I make no attempt to sit, prompting Mama to nudge Kaminde to shuffle along. I sit down next to her. A breeze from the open door flickers the wick of the kerosene lamp sat on a doily at the centre of a worn mica coffee table.

My eyes stray to the ghetto blaster, held together with tape, placed on the shop counter. The deafening gospel music vibrates the drab shelves populated with lonely bags of sugar and flour like old nuns, the dim light emphasizing the barrenness of the shop. I am counting the items on the shelves when the buzzing fly inside the glass shielding the wick of the kerosene lamp distracts me. It's flying round the glass wall of death looking for an exit from the hot vacuum. I hold my breath praying it finds a way out. I am engulfed by a suffocating feeling watching the fly fight against an invisible barrier into freedom. It's circling the glass in freefall until it's in the hot core close to the wick. Like the fly, I am trapped.

'I can't be that fly,' I think aloud.

Everyone turns to look at me. No don't look at me. Jane hovers around making herself appear busy. She thinks I asked her for tea, and she pours me a cup and hands it to me. I don't want it, but I take it anyway. I bring it to my face attempting to drink from it, but the rancid milk and layer of grease sat on the top is sickening. She turns away and hands new arrivals the remaining cups. I place the cup down. I don't want to be here. I would rather be in my bed planning my next step. My mind is preoccupied with the need to destroy my enemies but first I must get rid of my biggest enemy. This thing inside of me.

A heavy thud of footsteps walking up the steps makes Mama, Kaminde and I turn to look at the door. Gĩtonga walks in. I notice the buttons of his checked shirt are playing tug of war with his rounded belly. His sly face scans the room for a place to sit. I think of the lurid gestures he made at me at the ablutions and I look away. At the sight of Gĩtonga, Firifo's wife Jane freezes like Lot's wife turning to salt. He walks towards her. She drops the cups she is holding. She looks like she's going to faint. She can't seem to decide whether to straighten her headscarf or pick up the cups. I lean forward and help her with the cups close to my feet.

'Hello, welcome please, take a seat,' she says averting her gaze.

I watch him from the corner of my eye. He makes me shudder. A different kind of shudder than the one Jane has. With a wobbly hand, Jane gives Gĩtonga a cup of the milky tea. Gĩtonga pulls his tan trousers up revealing scuffed tan safari boots as he sits down, his mass overhanging the creaking bench. He sits next to Kaminde who turns to look at his face. I guess vile men gravitate towards each other. Gĩtonga maintains a downward gaze and doesn't look at Kaminde. His powerful boot sweeps black ants in a column out of the way. They re-form. Jane bends down, picks up the cups and dashes behind the counter. From where I'm sitting, I hear her quiet prayer and I lean closer to listen.

'You will not tempt me with lust Satan. I only have eyes for my husband.'

She sounds like she's begging someone.

'No one else. I will resist you like Jesus resisted you. "Turn the rocks into bread," but Jesus resisted, "jump from the temple and angels will protect you," but Jesus still resisted, "obey me and you will have everything you see, but still he resisted." I will shame the devil in the name of the lord.'

'*Hũdĩ?*'

A voice calls and I turn towards the door.

Jane is nowhere to be seen.

Gĩtonga returns the call, '*ĩĩ.*'

Wa Njũgũ steps in. My skin crawls with dread. I wished she wouldn't attend but knew, she being the compound news-agent, would be present. She steps over Gĩtonga's feet and sits in the middle of the bench opposite him. She hasn't seen me. I am glad to be out of her eye-line. Her presence makes me feel exposed. It's like she sees through me, reading my thoughts. From the corner of my eye, I can see her rocking her baby side to side. I look away. Looking at her is like looking at a mirror with a future I detest. She is the reason I worked so hard at school, so I don't end up like her. Her dark arms are poking out of a towel wrapped around the baby for an extra layer of warmth from night chill. Her unpredictability makes me nervous. Her vulgarity makes me squirm. She is everything I hate and yet she reads me like a book.

'I shan't be long my children are all alone,' she says as if reading my mind.

Gītonga smirks. He must be thinking what I am thinking. Her children are all alone is an understatement. They are the scavengers of the compound competing with stray dogs for morsels of food while she moves door to door spreading rumours. I'm glad Jane is standing between me and Wa Njūgū. She sips her tea, looking at Gītonga, hoping to start a conversation.

'Do you work for the Ministry of Works?' asks Wa Njūgū.

Gītonga nearly spits his tea out.

'The Ministry of Works was created because the colonial government was expanding the workforce for the occupied lands. Queen Elizabeth was supposed to visit it when she came in 1952 but it was delayed because we became ungovernable.' Kaminde burps and chews his imaginary cud.

How on earth does this creep know this information? I thought Kaminde's job is to hang around scrap metal.

'Very fascinating,' says Gītonga, full of sarcasm. He turns to the door, sipping his tea.

Kaminde sits on the edge of the bench.

'This was to be a very big site. They needed a compound to hide black workers out of their eye-lines as they played cricket.

But only months after her visit, Britain called the state of emergency, and the Kenya colony was over. Our governments are just as corrupted.'

Gĩtonga fakes a yawn. His head is bowed but his eyes are busy looking around as though in a covert operation. It's clear he's in no mood for a conversation.

'Did you know the Queen of England stayed at Tree Tops when my uncle worked there as a waiter? He was imprisoned for spitting in her food.' Kaminde burps again.

It clearly runs in the family, his family must all be vile. I turn to look at Gĩtonga who looks like a lion stalking prey.

'That man is up to no good.' Mama once said, watching him at the tap, shirtless, lathering himself with a bar of Lifebuoy soap.

No one in the compound can pretend not to be curious about Gĩtonga. He's to be found doing his ablutions around eleven o'clock when it's quiet. I see him loitering the compound like a lion at midday in the savannah, stealing looks inside people's houses before ambling back to his quarters. He doesn't appear to be employed, always emerging from his house after the hive of morning activity diminishes.

He is the reason Mama doesn't like me bathing in the pit latrine. Why are the men around me so abhorrent? There aren't any good ones. But then I remember Baba. A sweet gentle man without a bad bone in his body. I'm filled with sadness. His spirit must be sad watching us now, seeing what I've become and Mama with her heap of problems. She's fraught with the death of her friend and the looming homelessness.

My thoughts are interrupted by Ndekezie standing in the doorway. He seems ill at ease and could flee if anyone sneezes. It's as if he lives in his own world unable to see what's around him. Gĩtonga beckons him to sit. With his head bowed down, he sits at the end of the bench his weight making the other side tip up like a seesaw. That makes him jump. I feel like laughing. I think he'll run out, but he moves inwards and sits down again. One tip of his tight fitting buttonless shirt is in his hand and he keeps twisting it. He adjusts himself and spreads his legs, his wide shorts leave nothing to the imagination. He stares at his flip-flops. Uncomfortable silence fills the room.

I'm back to staring at the fly in the glass vacuum. Overcome by heat and drained of oxygen, the fly drops to the base where it settles upside down with its legs in the air. Its legs twitch with little drama as if to say a long goodbye. With the eviction looming, I wonder if this is our long goodbye.

The murmur of voices approaching eases the discomfort as we wait in anticipation.

'*Hũdi?*'

Calls a voice.

'*ĩĩ.*'

Everyone breathes out in relief.

Oh no. It's the gossiping trio. This is the worst-case scenario. It's just a matter of time before any one of these busybodies open their mouths. I will be their entertainment for days to come. My head stoops low. Jane welcomes the washerwomen pointing at the vacant spaces on the benches. They are already sniggering at the sight of Ndekezie's luggage. The thud and drag alerts us that Elephantiasis is arriving. He drags his leg across the floor to spaces further in the room.

'*Muriega.*' He sits with a sigh.

Everyone mumbles a response.

The forlorn face of the dying woman appears in the doorway. Her walk to the bench is humble, a hum from her throat barely audible. She sits opposite Gĩtonga. For a fleeting second, they exchange a look that cements the rumours that Gĩtonga has been knowing her in the biblical sense. The look on his face is nauseating. How can anyone want to be with him. I suppose the only person who is interested is dying anyway and so has nothing to lose. He looks smug, like a dog after stealing a piece of meat from the butcher.

It's obvious to anyone still up after ten o'clock that Gĩtonga makes frequent trips in the direction of the setting sun—to be precise to the house of the dying woman. I am kept awake by the giggling. Those of us living in close proximity to her house turn off their radio early for the late night extravaganza. He must be helping her with the dying because she squeals most nights. Whatever he is helping her with, he must be very good at it. Gĩtonga and the dying woman's escapades have sent shockwaves in the whole compound. There are hushed judgemental murmurs sprouting all over. No one knows what to make of it.

'He is risking her dying in his arms and touching a corpse is unclean according to the Gĩkũyũ tradition. Why would he risk that?' asked Mama in a discussion with Kaminde one evening.

'People do it all the time in hospitals and mortuaries and nothing ever happens to them. There's no need to discard the dying in the forests for hyenas anymore,' said Kaminde.

'Do you not see that the white man corrupted our way of thinking and devalued our customs?' replied Mama.

'His is an act of selflessness. Why can't a man offer his services to a dying woman? We are modern thinkers. Belief in spirits is old fashioned, and nothing will come of it,' said Kaminde.

'His actions are predatory,' replied Mama.

Tonight, giving Gĩtonga side stares, there's a glint in the dying woman's eyes. I look away. I want this damn meeting to be over. Usually I avoid all these people, now I must spend the evening with them. My nails sink into the bench in irritation.

The room is filling up and I am feeling less conspicuous. Jane is still fretting about making people tea but can't accept it's a bad idea as there are too many people and not enough cups. It's not clear who is leading the meeting. Avoiding everyone's eyes I instead focus on a picture of Jane and Firifo on their wedding day. Jane in her wedding dress is extending a fork with a cake at the end of it and Firifo's wide mouth is open, showing his teeth and tonsils. Jane looks happy and fatter than her current size, but Firifo looks distant. Once, I overheard the washerwomen say the reason she only has one child Ruth was because her womb was too thin to carry another baby. Another one suggested that his manhood doesn't rise for women which was met with screeches of laughter.

'Are you well?' Jane clears her throat.

'Yes, we are well.' Everyone replies in unison.

'Are you well again?' Jane's voice is croaky.

There are mumbles since many of us know Jane always greets people twice. I see her thin heart constricting every time she catches sight of the dying woman smiling at Gītonga. I don't understand her behaviour but these born-again Christians have bones in their closet.

'Yes, we are well.'

'Baba Ruth.'

With a meek voice, Jane calls her husband.

Firifo walks into the centre, hands in a prayer position like a priest whose sermon is about to begin.

'Praise the Lord.'

'Amen,' says everyone.

'Like Moses demonstrated to the cruel Pharaoh the divinity of God, we too shall conquer,' says Firifo.

'Thank you for coming—,' says a voice from the back.

I turn round to see Gathuki making his way to the centre of the room interrupting Firifo's sermon.

'Our struggle for our homes is just beginning. Like most of you, I am rather perturbed by the menacing note left on the toilet door. Whoever is behind the eviction has no value for us as a community and cares little for our plight. They think we, the little people, are powerless, but together we shall be heard.'

Gathuki looks irritable.

'I shall chair the meeting since bwana Gathuki's brain cells are not as young as they used to be.' Firifo moves forward in front of Gathuki in the process poking him in the eye. 'Let's begin with a prayer for Jesus to open the meeting.'

'The meeting is already open. Can't you see people need reassurance and not preaching. They want answers about the eviction. If they want to pray, they'll go to church on Sunday,' says Gathuki. 'We cannot allow this eviction to proceed. We will fight it tooth and nail.'

There are murmurs in the room. I see Kaminde stand up and hope he's not going to interrupt.

'Old man Gathuki was in the army and before that he was a *mūthamaki*. You must lead the fight bwana Gathuki,' says Kaminde.

I nudge Mama with my elbow, and she pulls him back down. Firifo stands back.

'We are humble people with meagre incomes, and we cannot afford to move anywhere else. I refuse to be destitute. We must fight this eviction,' says Gathuki.

Everyone nods in agreement. I look at Mama and she seems exhausted. Exhausted from the uncertainty that blights our lives.

'We need to establish who this so-called buyer of the land is and whether it's a legitimate purchase or just another government land grab,' says Gĩtonga, a menacing look on his face.

'Does anyone know who is behind the notice?' asks another voice from the back.

'Not a soul spotted the hyena. He knew that we would tear him apart, so he operates in the dead of night,' says another voice from the back.

'What if he had inside help, the gate is locked at night,' says Kaminde.

I can smell his bad breath from where I'm sitting.

'Who keeps the keys to the gate?' asks Gathuki looking at Firifo.

'I have a set, and the other set is with the fellow at number eighteen. He does a lot of night shifts so maybe he might know something,' says Firifo.

'Shouldn't we organise a committee to steer the residents into action?' asks Gĩtonga.

'I say we should hold regular prayer meetings asking Jesus Christ for his guidance,' says Firifo.

'I say we hold regular meetings with definite aims and Jesus can be present too if he likes. Who is to be in the committee?' says Gathuki.

'We need women, women are good at evoking sympathy of the masses,' says Gĩtonga.

'I bet you do,' I mumble to myself.

'Wa Njŭgŭ would be good as she has many children and people always sympathise with lone mothers with many children,' says Gathuki.

I choke at the mention of her name. She turns in my direction but doesn't see me.

'Why don't we divide up the roles so that we have someone to speak to all the night shift workers? They are bound to have seen the menace,' someone says.

'Hear hear.'

'We could also speak to the administrators of the approved school at the back of our compound to see if they might know something. They might have been approached by the same culprit. You know how the wealthy people operate, they want everything for themselves,' Gĩtonga is animated.

I am bored. I need to get back home and plot my future. If only I could find a way of sneaking out without alerting Mama.

'Oh yes, that's a good point,' Firifo has regained composure. 'I remember hearing that someone tried to get the approved school closed as it was built on contentious land. The case is still ongoing. You know how these government things are, they drag on forever. One of us needs to go to the Ministry of Lands and see whose name is on that register.'

'The fellow I bought my *matatũ* from works for the council. I could see if he knows anything,' says Kaminde.

An involuntary sigh escapes my throat. I can't bear the way he goes on about that ramshackle vehicle that has never completed one single journey without breaking down.

'My sister works there, maybe I can ask her to have a look,' comes an offer from the back.

'We also need to find out if he has court documents proving that the land is his and that he can evict us destroying our homes,' says Gĩtonga.

'We need to find out if there is a provision for displaced people provided by the government,' says Wa Njũgũ.

'We need to allocate duties if we are going to get anywhere fast,' says Gathuki.

Firifo opens a new page of his black book of credit and hands it to me to write. I stoop low. This is the kind of unwanted attention that I dread. He's bringing the focus on me. Unable to refuse, in a slanted handwriting, I scribble.

Objectives of the committee

To find and identify the buyer

To establish if there are court documents for eviction and demolition

Establish the legitimacy of the purchase

Understand if there is a provision for displaced people

'I suggest those with a good level of education undertake the legal matters,' says Firifo.

I keep my head down. These matters are for grown-ups. Mama is engaged in the conversation, and I can hear her breathing with a heaviness.

'I am happy to enquire about the court documents and the legitimacy of the sale. Since Mr. Gathuki is always talking about politics, maybe you would like to join me?' Firifo asks looking at Gathuki as if to offer an olive branch.

I think of last night and how they spent the whole time arguing about Gods. How will they complete a task if all they do is argue?

Gĩtonga puts his hand up. 'I will find out who that hyena is,' his face is full of menace.

'It is better if the women went to the city council to establish if there are facilities for the displaced. Act pathetic to invoke pity,' Kaminde says turning to look at Mama and then the dying woman.

'Ndekezie you go with Gĩtonga, your muscles will do a good job for anyone with ideas,' adds Firifo.

'We have five full days for the mission. We will report here on Friday at the same time. We have no time to lose,' says Gathuki.

There's rustling outside and everyone falls silent. There are footsteps approaching. It's as if the person is dragging their feet. The footsteps get closer. We turn round to see a haggard face partially covered by a cloth stained with old blood and brown caked matter. She looks familiar yet unfamiliar. The dim light is not enough to reveal her face.

She makes her way towards the centre as if in slow motion. Everyone is silent drawn in by the newcomer. I squint to have a better look and like a bolt of lightning, it suddenly hits me. It's the *chang'aa* seller! I'm hyperventilating, unable to breathe. She's come to finish me off. What on earth is she doing here? The image of her nakedness chasing Kīmathi, Wambūgū and I flash in front of me. Instinct tells me to flee but my legs are numb. Her curse has inflicted its venom on me and she's here to dish out some more. My body is shaking. My teeth chatter. I can't believe my eyes. She was the last person I expected to turn up here. Her home is closer to my ex-boarding school, at least three miles away. She looks confused and lost. Her face is scorched dark by the sun accentuating the sagging skin off her cheekbones. Under the weight of her droopy eyelids, bloodshot eyes peer round the room. Her gaze hovers then rests on the space above me. She looks like she is sleepwalking. She scrutinises everyone in the room as if looking for someone. Her enormous bottom lip trembles as if she's about to say something. Clasped in her enormous hands is a dirty gourd decorated with artwork and cowrie shells. She looks in my direction but doesn't seem to recognise me. Her eyes rest on Gathuki. She walks to the centre pushing peoples' legs out of the way and stands by the kerosene lamp where she stares at the fly. The stench of faeces and alcohol fill the room. The music on the cassette comes to an end as if to spotlight the woman in an arena of the macabre. There's a stunned silence.

There are puzzled looks as people try to recall whether she is a resident or not. She stands very close to Gathuki. It looks like her eyes, clogged with white gunk on the extremities are trying to focus on his face. Gathuki shifts, his discomfort palpable. She shoves the gourd in his hand.

'The gourd contains the riddle; the solution is four ridges to the rising sun as the crow flies,' she says handing him the gourd.

Gathuki stares at the gourd in confusion.

'Before seven days are over, one of you will be dead,' she turns round and walks out of the door.

My heart sinks.

Chapter Twenty-Eight

❧

It's gone midnight and I've just returned from the meeting at Firifo's shop. I'm relieved at being back in my room in the privacy of my thoughts. My mind is a carnival of the macabre, dominated by the *chang'aa* woman. She's the embodiment of the ghosts of the trauma of our people. I am spooked. *Before seven days are over, one of you will be dead.* Those words flash in my mind. I am convinced that she was referring to me. She must know something. I can't get that unsettling feeling out of my mind. Everything about her is terrifying. As if sensing my unease, the wick flickers a warning that the lamp is out of fuel. In my fogginess, I forgot to blow it out when going to the meeting. I need to save whatever little kerosene is left, so I raise the glass cavity and blow it out, leaving me to wrestle with my demons in the vacuum of darkness.

Before going to Dr Njaũ, I discounted self-abortion. It was a daily commentary at the tap, the hot topic for the washer-women. I heard the stories of girls haemorrhaging in their beds. Others were found dead with coat hangers still protruding out of their organs. I'd heard of girls that drunk bleach. I had ruled it out. But after taking the pills and the horrendous night I had, it couldn't get any worse. I expected one of two outcomes, the baby coming out or I'd die, like those girls in the clinic. I didn't die and neither did the baby. At least with the coat hanger it was bound to kill either me, or the baby. In the best-case scenario, both. The *chang'aa* woman knows something. She knows the end is near for me. There's no point prolonging the inevitable. I will go for the hanger. It's quick and decisive.

There's a finality to my thoughts. My decision is made. By morning either of us will be gone. It's then I remember we don't have hanging wardrobes at home and do not possess any hangers. The absurdity of this whole situation. I can't self-abort because we are too poor to afford hangers. I am stupid and angry. A fool tricked by my own mind.

At first rays, I jump out of bed, get dressed and wait for Mama and Kaminde to leave. Their door slams and I count to a hundred giving them a head start. Birds are beginning to fill the air with their morning melody as I walk to the phone booth. I dial the operator and ask for reverse charges to Bŭi. She accepts the charges.

'It didn't work. The baby didn't come out.'

I'm inconsolable.

'Oh man. What are you going to do now?'

'Hang myself?'

I'm half joking but that thought is appealing.

'I've run out of options. I must find something before the end of today,' I say.

'Go to Florida 2000. That's where girls go to find rich men,' Bŭi says.

'What?'

I think I misheard her.

'Florida 2000,' she says with a steely pragmatism.

'To find a job—oh you mean like a... you know a prostitute?'

It feels like someone poured a bucket of cold water on me.

Last night, my decision seemed final except for the coat hanger. I felt prepared to die if that was the price I had to pay, but in the cold light of day, the starkness of it is shattering. Bũi's suggestion is horrifying and nauseating yet feels like an option I hadn't considered. When Wa Njũgũ told me to spread my legs for money at the tap, I was too abhorred to even let myself think about it.

'That's what I did,' she says noticing my long silence.

'What on earth are you talking about?'

The phone goes dead for a moment. I can hear breathing.

'It happened in the *matatũ*, late one night when I was coming home.'

I don't understand what she is saying.

'The turnboy and the driver used to let me ride for free. I did it to escape boredom. They had the latest tunes. Me and other *chilays* rode that *matatũ* then one night I was alone. They said it was payback.'

'Oh Bũi, I'm so sorry,' I say.

'Don't let them defeat you. Go screw a rich man and get it sorted.'

Chapter Twenty-Nine

'Is your mother in?'

I turn round to see Wa Njũgũ standing behind me accompanied by the washerwomen. I stiffen. She's here to tell Mama. My mind is calculating whether to run away or walk back into the house and lock myself in.

'Last night's meeting was a disgrace. These men will not rescue us when they behave like children.'

Stifled air escapes from my lungs.

The events of last night's meeting come rushing back. After the *chang'aa* woman walked out, panic-stricken eyes stared around the room, blinking, unsure what they had witnessed. If it weren't for the gourd Gathuki was holding, we would have thought we dreamt it. We all stared at the gourd in disbelief.

'I would throw that out if I were you. She has been sent here by Satan to bring *ũrogi*,' Firifo said.

The mention of *ũrogi* sent everyone into panic mode.

'I am the one dying before tomorrow.' The dying woman began crying.

People shifted their bottoms further from her as if her dying was contagious.

'You've been pretending to die since I met you,' Wa Njũgũ said.

The dying woman began yelling obscenities and the two were about to fight and that's when Gītonga jumped up and separated the two.

'Everyone knows you have been sleeping together. You keep us awake all night. So, either die or stop wasting our time,' Wa Njũgũ said, accompanied by giggles from the back.

I was taken aback by this. I thought I was the one the chang'aa woman referred to. Firifo joined in, placing his hands on the dying woman's forehead as if he were a doctor.

'I command the devil to leave this woman right now.'

A voice from the back shouted, 'Amen.'

Grabbing Firifo by the neck, Gītonga shoved him away from her.

'Get your filthy hands off this woman. You say you are a man of God, but we all know you like men.'

Jane started singing.

In a loud voice Gathuki said, 'At the centre of her palm, lay the knobbly protruding mole that is the seed of knowledge.' He seemed hypnotised by the gourd.

'I said throw it out of my shop,' Firifo's face furrowed with anger.

Firifo lunged forward, snatching the gourd out of Gathuki's hand. 'I don't want witchcraft in my shop. This is the home of Christ.'

Gathuki snatched it back. 'You keep saying you are a man of God but never offer solutions to anything. The old hag came with an important message. Instead of using your brain you are always acting like a little child.'

Firifo boiled with fury. 'I am calling off this meeting right now you wicked man.' Fists clenched, Firifo edged closer.

The fly in the glass buzzed one more time in a final spasm.

'Now everyone calm down and think for a minute,' interrupted Gītonga standing between the two men.

'Whoever she is has come to bring us a warning and we need to think rationally. I recognise this type of gourd; it contains *gīcaadī*, my grandfather had one,' said Gathuki with a sense of urgency. 'Come to think of it, Mama Mūkami has a gourd with the same writing.'

Like everyone else, sitting in the dimly lit shop, we were stupefied. The power of the *chang'aa* woman to instil terror in people is immense. I was relieved she didn't recognise me because I would not have been able to escape the room crowded with the residents.

'This is a verse in hieroglyphics like our fathers used. It's a message. We need to decipher what it says.' Gathuki scrutinised the gourd.

We thought Gathuki had lost his mind. Standing there squinting and holding the gourd against the faint light of the kerosene lamp where the fly's body lay still.

'I am sorry old man. It's time for you to go home. This is no place for old traditions,' said Firifo.

'I am one,' Gathuki said, shoulders drooping as he spoke with reluctance. 'I too was born with a seed of knowledge in my hand. I am a foreseer, and she is one.'

'Are you impersonating the messiah?' laughed Firifo.

'Let him speak,' said Elephantiasis.

'There was a virulent curse cast upon Kīrigiti by my great uncle Kīmemia Wa Ng'ang'a, who squandered his gift of second sight. In hidden caves he cavorted with renegade spirits late into the night. Partaking in esoteric dances, stark naked genitals slapping thighs like colobus monkeys during full moon.' Gathuki appeared to be speaking to himself. 'Upon realising I was gifted with second sight my mother urged the midwife to baste my body in goat fat and to take me to the forest. She was instructed to stuff my mouth and nose with grass and leave me to be devoured by hyenas.'

I gasped in horror.

'Glad those days are gone,' said Kaminde.

There was a stillness in the room as we absorbed the words coming out of Gathuki's mouth. Words that judged me and my decision to poison the baby with Dr Njaũ's pills. Wa Njũgũ's baby started crying. She slid her leaking breast out and started to nurse. The thought of stuffing grass into the mouth and nose of a baby is the most disturbing thing I have ever heard, and incomprehensibly cruel. I thought of the baby in me. *It is not a real baby* I told myself. My grandmother told me that babies are not babies until they are colonised by the spirits of ancestors.

Kaminde burped, 'I am very gassy' he said, thumping his chest and continuing. 'If your mother gave you a death sentence as a baby, presumably you escaped as you are here telling us about it?'

'The midwife was barren, and she had been to a witchdoctor that day who predicted she would have a baby. She thought her prediction had come true and was joyous, taking me as her own. She suspended my sling in a tree in the forest, and pretended to walk away. When my mother and grandmother disappeared, she ran back and took me to her home.' Gathuki seemed relieved to offload his lifelong luggage.

Gĩtonga's buttocks shifted. 'If you really are a foreseer, what is our destiny?'

Chapter Thirty

'Good evening madam, welcome to ladies night?' A neck-less tower of a doorman leans over me pointing to a flight of stairs. 'Up this way.'

At the top of the stairs I pause and look back at the doorman. He is chatting to the watchman, and they are both looking up at me. Perhaps, noticing I'm a fake, they'll call me back. I turn round, unzip the *malaya* bag Bũi lent me and pull out the cigarette I bought for a shilling from a street vendor. I place it between my two middle fingers and bring it to my mouth. They are facing the street engrossed in conversation when I turn round again. Convinced I fooled them and that I look the part, I open the heavy metal and glass door and walk in. A wall of noise and music takes me aback. A sea of stilettos, exposed legs and red lipstick meet my eyes. Mama and the *kĩama* women would be horrified to see so many *malayas* together.

The stilts of my borrowed shoes are not enough, height must be a criterion as everyone towers over me. I'm wearing the required clothing, but I still expect someone to call me out and no one does. A boy carrying a tray and dressed in dark trousers, white shirt, and a waistcoat approaches me. He must be the waiter. His gaze brings out a feeling of shame. I'm sure he's judging me. He guides me to a table in the corner. Sitting down, I make no attempt to pull down my dress which is riding up. Bũi and I practised how I would sit and hold my cigarette, which should last all night in case anyone asks. To my horror, the waiter strikes a match and brings it to my face.

'For your cigarette madam.'

'What? Yes, I have one.'

'I am lighting your cigarette.'

I clamp the cigarette with my taut lips. He discards the burnt-out match and strikes another. His eyes bore into me as I wait for the cigarette to light up.

'Your first time here?'

Panic sets in.

'No. I am a regular here. I come all the time.'

'What would you like to drink?'

This is the only part of this plan I memorised.

'Tusker beer, small.'

Bũi's advice echoes in my mind.

'You don't need much money because entry is free for women. Just hold onto your cigarette and say to people you are trying to cut down, if they ask. You only need money for a small tusker, which you will pretend to drink all night.'

I nodded in nervous anticipation. So many questions went through my mind about Florida 2000. I recall a woman in the bus once pointing it out to her friend saying *that's where women sell their bodies,* but no one has ever explained to me how this happens. My thought was that the women sat on a platform like tomatoes while potbellied men walked up and down haggling. Who would do the haggling since I am not a tomato, and I don't have a seller? It didn't occur to me to ask Bũi.

The waiter takes me to a secluded dimly lit table. I sit down and observe. There's no one haggling. There are a few women surrounding two white men sat on bar stools. Each man has their arms around several women who seem at ease in their company. The men are blowing cigarette smoke into the women's faces. I'm surprised to see white men talking to the women so casually. I wonder why they would be here, and whether they keep *mpango kandos* too. Perhaps they are from Kitch Sarajevo, but they are not wearing the khaki and white uniforms of that place.

There are a few African men and countless women. The DJ plays all the current tunes to which some women are dancing. Then the music stops and the floor clears. Everyone gets back to their seats. Pounding drums herald an expectant silence. Beams of multi-coloured lights decorate the stage. A troupe of girls dressed in sparkly sequinned carnival bras with matching underpants, flounce to the dance floor and there is an eruption of whooping and cheering. I'm dazzled. I have never seen underwear that amazing. I want to move closer to the dance floor, but I don't want the waiter to get confused as to why I left the table he gave me.

The girls are mesmerising. They are the most beautiful and elegant women I have ever seen. They are clutching white feather fans with single loose ones planted in their hair, held in place by sequinned bands. Once on the floor, they take a bow, and the audience erupts again. A new song begins, and they all turn to the left and lower their bodies whilst wiggling their bottoms. They turn to the right and do the same. They turn to the front, stick their bums out and shake the tail feathers attached to their pants like glorious birds. Their faces are flawless, with red lips like that picture of Madonna Kĩmathi showed me.

The leader is encouraging the audience to clap. Cigarette still tucked into my fingers, I feel I should clap but I don't know where to put it, and I don't want to draw attention to myself for not having all the accessories. I couldn't bear it if I was caught and asked to leave.

'Can I join you?'

I'm startled and turn round, and my eyes roll up the plump body of a well-dressed man. I smell his perfume which reminds me of the roses my Baba grew. I say nothing. I didn't expect a potbellied man to come so soon. I don't know the process. And I don't know what to say, so I remain silent. Undeterred, the man pulls the chair and sits down close to me, the candle illuminating his immaculate navy suit and baby pink shirt.

'How long have you been coming here?'

Sweat begins to ooze from my palms threatening to destroy the cigarette. I had not thought of these questions. Did it matter the length of time I had been coming here? I am not sure what to say.

'Three years.'

My gaze is fixated on the candle on the table. I dare not look at him in case he questions my age. He leans over and flickers a light. I back away.

'Do you want a light for your cigarette?'

All the while I thought my cigarette was lit. I look at the charred end. He strikes the lighter again and brings the flame close to my face. I bring the cigarette to my mouth, I've seen Gītonga do it countless times, but I am unsure whether to blow or suck. I must think fast. When coaxing a fire to light, we blow through a metal pipe, and I feel I should blow on my cigarette. He is studying my face and brings the flame to the cigarette where it lights. He then pulls out a new packet of Marlboros from his pocket, draws one out, brings it to his clean-shaven face. His brown eyes study me as he parts his plump lips revealing his white teeth. He seems to inhale making the tip of the cigarette produce mini sparks. I do the same. He moves the ashtray close to me.

'The waiter tells me you must be here for school fees.'

Hot blood rushes to my cheeks and I hang my head in embarrassment. I thought I could pass for a grown up *malaya* but the rich man found out I'm just a school girl. I must be so obvious. That waiter, why did he have to open his mouth? This rich man will probably tell everyone about me. I wish I could run out and hide. Did the waiter act out of malice? Why would he snitch on me? I admonish the waiter in my mind.

'It's very noble of you wanting to pay for your education. It's nothing to be embarrassed about,' he says.

He smiles flashing white teeth with a gap at the centre of the top row. I thought he would call the bouncer, but he doesn't seem upset about my deception. I hadn't given much thought to the type of things *malayas* and rich men talk about. I assumed it would be discussions about short skirts, high heels, red lipsticks, necklaces, and belts. Now he wants to speak about education.

'What do you want to be when you finish your education?'
'Geologist.'

Uttering that word floods me with panic. I flinch at the memory of Wamakŭbŭ's caning and the headmistress yelling that I was expelled. Why is he asking these types of questions? My exposed legs or even the sunflower necklace or the fake diamond earrings I am wearing are more worthy of discussion. Maybe he is not a rich man. I look at his gold watch and matching gold ring on his finger. He leans over and pours my beer into the glass. I bring it to my mouth and the taste is repulsive. I don't think I can drink it, but he is watching me, so I bring it to my lips and swallow a mouthful whilst trying to remain expressionless. I mustn't give him more reasons to doubt whether I am indeed a *malaya*.

'I have a daughter nearly the same age as you.'

I choke. This conversation is throwing me off kilter. I don't know what to say about that information. There has been no mention of anything I prepared for. He has made no comment on the length of my dress or the high heels. The only *malaya* things he noticed were the beer and cigarette. He hasn't even noticed my red lips. Overcome by nervousness, I take another mouthful of beer. The waiter is coming to the table, and I am seething. Why he would tell the rich man I am not old enough?

'She just finished her mocks and did really well.'

I don't believe this. The mention of mocks brings me bad memories of Kīmathi holding my hand as we darted across the coffee bushes after skiving school. The bewilderment and a slight thrill of not knowing where we were going to celebrate. Then the stinging on my bottom from the cracking cane in Wamakūbū's hand. The way Kīmathi whimpered like a dog as he dragged his feet out of the headmaster's office. My heart constricts at the memory of being walked to the gate carrying my belongings, and the sight of his mother, as she sped past with him in a new Volvo. His gaze straight ahead, he did not turn to look at me. That was the last time I saw him.

'Her twin brother is something else.'

Anger is festering inside me, and I feel a renewed determination to see this through. I take another mouthful of beer. The rich man clicks his fingers, and the same waiter appears out of nowhere.

'Another round please.'

The interlude is finished, and the dancing girls are back on stage. We turn our attention to them as the lights dim and

the spotlight is on them. They are in a line, this time clutching red feather fans which cover various parts of their bodies.
They shimmy in unison and tease. I'm aghast. The audience
claps and loud cheers ricochet around the room. The troupe
turns round, sticking their rears out, and the feathers stuck to
their pants swish back and forth. The audience's excitement
is palpable. Reaching fever pitch. The girls step forward and
back, forward and back, they spin round. The music mounts.
The raucous cheering swells. They flutter their fans drawing
the room to a frenzy. To the left, then the right and in one swift
move they raise both fans exposing their breasts. The crowd
goes wild. I am stunned. They had their breasts out. I don't
understand why the audience is going wild over spotting their
breasts. Wa Njūgū walks around all day with her breasts out and
not a single person claps or cheers. They then shimmy again,
then flip their fans one more time and there is a crescendo. The
dancers snake off stage, stopping briefly to bow.

The music is back on and the rich man turns his attention
to me. 'You would look so much better without red lips.'

That's a slap in my face.

Short of time, we ran out of ideas on where to get lipstick.
At the bus stop, Būi saw a neighbour who works for the radio
station. She asked her if I could borrow her lipstick. When I
saw myself in the mirror, I thought I looked the part. I never
anticipated that anyone in Florida 2000 would reproach me for
wearing red lipstick, least of all the rich man. It's what I'd expect
from Mama and the women of the Ministry of Works. They say
only malayas wear lipsticks. Here I am in a *malaya* house with a
rich man who should be haggling with me instead he is talking
about not wearing lipstick. I say nothing and continue staring
at the space where the dancers were. I hope they return and I
don't have to listen to anything else from this man.

'I used to be a headmaster many years ago.'

I'm speechless. A headmaster? Why would a headmaster come to this place? A headmaster would never do anything like this. I doubt Wamakūbū would ever be interested in this place.

'That was before I started working for the government. I'm no longer a headmaster.'

He works for the government, like the potbellied men in Kīhoto bar with their *mpango kandos*.

'I'll order some food. Spareribs perhaps?'

All sorts of things are going round my mind. Puzzled by his not talking about anything I expected, I say nothing. He puts his hand up, beckons the waiter and sends him to get the menu. The waiter returns promptly, handing me the menu. My eyes are captivated, and all pride evaporates. I salivate at the pictures of ribs, *kachumbali* and *bhajias*. My stomach rumbles.

'What would you like?'

'Everything,' I say. I am mortified by my stupidity. How could I say everything?

'Okay, we'll get a selection of bites, *tafadhali* waiter.'

The rich man takes the ashtray and brings it closer to me. I look at my cigarette, I forgot about it and half of it is ash. I shake it off, bring it to my lips and inhale. My eyes water and I try not to cough. I feel him looking at me.

'Is this your first time smoking?

Chapter Thirty-One

Warmth from my seat reverberates through my body giving me a fuzzy warmness. The dashboard of the midnight-blue Mercedes Benz is slick and littered with different coloured lights. Kanda Bongo Man is playing as the car speeds down Uhuru highway. The rich man turns to hand me a chewing gum.

'Fresh mint is good after eating,' he says.

I take it and put it into my mouth. There's a tingling on my tongue as the sugary mint tickles my tastebuds. The memory of Auntie Eunice and her playful Wrigley's Juicy Fruit ritual fills me with shame. I dread to think what she'd think of me now. So far, this night is nothing that I expected. He has not touched my breasts as the rich potbellied men do with their *mpango kando's* in Kĩhoto bar, nor slapped my bottom. He hasn't mentioned any money despite that scornful waiter misleading him by bringing up school fees. His demeanour is courteous and I wish he could be lurid like other men I have come across. He is mystifying. I look through the windshield at the bright lights flying past me, wondering when the haggling will begin.

'We'll stop at Serena for a quick drink. What do you think?'

By now he should know I have no answers. Bũi made no mention of what rich men do nor how trading takes place when the *malayas* sell themselves. Maybe we are headed to the haggling place. I wish he would just stick to the rule book and not keep deviating. The car pulls up by the entrance of the Serena Hotel. A doorman clad in a crisp green uniform with gold buttons rushes to open my door and holds out his gloved hand to me. Puzzled, I give him my handbag. He takes it with a smile and reaches again for my hand which this time I sheepishly place in his and swing my legs out of the car. The rich man comes round to my side and takes my elbow, leading me down the steps to the saloon bar.

'*Mheshimiwa*, welcome, welcome madam.'

The doorman greets us and takes the rich man's car keys. We walk into the swanky lobby; the lighting is low and there is a gentle hum of voices. By a pillar, a man in tailcoats plays the piano softly. We head to the table discreetly positioned in a quiet corner. The waiter rushes ahead of us to pull my chair out for me. I sit down opposite the rich man.

'We'll take a bottle of your light white wine *tafadhali*.'

The rich man reaches over and takes my hand into his chubby warm hands.

'So, tell me, why do want to be a geologist?'

I tell him about my love of Geology, my dreams of the Rift Valley, my excellence in school. I don't tell him about the painful things, but about myself and my community, about Mama and useless Kaminde, the Ministry of Works, and it's characters.

'I climbed Mt Longonot for my geography class and since then I've wanted to understand more about the formation of the Rift Valley. I also want to know why the freshwater lakes are shrinking.'

'I like intelligent young women. That is what this country needs.'

I shrug.

The rich man pours what I presume to be wine into my

glass and I taste it. It's not better than the beer. I push my glass to one side, I was not going to drink its contents. He doesn't seem offended and doesn't try to force me to drink like Kīmathi did. He moves closer and his eyes as he is staring into mine sparkle. He is more interested in me than the handbag, or the high heels or short dress. He doesn't seem offended that I can't drink anymore. He tops up his glass again, then asks the waiter for more wine. He is relaxed.

'Like you, I didn't have much money growing up, and I loved school.' He smiles broadly as if suddenly flooded with good memories. 'I loved learning.' The intense stare returns, and he tells me, 'You must do whatever you can to remain in school.'

Knowing that I was expelled, his words slice through my heart.

'I nearly got into trouble. I got mixed up with the wrong crowd.' Tears are streaming down his face.

I stare at him, shocked. He is the strangest person I have ever met. I don't understand. I didn't know rich people could cry. What am I supposed to do? I have enough problems of my own and can't tell anyone. I want to run away. He should have haggled by now and he must have forgotten.

'I pulled the trigger. I regret it, it was I. J.J. was never meant to die. '

Reaching for his jacket he finishes with, 'I was only young. I never told anyone this before because I have carried so much shame, and guilt.'

'What price.' I think aloud.

'Indeed. What a price.'

He finishes his wine, takes my hand, and walks me to the lift. The lift opens and we step inside, his hand on my elbow. He presses number four and the doors close. Moments later, we exit and are walking down a corridor with a thick, patterned carpet, and stop at a dark wood door. He is wobbly on his feet. He swipes a card on a pad on the door, but he misses it, so tries again. Then we are in.

'Make yourself comfortable,' he says going to the bathroom.

He emerges with a robe fastened with a belt over his rotund belly, hands me another robe and instructs me to change. I walk into the bathroom and marvel at the smooth grey-veined white marble that covers the entire room, floor to ceiling, and the counter tops that surround the enamelled bath and sink. As I sit on the toilet, the cool feel of the seat caresses my thighs. There's no smell like the nauseous stench of the pit latrine at the Ministry of Works. It's true what people say; rich people shit does not stink. As a matter of fact, it smells like flowers. I stare at myself in the mirror. My lipstick has faded leaving a faint red streak around my lips. I take off my clothes. My eyes glide down at my belly. There's a definite roundness that is clearly visible. Seeing it is like being hit with a hammer. I can't bear to look at myself anymore.

I slip my hands into the robe and fasten it around my belly. This must be how the haggling takes place. It's not clear whether he begins or I begin. I think about what happens in the market. The customer asks for the price which instigates the haggling. Perhaps that's the etiquette. Taking a deep breath, I pick up my clothes from the floor and walk back to the room in preparation for what I have been waiting for all evening. I walk to the bed; he is already in it and his back is turned on me. Maybe it's a tactic. Sitting softly on the edge of the bed, I wait. Silence. He says nothing. Perhaps he's waiting for me to make a proposition. Maybe that's how *malayas* do it.

'Three for ten shillings.' I misspeak. What is wrong with me. What am I saying? I am not tomatoes. This whole evening,

I have been nothing but a disappointment. His broad back seems to admonish me and it's no wonder he can't even bear to look at me.

'Grrrrrrrrh.' He sounds disgusted.

'I'm sorry I am not what you expected,' I say. My mind races as I try to make sense of how to fix my misstep. Did I offer too much? Too little? Was he supposed to offer first? He knows. He knows I'm fake. I'm resigned to the fact that I am now exposed.

'Grrrrrrrrrrh.'

He's asleep. He was so disgusted he slept. I climb into bed still in my robe and stare at the ceiling. The crystals on the chandelier dazzle back at me as if trying to tell me something. Maybe I should turn off the lights. I look around but remember he turned them on by the door. I walk to the door and flick the switch. The room is pitch black and I feel my way back to the bed. I slide into the smooth cotton sheets feeling like I am being massaged by a dozen feathers. I try to go through the events of the last few hours but my eyes shut tight and I'm asleep.

A banging on the door wakes me up. My pupils are met by the chandelier, twinkling even in the cold light of the morning, cream walls and windows draped with opulent fabric, through which daylight is seeping, illuminating the room, and playing with the crystals in the light fixture above me. The room is cool and not sweltering like my room at the Ministry of Works. I blink thinking I'm still dreaming. I sit upright and turn to the hollow space occupied by the rich man the previous night.

'Housekeeping,' a voice calls.

Oh wait. 'Who is it?' I say.

The rich man is nowhere to be seen. I must have done something wrong. Maybe I was supposed to instigate the haggling and didn't. Did he become angry because of my stupidity and leave? Maybe he found out something about me. How am I supposed to find another potbellied rich man? Time is running out and my bump is getting too big to hide. I can't even go back to Dr. Njaũ's clinic because I don't have money for anything he can offer me now. I pace up and down wondering whether the rich man will return. Maybe he went for a walk to the shops. Why else would he just disappear? I knock on the bathroom door, push it in. He's not there. I look behind the door, he's not there. I look in the wardrobe, he is not there. I even look in the narrow space under the bed, a space clearly too narrow for him.

Another loud knock. I can't open the door because I don't know what to say and whoever is knocking continues loud and persistent. I attempt to walk toward it, then run back too frightened to open it and be seen.

'He is coming back. He just went out for soap,' I say trying to sound sure.

'Oh. I apologise you've run out of soap. The room should have been checked. Open, I will give you soap now.'

I head to the door, open it and the housekeeper hands me a bar of Palmolive soap. She apologises again and forcing myself to not look into her eyes, I quickly close the door. Breathing in the scent of the soap, I head into the bathroom, where the luxurious marble now glistens in the light of day. I touch the bath. Its silky sides feel luxurious, and I feel like I want wash myself. The bath has faucets just above it and I turn them on. A spray from above drenches me. I look up to see a large, flat, shower head spraying warm water. I put my hand underneath the flow and let the water soak it for a minute. My skin feels as if it's being massaged by invisible healing hands. I drop the robe I slept in onto the floor and I step into the shower. A thousand beads of water patter onto my back strumming my soul. I reach for the Palmolive soap and lather my skin. I watch the little bubbles drain into the hole easing my stress.

For a moment, time stands still as my body is caressed by the warmth. I'm motionless experiencing what I can only describe as heaven. My mind vacates all thoughts and worries as the water beats and dances on my weary body. The endless flows soak my worries away.

The steam from the shower quickly fills the room and it feels therapeutic as my skin, hair, soul, rinse and soften. Standing in the fog of steam, I'm unable to see anything, but in my heart, I am certain of one thing. This is where I want to be. My equilibrium is interrupted by another knock on the door. I step out of the shower and dry myself with a luxurious towel. In my robe once again, I walk to the door and ask.

'Who is it?'

There's no answer so I go back to the bed.

The rich man hasn't appeared. Then the housekeeping woman is back and says we must check out by eleven. She says it's almost eleven. I don't know what to do so I put on my normal clothes, stuffing the *malaya* things back in the bag. I am about to walk out when I see the note.

Dear sweetheart,

Last night, your beauty captured my soul. I have never been so blown away as I was with you. I couldn't stop looking at your beautiful face or bear to wake you, but I would like to see you again. I am off to the airport to catch a flight to Milan for business. When I am back, I want to see you. I must go for now but make sure you ring me on 2754 in a week's time. It's my direct line.

Bye for now.

P.S. I have left you some bus fare.

My mouth is agape. I stare at the notes in a neat pile. This must be a mistake. It can't all be mine. I've heard about the stupidity of rich people. The note says it's bus fare. Maybe he thinks this is how much it costs to catch a bus. Or maybe he just forgot. My mind goes through wild reasonings. Is it entrapment? What if he has called the police on me for theft? I read the note again but can't find the bus fare. Only a large stash of notes. This must be it. I have never seen so much money. I'm about to count it when there's another knock on the door. Stuffing the money into my jacket, I grab the note and walk out as the chambermaid walks in with a cleaning trolley. Afraid of the lift, I walk down the stairs. The doorman points me to the bus stop.

Midday traffic builds up as people head out for lunch. I'm still not able to process fully the past twenty-four hours, but the rich man's cash is adding bulk to my pocket in a reassuring, yet sobering way. Several buses go by as I stare, not seeing, while my mind sorts and stacks the last few days, and the preceding weeks and months.

As yet another bus moves past there is a sudden break in the traffic. I see across the road a sign that reads MARIE STOPES. The line underneath it jumps out. *Worried about unwanted pregnancy? Talk to us.* Have I conjured this? The last twenty-four hours have been strange; this would not be out of place. I've heard of cases where the mind can fool someone into conjuring something they deeply crave. I try to ignore it but it beckons me. I cross the road and walk up to the sign. It's real. I run my fingers over the ridged letters of the name. The words, 'unwanted pregnancy' keep me rooted to the spot.

I stand back and continue staring at the sign. I'm still staring at the letters when my eyes focus on a figure inside of the smart building. It's a *mzungu*. She waves and gestures me to go in. The door swings open and she stands there with a smile. I panic and begin to walk away. She steps out towards me. I begin walking fast, aware of her footsteps behind me. I walk even faster. My heart is pounding. Then the footsteps quieten. I turn back to look for her, and to my relief there's no one. That *mzungu* caught me by surprise. Just as I am deciding whether to turn back and clear up the misunderstanding or keep walking, I hear, in an American accent like Kīmathi's, 'Jambo, I saw you hesitate at the clinic and wondered if I can help you?'

I have never spoken to a *mzungu* before and I feel a mixture of fear and awe. I have only seen them from afar at Kitch Sarajevo. They don't seem to see us, but we see them. They never acknowledge anyone, and they just go about their business as if they live in a parallel universe. I am puzzled by why this *mzungu* is talking to me as if she was one of us. My grandma says they are terrible and cruel, but she seems nice. There are no words to describe what I want to say, so I say nothing.

'Come to the clinic, we help many girls like you who have nowhere to go and no one to turn to.'

I'm mesmerised. Something compels me to follow her. We head back to the glass door of the clinic and as we enter, we are greeted by a gust of cool fresh air blowing from above us. It's a refreshing contrast to the air outside which is sweltering in the February sun. I want to look upwards to see where the cold air is coming from but I'm aware of the woman watching my actions intently.

'Come this way for a glass of squash and we can have a chat.'

She leads me to a room with two chairs. I want the squash. Beer and wine are a mystery to me, but I love squash. She pours a serving of Tree Top orange squash into the white lid. It catches my attention as I remember it's the same lid Kīmathi had poured the *chang'aa* into. What is she trying to do? I leap to my feet and make for the door. She puts down the lid and rushes after me.

'Please don't leave. I can help you. We can help you. It's what we do. We help girls like you. If you suspect you are pregnant, we can give you a safe abortion.'

I pause. I don't turn around, but I absorb every word she says.

'We have doctors here and now who can give you a quick examination and book you in for a termination.'

'How much?'

'It's nine hundred shillings but the examination is free. Would you like to go ahead with the examination?'

I nod. I suppose I am already here now. This place looks so much better than Dr Njaũ's repellent clinic. This *mzungu* is my ticket to the other side. I think about the stash of money in my jacket left behind by the rich man. I didn't count it but I'm sure there's more than nine hundred shillings. She leads me to another room. Another *mzungu* man in a pristine lab coat walks over to me.

'Hi, my name is Doctor Albernack. I will give you a quick examination to confirm you are pregnant and then we will book you in.'

Before I know it, I am lying on the stiff hygienic paper covering an examination table, wondering how on earth I got here. The *mzungu* doctor inserts a cold instrument into me. Shutting my eyes tight, I breathe in deeply and imagine myself back on top of Mt Longonot inhaling clean air and revelling in the green valley vistas below. The instrument is out as quickly as it went in.

'The bad news is you are pregnant, but the good news is we can take care of it for you. We can see you next Thursday at two o'clock,' he says, placing what I presume to be the same item into a shiny stainless sink. This is the most important news I have ever received in my life. These clean people will help get rid of this thing for me. I'm overcome with relief. Nodding, I exit the clinic.

I pause at the bus stop, to take it all in. I'm reeling. Every turn presents something new, unfamiliar, and downright frightening. I am like a lone star hurtling in the universe to some black hole. Last night was the most puzzling experience of my life. The rich man was the opposite of what I expected. His line of questions and the things that interested him baffled me. Unlike other men I have encountered, not once did he harass me, lift me, or display his penis. Instead, he seemed vulnerable and was crying. If that was not odd enough, he left me a stash of money without haggling.

Now this encounter with the *mzungu* at the clinic, is compounding the strangeness of my life. She noticed me, followed me, and offered to help. When I looked into her eyes, they were the colour of the sky. They looked kind, not like the *mzungus* my grandma spoke of. The ones who got people mauled by ferocious dogs during the emergency. The ones who walked around brandishing whips and beating grandma and her friends for no reason. The ones who threw breast-feeding mothers into pits of cold water with rats and snakes. The ones who rammed sand into men's throats and anuses. The ones who punished women in my grandma's village by stuffing crushed chillies and petrol into their vaginas. The ones who made women dig their own graves into which, with their machine guns blazing, they toppled them like struck bowling pins. She didn't have a gun and neither did her colleague. They did not shoot anyone.

The receptionist was Gĩkũyũ like me. I saw her name on her

badge. It said Millicent Wairimũ. She was not frightened of the *mzungu* in fact she looked happy. Other workers in their clinic seemed happy and not sad like the slaves in my history books. She was not like the *wazungu's* predicted long ago by Mũgo Wa Kĩbiro. Above all, she was doing manual things for herself like putting money into the parking meter and mixing the squash.

I am relieved when the country bus finally arrives, and I get on. I don't mind it's not fashionable like the *matatũ*. It has no darkened windows or graffiti. There are no idlers riding for fun or mischief. It's full of serious country folk. Instead of the agility of the *matatũ* overtaking cars from either side of the road, the country bus chugs away slowly from the bus stop, swaying and lurching like an old woman going to market. The harassed driver keeps raising his hands in prayer, urging Ngai to provide rain for one more day before his crops die. When he isn't praying, he is bemoaning the state of the world.

'Pity we don't supplicate Ngai anymore. Now we must give money to a white God who doesn't know our language,' says the driver.

'True!' says the young turnboy with threadbare trousers. 'We'll be spraying mouthfuls of tobacco-stained honey beer to the ground for the spirits in repent.'

The driver agrees, 'Soon we'll be swigging empty calabashes with the poor sorghum crop that's predicted.'

I sit by the window listening to the stupid conversations.

'They are unlike us country folk, their lungs inflated with modernity and pollution, wrestling free from cultural chains, running fast from ghosts within,' says a passenger to the driver. His snoring soon harmonises with the engine.

I focus on the view from my window seat. My shoulders feel eased of the burden I have been carrying, creating space in my mind, as if the events of the last twenty-four hours have severed the chains threatening to drown me in the sea of life. The bus draws to a stop outside Kitch Sarajevo and I rush to get off.

A barely legible sign weeps with rust. The turnboy slaps the sign as if it were the thigh of his *mpenzi* interrupting my thoughts. A slap any harder and the aged metal would have given way but in the era of *kitu kidogo* giving up is no option. His greasy hand is imprinted in countless handprints on the decrepit metal like a dog marking its territory. The words mock me. *When women are done with men they turn to God.* I am not done with men the voice in my head rages. I extend my palm to him with my fare to pay, and he raises his hand and slaps it. I redden with anger. The turnboy hops back onto the step of the bus, his tan trousers tiled with threaded windows from which his dark skin peer. He holds the handrail beside the door frame, his lips melt away bringing to prominence fluoride-stained teeth, his young face full of mischief. With a poise of an ancient *gĩcaade* poet, the turnboy stretches out his hand and suspends my three-shilling change above my palm, then as the driver coaxes the bus back to the road like an aged concubine, he drops my change into my tense hand. I well up with irritation. I am in no mood to play games. He is unperturbed. These illiterate men have no concept of time or etiquette. He winks at me as the geriatric engine revs thrusting a cloud of fumes into my eyes. My eyelids flutter as the bus meanders back to the once smooth tarmac now reduced to asphalt and marram craters.

Stepping onto the dusty marram road brings back the enormity of my situation, and like an open window in a storm, blows away all the cosy warmness of the country bus. As I approach the gate of the Ministry of Works it suddenly hits me. If Mama finds out that I, Mũkami, sneaked out of school, purchased *chang'aa* from the mad seller, is pregnant, expelled from my new school after she forgave me for being expelled from my old school, and that I went to the *malaya* house, dressed in *malaya* things, spent the night with a potbellied rich man and that I am in collusion with *wazungu's* who promised to give me an abortion, she will be incandescent with rage. A bolt of fear shoots through me.

Chapter Thirty-Two

I stand still as I summon tears to wash away the dust in my eyes. I cross the road, the worn soles of my shoes grinding the gravel. Wilted maize stalks sway with disapproval as if wondering how I, Mūkami, in just four months, could go from an A-star student to a person expelled from two schools and a prostitute with a hit list. It's now February and my life is a mess. By now, I'd be well into my first year of A-levels but instead, I am crisscrossing all over the country and town, looking for an abortion. I am not ready to face Mama. I thought by now I would be without the parasite within me. The closer I get to home the more my clenched fists cause my nails to bite into the flesh of my palms.

As I walk up the curved road, guarded on either side by flaccid nettle, loud echoes pound my brain. Echoes of everything that's happening to me; my meeting Kĩmathi, Wamakũbũ's beating, Dr Njaũ and the headmistress's tirade, her huge eyeballs popping in and out of their socket to the rhythm of her cavernous mouth as she expelled me. I tried to add her name to my revenge list but, as if in defiance, the biro ink wouldn't transfer onto the paper.

My lead feet edge closer to the gate of the Ministry of Works compound. Its corroded spindles are twisted, almost spitefully, as if the world owes it an apology. It's slammed shut. My heart constricts jolting my soul out of my body, where it digs its adolescent heels into the terracotta earth refusing to join me.

'I just can't do it! I can't let her know,' I say out loud. The potential of Mama's anguish at my broken future is incalculable.

The man walking in front of me turns round to face me.

It's Firifo.

He stops. Firifo's mottled hands grip a Bible like an eagle in flight with prey. His claw fingers crawl on grubby pages pale with age, like a *thatu* caterpillar in metamorphosis. His concentrated eyes scour from left to right, peering into mine seeking my soul, but he doesn't see it, as it's now perched on the tall maize stalks taunting me.

He says, 'And Jesus said bring all the little children unto me.'

He edges closer. My face twitches from the warm breath his nose emits when he exhales from his bagpipe lungs. I can almost see his nasal hairs vibrate when he breathes. I lower my gaze to look at the passage.

'Parable of the Mount. It says Parable of the Mount,' I say.

Irritation crumples his long dark face, the moustache on his upper lip pulses.

'No. It says, "Jesus said suffer all the little children unto me," it clearly says so here.'

He is pointing and tapping at the words 'Parable of the Mount'. He does so with such conviction that I blink in doubt of my eyesight.

Then with an urgency as if time is running out, he says, 'For God so loved the world that he sent his only begotten son.'

A gust of wind blows the aroma of roasting meat into my nostrils. It's coming from Kīhoto bar where racks of meat sear, and crates of tusker beer are off-loaded in preparation for the Friday afternoon rush. Herds of double-chinned politicians and businessmen with distended bellies and gout ridden gaits will be flocking there soon. These notables fill the parking yard with imported cars. Pouncing around like alley cats, their chubby fingers will soon be fondling the perky breasts of their pubescent high school *mpango kandos*, whilst back at home their heartbroken wives soak their marital beds with tears.

Saliva oozes from crevices in my mouth as my thoughts torment me with images of the feast in Kĩhoto bar. Spitting golden ribs, side dishes of diced and fragrant *kachumbali* accompanied by refried *kĩenyeji* and salted *sukuma wiki*. An invisible fist intervenes, constricting my stomach.

'For all have sinned and fall short of the glory of God, for the Lord is my shepherd; I shall not want. He maketh me lie down in green pastures,' Firifo's Adam's apple ripples as he preaches and saliva pools in the crevices of his chin. I suspect from his gaunt frame that he too shared the same thoughts about the feast, and I cast my gaze to the wilted maize cobs.

'Why do the rich enjoy their wealth on earth, and we have to wait for ours in heaven?' I ask him.

He falters.

'God has a plan for each one of us.'

And what's mine? My mind screams, but nothing escapes my lips. My peripheral sight is on his drab ill-fitting suit, black, like a bat in slumber. Loose, worn cotton threads stick out of the neck rim of his shirt, once white now brown with age.

His enthusiasm to share the good news of Jesus gnaws my bones. Not even the disabled man at the crossroad, who tugs on the worn helm of his trousers, can distract him in his mission.

'Have you considered accepting Jesus Christ as your personal saviour?'

I notice the hand, tense with muscle and clutching a crumpled bowl, extend towards Firifo as he intones.

'Jesus died on the cross for your sins.'

The man's eyes squint from the sun as he waits in antic-ipation. Without averting his gaze, Firifo kicks the bowl out of the man's hand causing it to roll, wobbling, for a few yards. The eroded look of defiance on the disabled man's face is impenetrable.

I step toward the man and my hand unfurls revealing the three-shilling change from the turnboy, which I place in his twisted palm. He flings the coins back at me. I stare at his skin covered with weeping sores in shock, as he slithers his deformed body across the gravel to fetch his bowl, his ossified nails scratching around the red earth for any other treasure that might be strewn across his path.

Firifo edges closer to me, keen-eyed, proclaiming that Jesus is crying for me.

'I have knelt and prayed to Jesus from my heart, begged and cried and none of my prayers have ever been answered. Every time I pray the opposite happens. Jesus deducts some-thing from me.'

If Firifo heard me he doesn't show it and my disinter-est does little to dissuade his crusade. The charade is inter-rupted by the sound of quick footsteps coming up the dusty road. I turn to see Gathuki emerge from behind the maize, tight lipped, his sun scorched furrowed face hooded with unease. Firifo spreads his arms wide as if parting an imaginary sea leaving no room on the path for Gathuki to pass and I stand back. I must get home and face the music with Mama. I pray she is not back yet to give me enough time to compose myself.

'You too bwana Gathuki can see the eternal kingdom,' says Firifo.

Gathuki grimaces with exasperation. We are crowding the path. I step aside to allow his passage at the same time he decides to go around me. Our bodies bump. If he wasn't so advanced with age I would have exploded with anger. He is fraught as he jostles past me. Taking long steps, his cracked ashy feet are cushioned in tyre cut out sandals with toenails protruding at the front. He negotiates the narrowing path, the blanket he wears parts revealing wrinkled thighs. He pauses to look at Firifo, his curved back stiff with age. The bark string fastening his blanket dangles from side to side. A grid of his ribcage draped with saggy skin throbs with breathlessness. He reaches for the bolt with his dry mottled hands, slides it to the side, enters and bolts back the gate.

Before I can escape the gospel spreader, a man leaps from the maize like a deer in flight thrusting me to the ground. I land with a thud breaking a few stalks. Startled grasshoppers explode in the air like etymological fireworks. I look up in time to see the athletic frame of a shirtless Ndekezie fly past me carrying a bag. It looks like there's the tip of a snake sticking out but, then again, I have had quite a day. He stops at the gate gasping for breath. Then he leaps onto the gate. His fingers wrap themselves around the square mesh, the bag swinging. He heaves himself up, straddling the rusty metal, and is over, leaping on the ground. With the agility of a man in his prime, he springs onto his feet and runs into a cloud of smoke emanating from a pile of rubbish on the edge of the Ministry of Works.

Still dazed, I prepare to get up, feeling the stinging in my knee and elbow. I grab two maize stalks as leverage, and I haul myself up. The clunk-clunk of leather shoes on the gravel makes me freeze. Two muscled men run up the marram road and halt realising it's a dead end. They peer doubtfully into the compound of the Ministry of Works. There's no one in sight. They stare at the closed gate as if seeking an explanation. Finding none, they turn their menacing bloodshot eyes to me. The tall one with the Ray Parker Jr hair and thick muscles protruding from his sleeveless vest begins to walk towards me to the tune of my thudding heartbeat. His short accomplice with the face of a bulldog follows close behind. My veins throb giving me a headache. I close my eyes and swallow hard. A rough hand gathers the neck of my dress into its wide palm choking me and I feel myself levitate as the brute brings me to my feet. I open my eyes and see my frightened expression reflected in the satisfied looks on their faces.

'Which way did he go?' glowers the one with Ray Parker Jr hair.

My mouth is paralysed with fear. My lips quiver but utter nothing. He looks around as if contemplating his next move, shoves me to one side and rushes to the gate. For a moment he calculates whether to climb up, but a downward glance to his pointed leather shoes tells him otherwise. The shorter one, with the smaller frame, appears at his side. He pushes his hand through a small opening to undo the latch from inside, swings the gate wide open and they both run in. I am frozen by what just happened. I see Firifo, still standing at the side where Gathuki shoved him, seeming untroubled and appearing keen to resume talks of Jesus. He hesitates for a moment, then walks slowly into the compound. He heads towards his shop singing *wihoke mwathani rugendoini*.

I hurry towards the gate. These days, the gate is a prompt to any persons unfamiliar to the Ministry of Works, to drop any misconceptions they might hold about the compound in which I reside. I run past the amalgamation of clumsily constructed shacks that are only erect because there's no place for them to collapse onto. Oil drum walls flattened with giant hammers of frustration, stained black like the hearts of freedom fighters, absorb the heat from the sun as I go past.

I run towards the back row of the shacks stepping across a gully filled with human waste. Empty tubes of skin bleaching creams, and discarded matted hair, amongst the general filth, all cling to the side of the gully awaiting escape at the first sign of rain into Kīrigiti River, itself still tainted with freedom fighters' blood. Before its curse, the river nourished these hills, granted by Ngai Mwene Nyaga to the supreme ancestor Gīkūyū and his wife Mūmbi. But that was before the white man stained the land with insolence.

My nose twitches at the putrid stench as I cower under the suspended washing lines draped with garments, stained with privation. I pause and peep round the soft curved edges of the front row houses. My attempt to run is hampered by the uneven hardened earth. I take wide strides, peering through the chicken mesh windows covered with tattered blankets. A horde of children with earthy coloured hair appear from nowhere carrying bottle tops from Kīhoto bar. These are the only tools of amusement, which they use for pelting stray dogs and cats. Obsidian eyes of a little girl with a head covered with messy loose braids stare at me with curiosity. Her bony shoulders draped with a faded pink dress, riddled with holes.

The odour from the pit latrine filled with decades old faeces hangs around, choking me as I pass. Its corrugated iron sheets veiled with lavish vines, like a pregnant bride feigning virginity, do little to mask the smell. It's the only toilet serving the residents and built as an afterthought. Even after all this time, I am still unaccustomed to the suffocating air surrounding the toilet. I avoid the grassy swamp nourished by the copper pipe fastened to a wooden stump which protrudes like a cobra about to strike. I miss a step and my feet sink into the soggy ground, and I let out a curse underneath my breath.

The midday group crowd the ablutions area and I walk around them. A bead of warm sweat trickles down the ridge of my spine. Multicoloured plastic basins forming a queue for the tap monitored by a herd of washerwomen absorbed in conversation are in my way. I hesitate. I gaze at the women rubbing fabric between their clenched fists before dipping them into the mucky water. I should say something or even ask them for help, but they are engrossed in gossip.

'The so-called dying woman seemed pretty much alive last night by the noises coming from her bedroom,' says one as others unfold their backs bursting into laughter like raucous sea gulls.

I jump onto a mud island.

'I hear the resident of house number twelve was round her place giving her some sugar,' they laugh even louder, slapping the fabrics to loosen caked dirt.

'I'm making chapati, maybe I will borrow his rolling pin.' The laundry is forgotten, and they are clapping in amusement.

'He's what I need to massage my tiredness away,' one remarks.

'With that rod between his legs you won't be walking for a week,' says another.

They break into fits of laughter.

'I'll lock him in my place, and you won't see me here gossiping.'

More laughter.

There's still a queue of people from the mid-morning rush for the ablutions, waiting to fill their jerry cans. I proceed past the mound of smouldering rubbish and goats foraging for vegetable peels. A stray dog leisurely licks its anus as my footsteps quicken past Wa Njũgũ's house. She's yelling something about one of her children being just like its father. This is followed by the clatter of noises and a child crying. The dying woman is just spreading her mattress out on the grassy patch and doesn't look up as I hurry past. Elephantiasis sits pensively on his stool as if absorbing the perfume of hopelessness and doesn't turn as I run behind him.

As I approach my house, I see the door to the dual-purpose room I sleep in is shut. There's a padlock. The door for the room adjacent to mine which Mama shares with Kaminde is locked too. She is not back from the funeral. I know I didn't want Mama to be home but now I wish she was. I am not sure what's going on, but I am frightened. I scramble around but can't find my keys. My heart races. Kaminde has a set of keys but I'm certain he's loitering around the rundown garages striking conversations with scrap metal dealers instead of accompanying my mother to the funeral.

From the direction of the gate an eerie chant is encroaching, like the rising ocean tide to the shore. Hair follicles at the base of my neck constrict in agitation. My temples throb. With both doors locked, and the tempo of the chanting rising, panic bubbles from the well of my stomach compelling me to hide. Nowhere comes to mind. Then I remember that Mama keeps a set of keys in Firifo's shop.

I stride the few yards from our shack and I am relieved to see Firifo has returned to his shop. I pray he still holds a set of our keys. The door is ajar and I see the silhouette of his stooped shoulders. He is scowling at someone. I leap up the steps to the raised doorway and walk in. Tin shutters hinged on two small windows, sway with the gentle breeze, teasing the room with outbursts of light. When my eyes acclimatise to the lighting of the dark shop, I recognise the curved back of old man Gathuki. Gathuki's face is tilted upwards to Firifo like a giant sunflower, staring at him. They are in a stalemate, oblivious to my presence. I stand in the corner and await Firifo's attention.

Firifo leans against stacked crates from the rickety old delivery van that bounces in and out the potholes up the marram road every Monday to his shop. Then, ignoring Gathuki, Firifo drags over the tall stool he always sits on by the doorway, whilst his grubby finger scrolls through the list of his black book of credit, like an anteater scratching for ants.

Gathuki's stare is unwavering.

Firifo begins pulling things out of the crate with the same concentrated look he wears knocking on doors when he does his rounds at month end. He places the items on the counter. The shy light disguises the meagre brown shelves which blend into the darkness, making it difficult to see much else; which is just as well as there's not much in anyway. I press my back against the ridges of the dusty iron wall feeling its heat soothe my soreness away, but being in Firifo's shop does little to calm my nerves overall.

'Do you have our house keys,' I ask.

'It's a great day you have chosen for me Jesus,' Firifo breaks into a song taking no notice of what I said.

Gathuki, still without breaking his stare, shifts in agitation. I wonder what the hell is going on. Whatever this is, it must be serious. I fear my breathing must sound like a bellowing elephant but, engrossed in their stalemate, they take little notice of me.

Firifo tosses an empty crate aside which lands close to my feet. He pulls more items from the crate beneath. He walks to the shelves and begins placing them. Someone has entered. I turn and see Jane, Firifo's wife, glide in, her layered dress skirting the floor, with a cup in one hand and little Ruth, her big round eyes focused on me, anchored on her hip. Firifo stops briefly to sip the cup of milky tea handed to him by the twig-like fingers of his wafer-thin wife Jane. Stepping back, she now joins Gathuki in staring at Firifo and, I, unsure still of what is happening, stare back at Ruth.

Firifo brings the plastic cup to his mouth and drawing in the top greasy layer, smacks his lips in appreciation. Jane's face brightens with a broad smile, exposing yellowy teeth set in big pink gums. She turns round, weighed down by Ruth who's dressed in an oversized bridesmaid style dress, with hair braided so tight her small bald head looks like a miniature Firifo.

Gathuki's shoulders heave up and down as he holds his breath full of loathing. Firifo seems ground down by Gathuki's glare. He stops, feigning surprise as if he had been unaware of the old man. Their eyes meet. 'Whatever is the matter bwana Gathuki? Let Jesus take the burden off your shoulders.'

Gathuki walks towards him then hesitates before turning back and walking to the door which he slams shut leaving me struggling to see in the dim light.

'Do you mind not closing my shop, my customers will be alarmed if we are closed. I have many loyal customers you know. What is bothering you?' Firifo asks now that he is paying full attention.

'He is in here!' Gathuki responds, his wide nostrils flexing as if to smell.

'I don't know what you mean, who is in here? There is no one here. Mama and the little one have just left. They are travelling up country to visit her relatives,' says Firifo.

'I know that boy is hiding here; I can smell that dreadful snake,' says Gathuki raising his eyes in certainty. At the mention of a snake, Firifo jumps on the counter covering his face like a toddler. I am stiff with fear. My chest heaves up and down. The thought that a snake might be at my feet accelerates the sweat running down my temples.

'You saw a snake? In here? Oh Lord, I don't like serpents, they are the root of all evil, they are the reason man has to toil all his life, oh Lord help,' says Firifo looking around the floor to see if he can spot the snake.

My eyes gape around the edges of the floor.

'No. The snake is dead,' says Gathuki edging closer to look behind the counter.

Firifo jumps off the counter straightening himself. He looks embarrassed. I deflate.

'How do you know there is a dead snake in my shop?' asks Firifo.

It's now Firifo's turn to scrutinise the old man's face.

'I can smell it,' says Gathuki, moving to the other side of the counter to have a better look.

'You mean you can smell a dead snake all the way from your house?' asks Firifo who's expression goes from concern to questioning the old man's sanity. Firifo regains composure, casually walks over to Gathuki, and placing his hand on his shoulder laughs in feigned sympathy.

'Do you want a Fanta or Sprite?'

I could do with a drink. I've had nothing to drink all day but he doesn't extend his offer to me. I don't think he even knows I am here.

'No,' says Gathuki. He's adamant and agitated. 'This is not the time. That boy is in a lot of trouble, and we need to help him.' Gathuki flips the counter flap upwards and walks into the shopkeeper's side of the counter.

'Come out wherever you are.' There's a movement from

somewhere behind the counter and I turn to look. Whatever was moving becomes still.

Firifo arches his body with cautious curiosity and follows Gathuki behind the counter. He stares at Gathuki who appears in no hurry to enlighten Firifo. There's no movement and Firifo shakes his head at the old man.

'Your age is finally catching up with you bwana Gathuki. You've lost it.'

Gathuki's breathing is louder like a bull about to strike. Firifo stares at him with a look of patronising sympathy.

'Bwana Gathuki you should abandon your idol worship and come to the Lord God Our Saviour.' Firifo reaches for his Bible with the keenness I recognise from earlier.

'Not now,' says Gathuki. 'This is not the time. Listen,' his finger points into the air.

Firifo pays no attention.

'They are coming for him, listen,' says Gathuki.

Firifo opens his Bible and begins to read his paragraph. '"For God so loved the world that he gave his only begotten son...",' he stops. His ears pique to the chanting, growing nearer. Now he stands erect listening. I hear it too. I can't breathe.

'I told you he is in trouble,' says Gathuki.

'Who is in trouble?' asks Firifo.

'That Luo boy is in deep trouble.'

'He is not Luo. He is Rwandese,' says Firifo.

'That's irrelevant right now. I saw him at the market and there are dangerous men after him.' Before Gathuki finishes his sentence, there's a chorus outside the door. Firifo walks to the window, peeps, and freezes at the swelling mob outside. He marches to the door, but Gathuki jumps in front of him to stop him.

'Please don't open the door!' he says in a hushed voice.

'I need to know what is going on.' Firifo frowns with worry. He walks close to me and my muscles spasm in fear.

'Ndekezie is in trouble with dangerous looking men. That outside is a mob. Please don't let them in,' says Gathuki.

Oh no. What has Ndekezie done?

'How do you know all this?' asks Firifo in a low murmur, softening.

Gathuki moves closer and addresses him in earnest. 'I saw him at the market when I was buying mang...,' he stops, bows his head and stares at his empty hands. 'I bought mangoes,' he says as if to himself. 'Anyway, I saw him arguing with the nasty looking men, then he ran away. Now they think he stole something.'

Bang, bang bang! goes the door. I almost jump out of my skin.

'Don't open the door,' says Gathuki under his breath with great urgency.

The hairs on my back are standing up. I am now aware of a heaving type of breathing, coming from behind the counter. I stretch my neck to look in the direction and our eyes lock. The silhouette of tight biceps and chiselled body are unmistakable. From my position I can see his rounded eyes, the fear on his face palpable. Even in the low lighting of the shop I can see sweat beads glistening on his forehead. He looks at me expectantly, as if I will save him. I look away. Gathuki and Firifo, absorbed by the melee outside, are unaware.

Bang! 'Open this door or we will break it down.'

The voices yelling from outside startle me. I shrink, as does the sweaty head of Ndekezie behind the counter.

Firifo starts walking towards the door, but Gathuki grabs him. Firifo looks down at the wrinkled hands encircling his wrist and appears surprised by Gathuki's strength as he tries to shake him off. Firifo composes himself and again begins to walk to the door, this time half dragging Gathuki who is determined not to let him go.

'Don't open the door.' Gathuki's grip appears to be getting tighter. 'He needs your Lord and Saviour.'

Firifo stops to think. 'I do not consult with criminals,'

The mob chants.

'Hand him over, hand him over.

I slide further away from the door, feeling warm liquid running down my legs. Ndekezie's heavy breathing behind the counter alerts me to our synchronised fear. Firifo is close to the door. Gathuki makes a last-ditch attempt to stop him, standing in his way. He grabs him by the shoulders looking directly into his face.

'You are a man of God! That boy needs you now. Practice what you preach and show him clemency,' Gathuki yells.

Grinding his teeth Firifo stands firm, his upper lip scrunching upwards like a dog about to attack.

'Mine is the house of God, not the house of sinners,' says Firifo through clenched jaws .

Gathuki's grip is unflinching.

Bang bang bang! 'We know he is in there. Open the door now and hand him over,' says an impatient voice.

The two men stand in a silent stalemate staring into each other's eyes. I wish I could do something, but I dare not move. Outside the crowd swells up, yelling. Firifo's cold eyes full of contempt, move down to look at the fingers digging deep into his flesh, then back up to Gathuki's eyes.

Firifo wrestles the old man.

'"And as Moses lifted up the serpent in the wilderness, even so must the Son of man be lifted up; that whosoever believeth

241

in Him should not perish, but have eternal life," John 3:14.'
Gathuki speaks, unflinching, quiet, and determined.

Firifo appears paralysed by those words. He eases his grip
on Gathuki's arms.

'You do know the Bible,' says Firifo confused.

Gathuki just stares back at Firifo, his eyes burning with
fury.

Chapter Thirty-Three

I am in the corner, trapped, not daring to draw attention to myself. Firifo and Gathuki seem frozen in time. The stillness of the stark room magnifies the furnace of anger outside, now reaching fever pitch. I fear I will vomit. The discoloured weighing scales on the counter seesaw softly; a metronome to my fear. Even the miniature bags of sugar seem to quiver in anticipation. The two men are breathing stale air into each other's faces. Firifo towers over Gathuki, his lanky limbs dangling, his scrawny frame hunched forward. Gathuki's body is stiff with age. He is semi-upright, his furrowed forehead tilted upwards with a stern look of reproach.

There's a movement and I turn to see Ndekezie's chiselled body, stock still like a mime artist. The only part of him that seems alive is his eyes. They are oscillating between me and the two men as if my input could diffuse the situation.

'Give us the thief! Give us the thief!'

The mob chants banging on the door.

Ndekezie's limbs cave in knocking something over, making the two men turn around, easing the stalemate.

'You have the power to calm the crowd down. They will listen to the man of God. Jesus himself bathed the feet of a prostitute and you won't follow in his footsteps,' says Gathuki.

'Give us the thief!' The anger outside the door is reaching a climax.

I stiffen.

'God's eighth commandment, "thou shalt not steal",' says Firifo. 'The man broke the commandment. Blessed are they who observe justice, who do righteousness at all times.'

'How can you know this if you weren't there? I was there and all this boy did was take a *mandazi* to quieten his hunger,' says Gathuki.

Gathuki looks like he's at the end of his tether. 'Thou shalt not kill. The sixth commandment. They are going to kill him!' he says.

'That boy is a sinner,' says Firifo.

My tummy bellows reminding me I haven't eaten all day.

'You know he's mentally challenge-.' Gathuki tails off. 'He is not like us.' He stoops forward looking a lot older.

'He who walks with the devil shall be slain like the devil,' says Firifo.

Gathuki's raging. I feel it too. It's as if there's a wall barring Gathuki's words from penetrating Firifo.

'Please listen to bwana Gathuki,' I say. It's almost a whisper. I am nauseated by Firifo's wickedness. He has the power to save Ndekezie instead he chooses to side with people whose cause he knows nothing about.

Bang bang bang!

I shudder.

'You call yourself a man of God yet you are gleeful at injustice,'

I am trembling.

'Do you have no mercy! Why can't you people of God inter-pret the Bible correctly? You have the power to save that boy.' Gathuki is tense with impatience.

Face contorted in fury, Firifo shoves the old man out of the way. Gathuki lets go of Firifo, walks to the door and opens it, facing the chanting.

'Thief, thief, thief!'

'Wait a minute. None of you saw what happened today, I did. Let he who has not sinned cast the first stone.'

Bang! A stone lands on him.

I can just about see Firifo standing at the door with his Bible.

'Leave the old man alone. He has lost his mind. I will bring you the man you seek. But please leave the old man alone.'

Firifo pushes Gathuki out of the way of the mob. I catch sight of them. Eyes popped out and snarling teeth, salivating, like police dogs about to pounce. Their faces filled with hate; bodies poised ready to attack. They are like soldiers in combat, brandishing stones and sticks. There is a vacuum of fear and stillness in the room. A quick glance at Ndekezie, glistening with sweat, looking like a moulting snake. My breathing is in slow motion.

Firifo returns to the door. A barrage of chanting is unleashed. They mob surges forward. Gathuki is pushed. He looks defeated. They make for the steps like an angry flood. The henchmen from my encounter outside the gate run into the shop like sniffer dogs. I freeze. They move past me. Bodies are squeezed in at the doorway all pushing to get through. Some men are trying to hold off the mob from entering the premises.

'Come out now, you have run out of options,' says the man with Ray Parker Jr hair.

He kicks the crates out of the way. Ndekezie who has been cowering like a little mouse bolts from his position and leaps towards the window. The ringleader too leaps and grabs Ndekezie's wide oversized shorts which slide down his legs

245

with ease leaving him stark naked. His dark skin is wet with sweat. The man with Ray Parker Jr hair tries to grab onto him but he hesitates not knowing where to hold him. Ndekezie seizes the opportunity and jumps out of the window.

'Run,' I say softly.

Dust particles settle on the ledge from which Ndekezie jumped. I'm tense with anticipation praying he gets away from the marauding mob. The man with Ray Parker Jr hair snarls, punching the air. His eyes scan the room and settle on me. My bladder slackens. His accomplice grabs his arm.

'Don't let that rascal get away.'

He hesitates and runs out, joining the chanting mob. The door sways at their departure. I am left reeling, almost levitating in fear. Surrounded by a stillness as disturbing as the chaos that preceded it. I sit still. Close my eyes.

'Dear God, please let him get away.'

Like a herd of elephants, there's a scramble outside as the crowd moves away in pursuit of Ndekezie. Menacing excitement is coming from the other side of the window. I edge closer to the window, sitting on my heels. My ears take over, picking up fragments of information. Ndekezie can't have run far from where he landed because I hear him whimpering. He must be hiding but his sobbing is loud enough for me to hear. He sounds frightened, like a cornered, injured antelope. If only he was still under the counter, I could reassure him with my eyes.

'Wait he's here,' a voice calls.

The mob bays like wild dogs at a hunt. There's scrambling and I think Ndekezie is trying to get away.

'He's broken his leg,' laughs a voice.

The mob jeers. I bow my head.

'What do you have to say for yourself,' another voice demands.

'I did not steal anything.'

'If you were innocent, why would you run?'

'Because the men frightened me,' Ndekezie's voice quavers.

If only I could hold his hand and make everything okay for him. I want to go outside and order those hooligans to leave him alone. I realise there's nothing I can do. I'm paralysed by fear. For him. He must know that I feel it for him too. The way his eyes pleaded with me.

'Just admit it, you are nothing but a petty thief.'

Silence.

'Say I am just a petty thief.'

More silence.

'The market seller said you stole a *mandazi*,' a voice says.

'No. I am not a thief. Please.'

'You stupid man taking us for fools. The reason you ran was because you were guilty. The guilty will pay for their sins.'

There is a thud. A distressed squeal pierces my ears. I stop breathing. It sounds like a lamb caught a hyena's jaws. The crowds cheer. I'm drenched in sweat. The fear is morphing into anger. Who made them judge and jury? Even if he stole, why can't he be tried in a court of law?

There's another thud. Amplified by the hollowness of the shop which shocks me to alertness. What on earth was that? There's a squeal which turns into a scream. Droplets of a liquid lands on my hands. I think it's rain but when I look and see its blood. It must be Ndekezie's blood. Oh no. They are hurting him. What sort of people would go out of their way to come all the way from the marketplace to hound a man?

There's another thud followed by a shrieking sound.

'Please stop!' I say.

My voice is feeble and inaudible amongst the chants. I cover my ears. I can't listen anymore. The crowd outside is ecstatic.

How can they delight in their grotesque viciousness? How can they go back to their normal lives and pretend to be normal people to their neighbours after this? These Christians like Firifo are hypocrites attacking a poor man for no reason.

It is then from deep within my womb I feel a movement. It's almost a nudge. Oh God, there's a life inside of me. A human being like Ndekezie. Maybe the fear I feel made it move. I wonder whether it knows what my plans are. I wonder if it's cowering like Ndekezie fearing for its life. I wonder if it feels the same fear I feel now. Then it occurs to me, I am no better than them. I am hounding this life inside of me with the evil callous plans to terminate it. I slide onto the floor and begin to weep.

There's a wail. It's about to tail off. Then another thud brings out more squeals. I feel each one of them as if it were me. There's another thud.

'You've punctured his eye!' a voice says.

There's a scream. The crowd cheers.

Thud. 'Take that you monster.'

'Mama, Papa!' that sounds like Ndekezie.

Thud. 'Not even your parents can save you now.'

The squeal turns into a wail, then a whimper as the crowd swells with excitement.

'Asiefunzua na mamaye hufunzua ni ulimwengu.' Yells the high-pitched voice of a woman.

'Get his big head.'

There's a thud and another. It's almost a rumble. I lose count. Out of nowhere the bellowing of horns silence the compound. I freeze unsure about what's happening. The horn blares again, this time with great urgency. A stillness envelopes. No crickets, birds or planes break it.

'You are doomed.'

It sounds like Gathuki.

'We are about to lose everything. Our homes and everything we've ever worked for, yet it's a poor man child who you attack?'

'Shut up old man,' a voice yells.

'He's gone! The thief is gone.'

I hold my breath.

My head is spinning, everything becomes a massive black hole. The room is swirling, and I can't breathe. My stomach constricts. I retch. It yields nothing but slimy bile. Everything falls silent.

Chapter Thirty-Four

A gentle stroke on my cheek rouses me from deep sleep. Mama is towering over me. I blink, blinded by the light from the open shutters. I am dazed and disorientated. The last thing I remember is her going to the funeral. Then I was out with the rich man. *Ndekezie.* The events at Firifo's shop gatecrash my mind. Then the floodgates open and I remember the worst of it; his voice whimpering outside the window, him getting away from the mob. How I got home and into my bed, I don't recall, and conclude Mama must have brought me.

'What day is it?' I ask feebly.

'Today is Sunday. I couldn't go to the kiosk and leave you like this,' says Mama.

Thursday is important and I can't remember why. All I know is that the day is etched and circled in red in my mind's diary.

'You have to wake up and eat something.'

My head throbs. She brings a glass of cold water to my lips arousing my thirst. I drink it all and ask for more. The hydration eases my mental fog. Fragments of memory are littered in my mind like a patchwork quilt. One minute, I am lying on a bed with a white doctor towering over me, next I am hounded by a mob who mistake me for Ndekezie. I can't focus.

'You have to get out of bed. It's not healthy. Come sit with me outside.'

Mama walks outside taking an extra stool for me as I sit up to get dressed. I have lost track of time. I reach under my pillow where I flatten creases out of my neatly folded dress. Something sharp pokes my finger jarring my memory. It's the pencil and stash of notes. I pull them out and display them on my bed. The first one reads:

List of my enemies
Kīmathi * —physical punishment and prayers for bad things to happen
Wambūgū * —physical punishment and prayers for bad things to happen
Geremani* —physical punishment and prayers for bad things to happen
Oily Man in jungle lair —physical punishment and prayers for bad things to happen
Eastleigh turnboy —prayers for bad things to happen
Kaminde *—physical punishment and prayers for mangoes to fall on his pointed head or his matatū to get stuck in the mud

The second note is from the headmistress to Mama. It reads:

To Mūkami's mother,
    In life, not many get second chances. I gave one to Mūkami. She squandered it. Today, I have expelled her. She was unable to keep her legs shut. I am sorry to say this but your daughter will NEVER amount to anything. At best she'll become a market trader, but I would not hold my breath. Her only hope is to become a prostitute or chang'aa seller.

This is the first time I read this and my blood boils with anger. Who is she to determine my future? She barely knows me. In my previous school I was a well-behaved prefect with a goal of becoming a geologist and dreams of buying a house for me and Mama in the Rift Valley. My dreams have been hijacked and diverted off course. My heart is full of sadness. As I unfold the third note, tears roll down my face.

Dear sweetheart,

Last night, your beauty captured my soul. I have never been so blown away like I was with you. I can't stop looking at your beautiful face. I couldn't bear to wake you but I would like to see you again. I am off to the airport to catch a flight to Milan for some business. When I am back, I want to see you. I must go for now but make sure you ring me on this number in a week's time 2754. It's my direct line.

Bye for now.

P.S. I have left you some bus fare.

These three notes define my life. I put the two back under my pillow and stare at the list of my enemies again. I get up and get dressed. Once dressed, I step outside. My eyes flutter in the deluge of sunlight. Mama hands me tea and *mandazi*. I devour it and swig my tea.

'I'm going to stretch my legs.' I excuse myself to Mama who is relieved that I am finally out of bed and engaging with her.

'It will do you good.'

As I walk past his house Gathuki is sunk low on his *njũngwa*, his head stooped like an old crow, knees bent, touching the wisps of hair on his chin and excess folds of skin that hang at the crook of his neck. He doesn't look up as I approach. His face is etched with pain. He wears the vacant look of a man whose world has ended. He mumbles something, scratching the upper cartilage of his ear that he has decorated with bone, in the old traditional way.

'I could have stopped it. I could have saved him,' he says.

I get closer and stand still unsure whether he is speaking to me or himself. He is staring into a space between the mucky soil and his pointy nose, anguish imprinted on his face accentuating deep wrinkles. Sensing me, he turns slowly and our eyes lock, dragging us back to the depth of events at Firifo's shop. I think of the effort he'd put in convincing Firifo to spare Ndekezie. Now he's sunk into a void of hollowness. His mesmerising obsidian eyes, with a narrow streak of silvery catarrh and clear teardrops in the corners, draw me closer.

'I could have prevented it, but I am a coward.' A mask of gloom clouds his face.

I absorb his words.

'*Sielewi bwana* Gathuki, but you did save him,' I say.

'All my life I have fought it. Deep in the nights, long after the sun sinks into its cavernous hole and the owls hoot their final lullaby, he appears to me in my sleep. All my life I have fought it, and it's my weakness that caused that boy harm,' he says rubbing his eyes in sorrow.

'He got away bwana Gathuki,' I say but he doesn't seem to hear me.

I shift, listening, but it makes no sense that he is blaming himself for the attack on Ndekezie. He draws a long, deep breath and begins to speak, with resignation. 'A few nights ago, Ngai Mwene Nyaga appeared to me in my sleep. From a place far beyond the precinct of the human ear, he spoke to me and I listened. Light as a feather I began to levitate, and we floated away to a marketplace. It looked very familiar. I could see traders chatting noisily, haggling with customers, the sun was shining, and nothing was amiss. Then I spotted him. A hapless young man, looking distraught. He darted across the market in search of cover. My eyes had the clarity of daylight and I saw it was Ndekezie. He crashed into a sack of potatoes, then jumping back, crouched down behind it. An angry mob pursued, vying for his blood. I saw his peril and I tried to warn him his assailants were lurking about, but even as I shouted at the top of my lungs, my voice simply melted into the air, like ice in the midday sun.'

I stand still, unsure whether the story is finished and whether I should go or stay.

Big, anguished tears roll down Gathuki's worn, creviced face and he wills himself to carry on.

'Unwittingly, the young man got up from his hiding place just as the leaders of the mob turned in his direction. They spotted him, and the angry mob flocked to him, ravaging him like a pack of starving hyenas.'

Gathuki stops, wiping his weeping eyes with the back of his hand.

'I tried to shoo them away, but it was too loud. The mob dispersed as quickly as they came leaving nothing of the young man.'

Shaking violently, Gathuki finishes with, 'I am a coward.' He inhales a stringy mucus loudly, then wipes the remainder with his hands and transfers it on to his heel, drawing my gaze to his cracked feet.

I am dumbstruck and shudder, feeling the depth of his trauma. In an effort to reach through his torment I extend my hand, touching his thin bony shoulder. His soul is broken, unlike mine that's just dormant.

'Be on your way,' he says. 'We all have our crosses to bear.'

Walking out of the gate, I hurry to the phone booth, moving automatically, without thought or reason, my mind clear.

As I arrive, I see a man who is in a heated argument with an entity on the other end of the line, thrashing his finger in the air, splashing spittle onto the glass. His anger mounts, but it appears he has been cut off mid conversation. He bolts from the phone booth leaving the handset dangling and before I enter, I prop the door open to dispel the lingering odour of stale sweat. Satisfied the air is clearer I enter and sliding a shilling into the coin slot, I dial.

'Kĩrigiti high school can I help you?' a lady's voice answers.

'Good afternoon, my name is Mama Mũthoni and I would like to speak to the headmaster please. It's very urgent.'

There is a clicking noise and the unmistakable voice of Wamakũbũ comes on.

'The headmaster, may I help you?'

'Yes, good afternoon this is Mama Mũthoni, I don't know if you remember me.'

'I meet many people Mama Mũthoni, so please excuse me if I forget who you are.'

'I am the lady that cooks the *sambusas* for the carpenter's shop.'

'The carpenter doesn't have a shop.'

'Yes he does, I supply him with the *sambusas* he sells to the students. Could you please pass on a message to him?'

'He does what? In his workshop?'

'Yes, it's a very profitable business. Please can you tell him that I am running a bit late, the rain has messed up all the roads and I will not be able to get there until four o'clock today.'

The voice turns hard with rage. 'I shall make sure he gets the message.'

I hang up the phone and pull out the list of my enemies. My heart is pounding as I tick off the next name on the list.

Chapter Thirty-Five

⌒

My feet crunch the gravel with renewed vigour. I see the obscured PCEA church sign and walk to the gate next to it. The voice on the telephone had sounded sympathetic and eager.

'Come straight away. I am home today.'

I knock on the chequered gate with a small stone. A dog barks. It takes less than two minutes for the gate to swing open. In front of me stands a lean man with the demeanour of a middleweight boxer. He is in a vest and shorts as if I have called on him mid-dressing. His wide face scrutinises me as I step into the front yard, grey with concrete paving. A geriatric dog is sprawled in the shade of the house. It acknowledges my arrival by slapping its tail on the concrete but doesn't bother to open its eyes. There's a woman in a maid's uniform coaxing a toddler to eat some pawpaw mushed up in a bowl. The little girl smiles at me, and I nod. From the corner of her eye, the maid stares at my abdomen.

From inside, I see two small identical faces peering at me through the curved floral spindles protecting the window. They disappear as quickly as they appeared. We walk to the front door which is ajar, and he invites me in. I stand by the door and look round the large room. Close to me is a dining table whose polished edges are visible underneath a white linen tablecloth.

Opposite, a wall unit houses a tv with the volume turned low, and football playing in the background. There are several sofas situated around the room.

'Jeremiah! My name is Jeremiah,' the Editor of the Standard says firmly, extending his hand in a jolly, comforting manner.' His eyes dart over my appearance. 'Well, well. It's not every day I get visits from high school students.'

He walks to the dining table where he must have been working and picks up a notepad with some squiggle writing on it. I look at it in confusion, wondering what language he writes. Seeing my concern he tells me with a wry smile, 'That's short-hand. It's how we jot down stories quickly.'

I nod remembering I have seen Wamakũbũ's secretary take notes with the same type of writing.

'It's rare that I invite clients into my home, but since your phone call, it is clear this has to be done, and quickly.'

Feeling an overwhelming sense of calm, I shrug.

He picks up a camera from the table and walks to the door.

'We need to take some pictures of you ideally in your uniform, have you brought it with you?'

I nod and he points me to a toilet next to the corridor. Orange walls make the space feel claustrophobic, as I get out of my dress and put on my school uniform. I tuck in my shirt and wear my skirt just above my stomach accentuating my rounded bump. I step outside the toilet to find him waiting for me with his camera in hand. He walks me to the back, to a courtyard with better lighting.

'Stand by that wall.'

I walk to the whitewashed wall and lean against it bowing my head. There are a few clicks of the camera.

Staring intently, he says, 'I want to catch the side view, so pause there, now turn slightly to the right.'

I stick my belly out and I catch a reflection of myself on the window. I had not realised just how big my belly was. It's alarming and I blurt out, 'Please don't show my face, my parents will know me and say that I am bringing shame to our family.' I try to sound convincing.

His arms drop and the camera sways as he says with determination, 'I understand. I need to nail these men who are ruining our country by impregnating young schoolgirls.' His disgust is palpable. 'At least with our newspapers, we can and must, hold these hoodlums to account.'

Click goes his camera. After several shots, he points me to a chair at the kitchen table where he tells me to sit while he retrieves a beaten up recorder and small microphone. He motions to the mic and says, 'Now we are going to do a recording. Just tell me exactly what happened. Don't worry we will protect your identity.'

Sitting comfortably, I begin and let my imagination run. Once I finish, I stand up in silence as he fumbles with the recording equipment. I gather my belongings, hastily changing out of my uniform, thank him and rush through the gate. I make my way home without a single thought in my head. I feel unburdened and have a growing satisfaction of having reduced the number of names on my revenge list by one more.

Mama is still sitting outside as I walk back into the compound.

'You look more alive after your walk.'

'I am,' I say.

Chapter Thirty-Six

The pattern of criss-crossed sisal and vibrant pea pods keep morphing as Mama scoops the handful of yet more peas and tops up my *gĩtarũrũ*. The tray balances on my lap as we bask in the early afternoon sun. I pick one pod, twist and extract the round globules putting them into the *sufuria*.

'You look so much happier today," she says sweetly, but she still seems distracted, more focused on her task at hand than me, for which I am grateful. She continues, 'I too have benefited from taking a few days off work.'

We are interrupted by a pair of tyre sandals in front of us. We look up to see Gathuki standing with a distraught look.

'Bwana Gathuki, you mustn't blame yourself for what happened. You did everything you could do. We have a problem with our mentality. A poor boy can lose his life for a *Mandazi* and a rich man can steal homes with impunity,' Mama chides.

'That's why I am here. We need to gather everyone as soon as possible and congregate by the mango tree now.'

Mama gestures to me to move and I immediately jump up ready to join everyone. We put the peas back in the *kĩondo*, lock the door and walk to the mango tree with our stools in tow. Several people are already gathered under the tree. Gĩtonga looks up from the daily newspaper he's reading as we approach.

We position ourselves next to him. I take a glimpse of the headlines. 'Kīrigiti High School Headmaster fired for impregnating schoolgirl.' A shiver runs through my body. I don't know if that's the feeling of revenge, but it thrills my heart a little to think his life might be destroyed like the way he destroyed mine by quashing my dreams. I have an incredible urge to pull out my list of enemies and cross out Wamakūbū's name but decide to wait until later when I'm in my bed.

I sit next to Mama and when everyone settles Gathuki stands up, unfurls his arched back, and begins to talk with urgency.

'During the meeting, I let it be known that I was a foreseer. All my life, I run away from the messages delivered to me by Ngai Mwene Nyaga. But time has come for me to take on the responsibility he bestowed upon me. I had a vision about the notice, I did nothing. I had a vision about Ndekezie's attack, and I did nothing. If only I had done my job.'

The mention of Ndekezie clouds the warmth of revenge. My head droops with sadness as others bow their heads at the horror that manifested in our compound.

'The old hag warned us but we did not take heed. Some people mocked her thinking she was mad, but she bears the same gift as me. Her words were nearly realised.'

I don't know why Gathuki is talking about these things that drag me back to the pit of gloom. The numbness that enveloped me during Ndekezie's attack was crippling, but I was just beginning to feel human, and now the thought of the *chang'aa* woman fills me with discomfort. I'm consumed by a contradiction of feelings; the victory of my revenge, sadness for Ndekezie's attack, and fear for my life. *Before seven days are over, one of you will be dead.* Does Ndekezie's attack qualify as a death? Will the *chang'aa* seller's curse be absolved? I still have a baby inside me so I could die. I am horrified by that thought, and every time I close my eyes, I see Ndekezie's eyes looking back at mine, pleading with me to help him.

'I had another visit from Mwene Nyaga and it's not good. None of us is safe. We have scorned our ancestors and they are lashing out. All the predictions of Mũgo Wa Kĩbiro are coming true.'

'Tell us about your vision. What was it about?' asks Elephantiasis?

My gaze is fixated on Gathuki's overcast face.

'A few nights ago, as we made our rounds inviting people to Firifo's shop for a meeting, I shared with Firifo and a few others that I had a nightmare in which his wife Jane and little Ruth turned into devils. That's always a very bad sign.'

'How does your dream concern us, Bwana Gathuki?' asks Gĩtonga.

Gathuki hesitates and I am wondering the same.

'I dreamt that we were at Firifo's shop for a meeting and a fire began.' Seeing the terror in people's faces, he pauses. 'It's nothing to worry about. We need to reach out to our ancestors and apologise to them for shunning them. We need to slaughter a *ngorima* to cleanse ourselves.

'You can slaughter one of the goats in the compound,' says Gĩtonga.

I squirm in disgust. The goats in the compound are sustained by filth and prevent us from drowning in rubbish. They would probably be rejected by the ancestors.

'It has to be a special one from a special herd. It must be unblemished,' says Gathuki.

'I suggest we fundraise to buy one if it's for the benefit of the whole compound,' says Elephantiasis.

I don't know why they think this is a priority. I have more pressing matters. I still have a baby to get rid of and Mama must find somewhere to live. Fundraising for a goat is the least of our concerns.

'We must do it in haste. We have no time to spare. Something terrible awaits.'

Chapter Thirty-Seven

Bodies ripple with rhythm, like shifting dunes in the wind. Restless feet pattern the dance floor, limbs swirling in tune with the DJ's mastery. He ensures no feet get an ounce of rest stealing the show with one hit after another, the crowds lost in the beat. The flickering lights shower the revellers with bursts of colour, highlighting merry faces gurning with delight. The hairs on my skin are erect with nerves as I, hawk-eyed, watch a group of young men as the waiter serves their drinks.

Resembling a girl band, three girls join them clad in tutu skirts, leather jackets and bangles. They exchange hugs and kisses on the cheek, as I move closer to the dimmer part of the sitting area. My heart pangs as Kīmathi puts his hand around a slight girl with braided hair and hoop earrings, drawing her closer to him. Throbbing pain in my nails alerts me to the fact I have dug them into the wooden table. My other hand clenches the tray I'm holding so tight I fear it will break.

The girl with braided hair reaches out with delicate fingers and touches his face. He leans forward, his nose tucked into her neck as if to absorb her perfume. I'm about to combust in anguish. She gazes into his eyes with a tenderness I thought only I possessed. I desperately want to warn her about him. Tell her that all that affection is fake. That he will destroy not only her present but also her future. That if she doesn't succumb to his demands, he holds no barriers and he will go to any lengths to forcefully take away what he can't have willingly. A tap on my shoulder makes me jump with fright.

'Excuse me please can you take our orders?' says a man in a coarse voice.

'Sorry I don't work here.'

The man looks at me with a raised eyebrow, as his eyes shift to the name badge pinned above my breast, stolen by Bũi from her work whilst I kept watch. He rolls his eyes to mine, and I stare back in confusion. The absurdity of the situation is laughable. Resembling the waiting staff, I am wearing Bũi's waistcoat, borrowed from her saloon, and my white school shirt. I burst out in a nervous laugh.

'Of course, sir, please give me one minute.'

The man walks off and I continue the vigil. I scrutinize Kĩmathi with the keenness of a bird watcher spying on a flock. He's relaxed and his smile is tender. I wait until they have had a few to dull their awareness. So far Kĩmathi has drunk two large bottles of Tusker and he's on his third. Everyone is engrossed looking at him in adulation. He appears to be telling a hilarious story only pausing to swig beer from his bottle. They throw their heads back, their raucous laughter rising high above the already loud room. I am filled with jealousy. I'd give anything to trade places with his companions. Sitting at that table laughing at his jokes. I think of the way he fed me *bhajia's* as we gazed into each other's eyes. I think of our dancing and how he took my breath away. The smell of his perfume is imbued into my being. My heart weeps at those memories.

Kĩmathi's girl leans over, and he kisses her lips. I could throttle them both. I want to run and never stop. I need to abandon this mission. I am not cut out for this. A kick in my abdomen shocks me back to reality. I remember the hostility on Geremani's face as he walked me out and closed the gate on my future. I think of how the headmistress slammed the door in my face for being pregnant, destroying every ounce of who I wanted to become. I think of how I came face to face with death at Dr Njaū's clinic.

Bile bubbles from deep within and my heart throbs, flaming with raw anger. I am here and force myself to concentrate on the task ahead. Two more days. Just two more days until the clean people in the *mzungu* clinic take this alien out of my body. And then can my life get back on track again.

I force the green monster back into the pit of my stomach. I can't allow jealousy to derail me now. My observation continues. Kīmathi has been drinking beer straight from the bottle and no one at the table is using a glass other than the wine drinkers. His bottle is almost empty, and I must move now before another waiter walks over. Pushing the borrowed spectacles up the bridge of my nose and pulling my headscarf down to my brow, I make my way to them, holding the tray I lifted from the table next to me.

A tug of my shirt and I am swung round staring into a dark burly puffy face.

'What do you think you are playing at?'

I gulp for air. I'm paralysed.

'I've watched you all evening and you've been trying to do as little work as possible. The place is littered with empty bottles, and you are just standing here enjoying yourself.'

It takes me several minutes to realise he must think I am staff. A choked laugh escapes and I apologise. I busy myself wiping the table and when he's gone, I make my way to Kīmathi's table.

'Same again?' I say in a low tone and broken accent shaking the bottles and collecting the empties.

They nod without glancing at me. I am about to walk away when Kĩmathi calls.

'Waitress?'

I stop. Did he recognise me? I have his full attention. I can't risk turning round. If he looks into my eyes, he will recognise me. I'm drenched in sweat. I keep walking disappearing amongst other waitresses at the bar. Shuffling behind a pillar, I give them a quick glance and see they are back in conversation. Tucking the tray between my legs, I order four beers and two wines.

'You must be new, I haven't seen your pretty face here before,' says a man behind the bar.

I scowl, give the table number and order. He is swift, preparing the order without the need to check or second guess his concoctions. I soon have the four drinks in front of me and placing them on the tray, I walk to the other end of the counter and with my right hand obscured, I pull out three pills and drop all three in the bottle one after the other. I watch as they dissolve and once the drinks look normal again, I walk back to his table. Keeping my glance down, and aided by low lighting, I place the drinks in front of each person. Kĩmathi's drink I place closer to him. I thank them and wish them a good night, swinging the tray up under my arm as I leave, making sure I give their table a last quick swipe with my cloth. I drop the tray at the workstation and then, from the shadows I watch.

Kĩmathi must have many stories to tell. Everyone is still listening and laughing. He lifts the bottle and raises it to his lips. I inhale. He pauses, I bite my lip. I wonder if he smelled anything different. I can't remember if the pills I stole from

Dr Njaũ smell. He places the bottle back and raises his hand for a waiter. My heart sinks. He is suspicious. I have failed yet again. I watch as another waiter comes over, listens to him, and scribbles something down. I think he's calling the manager, but the waiter walks away. He leans forward, takes the bottle, and brings it back to his mouth. My heart stops. He takes a big swig. My heart pounds. He takes another, still telling his story. I watch. He takes a couple more swigs. I keep staring as he empties the contents into his mouth, just as he did with the *chang'aa* seller. Satisfied I ditch the cloth, walk to the bathroom and peel off my disguise.

I stare at my face in the mirror. All that looks back at me is ugliness. I'm consumed with self-loathing. My face is shrouded in bitterness, jealousy, and scorn. I think of the old *chang'aa* seller and her hideous face. This is how people become ugly, through the ugliness of life. She was probably once a beautiful girl with dreams of a brilliant future, and not a urine-soaked old age. This is who I have become. A jealous scorned girl with a bleak future. I am so jealous seeing him look at that girl. There must be something wrong with me. I think of the last thing his maid said to me on the phone at the crossroads after my expulsion. *'He's fucking another girl.'* The pain in my chest is as raw as on the day those words were said to me. I'm to blame for my weakness. That's what landed me in his arms after the school disco. It was my weakness that made me walk to the barbed wire fence at the end of the mocks, but it was he and his protégé that forced me to do things I can't comprehend. It was his cruelty that landed me in this predicament. He is the architect of my demise. He deserves everything that comes to him after everything he did to me. I stuff the glasses and scarf in a bag and walk to the dance floor.

The DJ announces it's the end of the night by playing 'Lady in Red' and couples embrace in the slow dance. I lean against the pillar watching him dance with the girl in braids. Tears roll down my cheeks remembering that moment during the school disco. When the song is over the group walk to their table, empty their drinks and head out to the car park. I follow at a distance, careful to remain under the shadows.

I notice his feet begin to drag, and he is clearly staggering and struggling to remain upright, but he makes it into the driver's seat and his girl sits in the passenger's side. I watch the lights come on, the engine start, and the Volvo jump as he accelerates out of the compound onto the main road. I turn and walk away and don't look back to see the car collide with another car. But I hear the screech of his tires and the crunch of metal on metal. Keeping my head down, I make my way to the exit.

Chapter Thirty-Eight

The car revs as I step in. The driver steps on the accelerator and we skid off.

'Another one bites the dust,' says Būi, turning round to look at me. 'How does it feel?'

'Revenge is meant to be sweet, but I feel nothing,' I say.

'So, we are not going to Annabel's?' asks Būi's friend, the driver.

'You bet we are. Just because I don't feel anything doesn't mean it's not payback time.'

They both cheer. He steps on the gas, and we are flying down Lang'ata road. The roads are clear at this time of night as clubgoers are still in the throngs of fun. I think about what just happened with Kīmathi.

For hours, I fantasised about what I would do to him if I ever laid eyes on him again. I don't know if he'll live or die in the collision, and I don't care. I am numb to logic. I seem to be fuelled by two things, getting rid of this baby and revenge. A small part of me wishes he didn't suffer. I wish I could drag out the love still hiding in the crevices of my heart and crush it under my shoes. But it still hangs on.

I look out of the window as the car spins to the left by the stadium. Big drops of tears roll down my eyes. I don't know if they are tears of joy, relief, or sadness. We are on Uhuru highway when Bũi turns round and says as if to remind me, 'revenge is getting even. Sharing the pain that was inflicted.'

I have to agree. The caning by Wamakũbũ was the worst pain I've ever experienced. It wasn't just physical pain Kĩmathi inflicted on me, it was also emotional and economic. It's as if he was on a quest to destroy every aspect of my life. What I have done to him is only a tiny fraction of what he has taken away from me. He's taken away my present and future. He's taken away my innocence, propelling me to have to go into worlds that up until now would have been inconceivable. I should be in my school dorm reading for my A Levels, instead I am wandering from place to place dishing out revenge. I could find other ways of inflicting more pain and suffering on him, but I have no energy or know-how.

The traffic is clear, and we are at the museum roundabout. The brakes screech to a halt and we get out of the car outside the big dome building painted in black. Bũi and I walk to the door. A burly doorman emerges from boredom to give us a sly smile.

'Our friends paid for us, and they are already inside.'

Staring at her cleavage, he smiles and nods.

'Stop by at the end of the night and I will give you some honey,' he says and winks.

We are in. The club is nearly empty.

'There is only one hangout joint for trendy people. And that's Carnivore. I guarantee you will find Kĩmathi there. This Saturday is Super Soul. Everyone is guaranteed to be there,' said Bũi on the phone.

'I don't think he's still friends with Wambũgũ I doubt they'd go to the same club,' I said.

'The only other place is Annabel's. It's the loser's joint,' she'd laughed.

The ambience in the club is subdued. It's as if the DJ has quit enticing people with hit songs. Kenny Rogers and Dolly Parton's 'Islands in the Stream' plays. There are a few people swaying reluctantly on the dance floor. I look around. The club seems populated with potbellied men and their *mpango kandos*. On the third table after the door, I spot Wambũgũ. He's sat in a booth with a girl. He is looking at her tenderly and she leans over gazing into his eyes. In front of them is a tray of lamb chops. She cuts bits and feeds him as if he were a toddler. I nudge Bũi and point. From her carrier bag, she pulls out a pair of high heels, slides them on and approaches them with a swagger. I sit at a vacant table close by.

'I knew I would find you here. You knew the baby had no milk and instead of bringing it you are out with prostitutes.'

Startled, the two jump to their feet. I strain my neck to have a better view.

'What on earth are you talking about?'

'You are now going to play that same game that you don't know who I am,'

'I have no clue who you are.'

'That's not going to work this time. I am collecting my things and heading back to my mother's. You are a no-good cheat. How many of us are you going to impregnate? Sweetheart, you better join the long queue because you are last.'

I am impressed by Bũi's performance.

'Please leave us alone. I don't know who you are or what you are talking about.'

'Don't worry, I will leave you alone and don't come begging me like you always do. This time is for good.'

I want to jump up and clap for a brilliant performance. Bŭi's ingenuity has no bounds. I watch her with pride, as she swaggers out into the darkness. Turning to look at the table, I see Wambŭgŭ's girl toss her drink into his face and walk out.

Chapter Thirty-Nine

⌒

I lie in my bed listening to Mama and Kaminde snore, alternating like frogs in a mating dance. Having pretended to be having an early night, I feigned calmness as they stood up to leave the room. I think back over the events of the day. How once they were settled, I pinned my ear to the barrier wall and listened. They were discussing something in low tones. Placing a stool underneath the window, I unlocked the shutters and blew out the wick of the kerosene lamp. Slowly I climbed out of the window, cowering in the shadows. At the gate, the watchman was settled for the night. Taking off my shoes, I climbed to the other side and hurried down to the bus stop outside Kitch Sarajevo to find Būi and her friend waiting for me.

Mama's words before she left for her room ring in my ears.

'Your school starts on Friday. Make sure you wash all your uniforms, and I can help you iron them.'

'I will.' I bolted the door from inside like I normally do.

Even if the *mzungus* from the clinic take out the alien invading my womb, how will I explain to her about the school situation? Being expelled twice from different schools is a crime worse than murder. How will I ever get back to education?

I am peering into the deep well of my problems, and I can't see a light. I am unable to accept that I will never sit in a classroom again. That I will never read books from a school library again. What will I do for a job? Join Mama to sell white people charity clothes in her kiosk. What other options are there? Maybe I could attend a secretarial college. But the fees are astronomical, and I'd have to have finished school.

I am in a vicious cycle, and I can't get out of it. I turn over, bury my face into my pillow, and weep.

I'm back staring into the hollow darkness of the night. It has become my companion as my mind duels with itself. I remember that I forgot to do the most important task. Update my list of enemies, but I am already drifting off to sleep.

Chapter Forty

⌣

In my dreamy state, I hear drumming. At first, I think it's Jane and Firifo doing their Sunday ritual when he marches to the pit latrine for his weekly bath wearing a sleeveless vest, his biceps sticking out like sundried lemons. She drums, singing her love for him, until he returns from his bath wrapped in a threadbare towel. The sound is getting louder, and I bolt upright. It's Mama knocking.

'We have a meeting at Wa Njũgũ's,' she says walking in.

The mention of Wa Njũgũ leaves me cold. Mama knows. She must, otherwise why would we be going to her? She isn't friends with Wa Njũgũ. There's no other reason to be visiting that vulgar woman other than for her to blurt out my secret. She is taking me there to get a testament. That has to be it. My heart thuds and I fear she can hear it. My mind is racing wondering what I should say or do. A thought flashes through my mind. I'll wait for her to walk out of the room and then I'll run. She turns round and before she exits, I am already taking off my nightdress.

I put on my dress and reach for my bag. I am leaving home. It's getting harder to hide the bulge, it's becoming more prominent by day. The stress of keeping the secret is consuming me. I am shocked Mama hasn't noticed before. She's blinded by

her own pile of problems getting bigger. Her kiosk was bull-
dozed and now she displays her clothes on the floor with no
shelter. She's still sad about losing her friend, and the crossway
tailor keeps threatening her if she doesn't make her monthly
payments. I've been refusing to get out of bed or eat, leaving
her fraught with worry. I must think fast. I tiptoe to the door
and look out. No sign of Mama. This is my chance to flee. I'll go
to the *mzungu* clinic and beg them to get this thing out of me.
I can't carry on with the pretence. I will not let the residents of
the Ministry of Works humiliate me and possibly beat me like
they did with Ndekezie. I step back inside, grab a few things
and stuff them in my bag. I take a big breath and stride outside.
I halt mid-step coming face to face with Mama.

'I didn't expect you to get dressed so fast,' she says.

I'm gripped by fear. I can't think, so I stand still.

'Come my daughter, we won't be homeless, God will give
us a way,' she says, leading me in the direction of Wa Njũgũ's
house.

I'm breathing shallow and fast. I can't speak in a normal
tone, so pretend to cough.

'Why, what's this about?' I ask.

She's holding my hand. Is this a plot to get me there? She
must suspect my plan and I want her to let go before she detects
the tremor going through me. Oh God I need to get away. I drag
my feet. My body is reluctant.

'Women of the neighbourhood are gathering there to come
up with a plan for the eviction,' she says.

I grunt. She's lying to trick me into going without drama.
I'm caged in a never-ending nightmare. The humiliation of
being dragged by Wamakũbũ to his office in front of everyone washes over me. I can already visualise the washerwomen
and Wa Njũgũ cracking their jaws with laughter, uttering snide

remarks; *I hope she enjoyed herself* or *she couldn't keep her legs together.* I'm dripping with sweat at the thought, exacerbated by the intense morning sun. I walk alongside Mama like a lamb to the slaughter. We turn the corner in the direction of Wa Njũgũ's house. I imagine laughter will emerge anytime soon. I close my eyes in anticipation. I hear nothing and when I open them, I see Wa Njũgũ perched on her *rĩthũ* with her baby sitting between her legs playing with a stash of bottle tops. I am filled with trepidation.

Mama tugs me to carry on walking. The washerwomen are congregated around Wa Njũgũ and their presence makes my face burn with anticipated humiliation. Their buttocks are spread out on their *rĩthũs* like picnic blankets. The dying woman picks twigs from her sponge mattress as we approach. Residents of number twenty-one, fifteen, eighteen, thirteen, and six all scan the ground for a space to perch on. This is the worst place for me to be under the scrutiny of all these women. Women are sharp at deciphering, and they'll see right through me. Even the *mzungu* woman read me like a book. I sit as far away as possible obscured by Mama. My only defence is denial and if that fails, I'll flee.

Jane appears carrying Ruth on her hip. She finds a patch of naked ground to spread her *rĩthũ*. All the houses at the Ministry of Works have a similar design and everyone knows that no one house has enough space for entertaining guests. Before, if anyone had guests, they would borrow stools, but seeing that people forget to return them they've stopped lending. Everyone knows to bring a seating plan. Wa Njũgũ clears her throat to speak and my heart stops pumping. I am having a heart attack.

'*Mũrĩega*,' Wa Njũgũ says.

Her voice fills me with horror. I am numb awaiting my condemnation.

'These useless men decided to go on a journey in search of a medicine man, how is that going to help us?' she says.

My mind races through the dictionary in my brain trying to decipher what she's saying.

'*Ehe*! Today is the day our compound is meant to be demolished and it could happen any minute now. We have no time to waste,' says the resident of number fifteen.

Wait a minute. I thought this was about me. In my quest for an abortion and revenge, I forgot about the notice. I thought we were here so that these women could laugh about abortions. Why else would they have a women's meeting?

'That's why I have called you here. Our inaction risks our homes. That last meeting achieved nothing,' says Wa Njũgũ.

'We need concrete action,' says Mama.

I wasn't prepared for this. I am weighed down by my problems, and I cannot engage with this conversation.

The woman from house number eighteen leans forward. 'It has to be a politician behind that note.'

Wa Njũgũ says, 'This meeting has already yielded more action, and we are only five minutes in. We all know who the land grabbers are. I say turn up at his house and demonstrate.'

This is not helping me. I cannot process what they are saying. I need to quieten the demons in my head. I need to find solace. This conversation is causing me more distress. Homelessness is something I can't fathom right now.

'Yes, let's take all the women and children and protest outside his house. If he doesn't listen, we take drastic measures and throw *maii* at his house,' says number fifteen.

'We need to conduct ourselves as decent citizens if we want public sympathy, throwing faeces isn't going to work in our favour,' says resident of house number six.

Wa Njũgũ looks at the woman with great interest.

'Do you think they are throwing us out because the place is very dirty. Look at all the rubbish dumps infested with rats. How will anybody respect us if we don't respect ourselves,' says number thirteen.

I look at the pile of stinking decomposing rubbish strewn all over the place. This reflects my life. Chewed and discarded to rot. Like the residents of the Ministry of Works. Fighting crows merge into the battle in my mind. The stench of urine and rubbish makes itself more prominent in my nose in agreement.

'We need to show value of this place by clearing all the rubbish,' says a voice from the back.

'We don't want to waste our energy on clearing the rubbish, first things first, otherwise we will be just like the men, useless. We should dedicate our energy on getting that *kĩhĩĩ* who placed the notice in the first place,' says Wa Njũgũ. 'It's unanimous we will get there first thing in the morning before he leaves for *mbunge*.'

Everyone nods in agreement.

Chapter Forty-One

⌒

The rousing women liven the compound, putting the resident cockcrow to shame. I sit up from another restless night and rub my eyes. Mama is waiting for me to open the door so she can use the kitchen space. I let her in and head to the pit latrine. The cool morning air chills me to the bone. There's no queue so I am in and out. I stop at the tap and wash my hands and face with the ice-cold water. I gargle, spit and walk back to the house to find Mama boiling water for *turungi* as there's no milk. We eat boiled sweet potato for breakfast. I relish being with her without Kaminde. There's a calmness that engulfs her when he is not around. She is softer and more perceptive. It's as if he sucks all her warmth when he's around. His constant need to talk about his plans which involve unroadworthy cars and lame duck projects. It's as if he lives in an alternate reality where junk is a viable business option. He drains me too, always creating a barrier between Mama and me. Our equilibrium ends when she stands up in time to go to the protest.

Wa Njũgũ and several women and children are already there when Mama and I arrive at the meeting point by the gate.

'*Gĩchamba nĩkĩrũaru ni gitũaruo thibitarĩ.*'

Wa Njũgũ begins the chorus once everyone is assembled.

Stomping like a herd of elephants, our human bus

mobilises, leaving clouds of dust on the marram road. Jane beats her drum. I don't want to be here, but Mama needs me. The women and children sing with vigour, and I join in reluctantly. It's difficult to keep up with the animated crowd but I push myself. This thing inside of me moves all the time now and it's difficult to ignore. Its kicks intensify as if to join the protest. Why can't I have my own space where I don't have to participate in any of this? I don't want anyone to turn their attention to me.

We arrive at the crossroads. Reminders of my predicament are ubiquitous. The goat which tempted me to hang myself is still tethered to the tree. It circles the tree trying to reach greener grass outside its perimeter. It's stuck unable to break free from the noose around its neck, mirroring my life. I walk past the phone booth in which Kīmathi's maid informed me he was fucking someone else. My heart wrings out pain. His torment is inescapable. My revenge does nothing to soothe the pain I feel. Not only that, but he also planted an evil spirit to haunt me from inside. I am trapped.

Mama holds my hand as the human bus veers left in the direction of the formidable mansions. Cars toot their support as the march proceeds fuelling the group's momentum. By the time the first *matatū* begin their schedule, the troupe is approaching the palatial gates of the MP's house, and I am out of breath.

'He already lives like a *mūthamaki,* look at all this, and still he is not satisfied, he has to evict us to grab more land,' wails a woman from the back.

I want to sit down already exhausted from the walk. No one else is sitting so I look for something to support my weight. A hedge of pristine bougainvillea beckons, and I lean against it.

'It's all stolen money,' says another.

I look at the sprawling mansion hidden by bougainvillea and wonder what it must be like to live in this peaceful oasis. How do people get to this destination? Before I was derailed, I dreamt of living in a small house with Mama in the Rift Valley breathing all the fresh air. I draw in a sharp breath, the air here is different from the air in our compound in Kĩrigiti. There's no stench of toilet and rotting rubbish. Just flowers.

'*kĩrũtindũrũ kĩrũtindũrũ giataga rũta,*' the chorister rouses the sleepy guard. Red-eyed faces peer from a cutout in the gate.

'What do you want,' he grimaces in disdain.

He reminds me of the compound dog that sleeps all day when it's not eating or licking its scrotum.

'We demand that the minister comes to talk to us about the Ministry of Works. We believe he is behind the eviction notice and we demand an answer,' says Wa Njũgũ.

She's forthright and vocal. Her voice is commanding. If I didn't loathe her so much, I'd think it's admirable. I'm glad she's far away from me. She makes me want to curl up and hide.

'Tell him to come out here and see the mothers and children he is throwing out,' she says.

There's a loud cheer.

'It is women and children. These greedy politicians have no mercy,' says the dying woman with more passion than I've ever seen in her.

A chorister sings and everyone except me joins into the sound of the drums. I am drained, thirsty and my legs are swollen. I fear they'll give way if I don't sit down.

The gate swings open and out protrudes a belly covered with a tent for a shirt. He toggles the braces supporting his extra wide girth which resembles the belly of a pig. I gasp. He's grotesque. Small reptile-like hands reach to his neck to adjust his tie. I stand straight to get a better view. He has a glass eye.

I know which one it is because it's the one that looks at us with sympathy. He swivels his tiny face making his huge nose protrude. He resembles an anteater. I want to laugh. He stares at me and then the others with hostility.

'You can't move us because we have the strength of Jesus,' says Jane, Firifo's wife.

'Quiet!' he says with a squeaky voice.
The women throw their heads back with laughter. I snigger.

'I can reassure you that I am not the one behind the eviction notice. It's lies by my enemies,' he says.

'In that case, how do you know about the eviction notice?' a voice calls.

The boisterous women jeer. He shifts in discomfort. How can a man like this thing, without any redeemable qualities, reach such heights? He's not articulate, or personable, and yet he's at the top of the pecking order. And we are at the bottom, caged like chicken in a coop, living amongst our filth. I am filled with bitterness. I tried my hardest. Revised and did all my homework, was obedient and now look at me. Where do all these qualities get me? Nowhere. Two expulsions and pregnant against my will. I look at all these women weighed down by societal breakdown and yet they are still fighting.

'How could you take the homes of women and children whilst you already live like a king?' says Wa Njũgũ.

'As your MP, I demand you show me respect.' His voice tails off.

There's a loud booing.

Chapter Forty-Two

⌒

A whispering wind concurs I should stay in bed. I turn over but my bladder protests. I throw off my blanket and slide to the bottom of my bed. In my stupor, my fingers glide over the ledge of the cupboard. Using it as leverage, I haul myself to my feet. I feel for the table on which our two-ring burner sits. Like a nocturnal beast, my nose twinges in search of my plastic basin, half-filled with water to dilute the stench of urine. I feel the rounded edge of the bucket, back up my bottom and suspend it in the air like an insect, over what I suspect to be the centre. I stoop and lift my nightdress. Fingers digging into my thigh, I reach between my legs and peel the limp elastic of my pants to one side creating an opening. This saves me from pulling my pants down. Like a geyser projected by a majestic force, my urine drones into the water splashing my legs. Eyes still closed; my bladder deflates filling me with a lightness. I am halfway through my release when a blood-curdling scream stops me mid-flow.

I'm now wide awake.

'Help me,' a harrowing voice calls.

Grabbing my jacket, I unbolt the door and step outside. I'm immediately overpowered by a smell of burning wood and plastic choking up my lungs. My eyes tear with smoke. There's

285

a bright glow coming from the back of our house. The wind blows a whirlpool of sparks, peppering the night with infinite shooting stars. Frightened voices fill the air.

Panicked residents fly past like stampeding wildebeests. Mama's door swings open. I'm blinded by the light from the torch Kaminde holds. We are immobilised by confusion. Another scream emanating from Wa Njũgũ's house interrupts our perplexity. As if drawn by a magnetic force, we run in the direction of the scream. Flames are creeping out of every space of Wa Njũgũ's house. The door is open and from behind a curtain of flames a figure emerges, as if in some apocalyptic film, flinging a baby into the air. If I had blinked, I could have missed it. I grab it.

Before I can catch my breath, another flaming child comes our way and Mama jumps to catch it. One by one Wa Njũgũ flings out more children. Out of nowhere people scramble to grab one. Someone takes off their coat and covers one child stifling the flames. Another person is rolling another burning child on the grass. Holding the baby up with arms raised, I run in the direction of the tap. By the time I get there, the sleeves of my jacket are on fire. I twist the faucet and place the baby underneath it and slap off the flames on my jacket. Her crying is piercing my heart and deafening my ears.

'Don't cry you will be okay,' is all I can say.

I want her to stop hurting. I continue dousing her with water hoping it will soothe her. Then I hear her teeth chattering. From the glow of the fire, I can see her raising her little hands to me to pick her up. I pick her up and she holds me close. I feel the thud of her little frightened heart. I hug her closer.

Kaminde arrives carrying another child. A flashlight beams on us, and its carrier is running. It's Mama. She has another child. Others do the same. We are competing for handfuls of water to put out the fire on the children's clothes.

With all her children rescued, Wa Njũgũ collapses outside her house, clothes still on fire. Gĩtonga runs to her and begins emptying the contents of his two jerrycans on her, dousing the remaining wilting flames on her clothing. Then tossing them to the side, he lifts her into his arms and runs in the direction of the gate like a man possessed by demons.

Above the roar of the inferno, the voices of the washerwomen chorus, ringing out a powerful alarm call. From all directions people are attacking the raging fire. The dying woman is running between hers and Wa Njũgũ's house carrying two *sufurias* full of water, spraying the loads through the windows. Elephantiasis, dragging his leg, is brandishing a large cylinder which he is rolling towards the fire. Gathuki clutches two gourds of water which he points to the fire, shaking them. Firifo runs to us in his underwear, a hosepipe flung over his shoulders. His wife Jane with little Ruth strapped on her back, bears two small pans whose tossed contents evaporate before hitting the flames. Firifo is unravelling his hosepipe. Someone grabs one side of it and attaches it to the tap. Firifo runs to the fire pointing the hosepipe as the water just trickles through. The fire roars like the *Ndamathia* monster about to be stripped of its magical rainbow hairs.

'Turn on the water,' says Firifo in the direction of the tap.

'I'm trying,' the man curses. 'Nothing is coming out.'

'I don't believe it.' Firifo can barely disguise his weary disappointment.

Across the compound torches flash like fireflies, as people run around fighting the fire, itself now deranged, infecting other houses like a contagious disease. The hosepipe only produces a pathetic dribble and Firifo abandons it. Bodies crisscross one another in fright. Someone is yelling. Like a scorned dragon, the fire retaliates to our meagre efforts, spitting out sparks, exhaling a huge fireball which jumps to our house. I scream. Mama screams. An explosion of a gas canister sends an array of fireballs in all directions. The sky is lit like some mighty beast has been roused, and the flames grow taller illuminating the horror on our faces.

'Run to the gate, run.'

Still holding the baby, I run towards the gate blinded by smoke. The fire is spreading. We are engulfed. At the gate, the night watchman is struggling to insert the key into the padlock. His hands are shaking. I take the key, insert it and twist. It's unlocked. I throw the padlock to the ground. Everyone is pushing behind and there is a stampede as the fire is getting closer. The rusty gate gives way. We run towards the maize stalks.

As we move away from the flames there's a chorus of names. People searching. Fathers, calling to children, children calling to their mothers. Others simply run around too stunned to speak. Eventually, we fall silent and stare. We are the audience watching a fiery performance played out on a stage of smoke. The fire roars, swallowing anything still standing. The baby on my chest is sniffling, terrified of the beast we see before us. I am crying.

We are defeated. The fire is of biblical magnitude. Villagers arriving from the surrounding areas are rendered speechless by the spectacle. We have succumbed to the ferociousness of the fire. All we can do is stare as our lives evaporate into nothingness.

Chapter Forty-Three

Pushed by the intensity of the fire, people crowd the Kitch Sarajevo bus stop. They've run out of tears and are now gurning with shock. I am circling them, inspecting their faces in the glow of the fire. None of them are Mama or Kaminde. I'm filled with fear. My throat is sore from yelling. The baby mimicking the sound emanating from my throat. I don't know what to do. The last I remember is they were by the tap dousing some of Wa Njũgũ's children. They couldn't have gone far. There's no public transport at this time of night and the road is silent.

'Come this way. There's a car taking people to hospital.'

Turning round, I follow the speaker to a pickup truck. The engine is revving. By the driver, a group of wailing people sit. The truck bed is overcrowded. I think there's no space for me. I try to hand the baby to someone to take her to hospital, but she refuses to let go of me. There are more groans as people huddle tighter to free up a space for me. I squeeze in at the back of the pickup truck and sit on the floor with the baby sitting on my lap.

Bobbing up and down in the ditches of the worn tarmac causes whimpers from the casualties and the car's tired suspension. The journey takes an eternity. We arrive at the hospital and there are nurses and hospital staff rushing back and forth with trolleys filled with the injured. I walk into the casualty department and there several residents are sat on benches. I see Wa Njũgũ's paler bleached skin now scorched and blackened. She is lying on a trolley staring at the ceiling teardrops flowing from her lash-less eyes. Her mouth is quivering, as if she is trying to say something. I edge closer to her. She's barely recognisable from swelling.

For the first time she is not the centre of attention, overpowering those around her with the speed of her words. In front of me is not the obscene woman taunting me. She is a shadow of the fierce matriarch striding around the compound of the Ministry of Works disseminating gossip. She looks vulnerable. I feel a pang of sympathy for her and think of her bravery running in and out of a burning building to save her children. I see a woman who perhaps had dreams before she was broken by life. Why do I fear her so much? Maybe I am afraid of being consumed by life and she is the embodiment of that.

A voice escapes from her blistered lips. I lean forward to listen.

'My baby.'

'I have your baby,' I say.

She begins to cry. Her tears seem to be stinging the burns on her face. The baby sees her mum and she wants to go close to her. I move closer, but hold onto the baby.

'It's okay. Mummy will be well. She's tired now.'

I whisper to Wa Njũgũ's ear, 'don't worry your baby is safe with me.'

I look around. I am expecting doctors and nurses to be fussing around Wa Njũgũ and the baby. There's no one. A nurse in a starched hat and flat ironed uniform sits behind a desk. I show her the baby.

'She is badly burned. She requires urgent treatment.'

I expect her to take the baby, but she just stares at me.

'And the woman lying on the trolley, why isn't she already receiving treatment?'

The nurse's face clouds over. 'She has no money. We only begin treatment once a deposit has been paid.'

'How about the baby, surely you can begin treating the baby?' I ask.

'Rules apply to everyone.'

'So, you are saying that these people deserve no help because they haven't got money?

She shrugs and carries on doing whatever she was doing.

'Please don't just sit there, help this woman and her baby!'

My pleas are met with a blank expression. There must be another way. Wa Njūgū and her children need urgent medical help. We can't just sit back and let them die. I walk round the casualty department calling for people with money to help with a deposit. My request is met with apathetic glares.

'Only the saviour can perform miracles here. We are poorer than mice,' says a man holding onto his bleeding forehead.

I go back to check on Wa Njūgū. She's gasping.

I run back to the desk and plead with the nurse, 'She's dying. Please help her she's dying.'

The nurse rolls her head as if I am wasting her time. I see an oxygen mask, take it, and place it on Wa Njūgū's face. The baby is still sniffling, but she is distracted by the flap of my jacket pocket. I look at her fingers flipping it up and down. Something falls on the floor with a thud, and I look. It's the rolled-up banknotes the rich man had left behind the morning after I went to the *malaya* house. I had stuffed the notes into my jacket pocket but distracted by the events of the last few days, I had forgotten about the money. I pick up the bundle and run back to the nurse.

'How much deposit do you need to begin treatment for this lady and her children?' I ask.

Without looking up she says, 'Five hundred shillings each.'

I hold out the stash of money still rolled up like the day the rich man left it.

At the sight of the money, she looks up. 'Is it just the two?'

'Start with the woman and the baby,' I tell her, in that instant feeling the power of what money can do. 'I will find her other children.'

I am about to go around the cubicles in search of Wa Njũgũ's children when Mama rushes in with two of them, followed by Kaminde with another two. I call them over and the desk nurse, now attentive and conciliatory, questions them on the condition of Wa Njũgũ's other children.

'These two, they are urgent,' Mama says, her eyes wide at the sight of the money at hand to me. There is so much money, there's enough to begin treatment for Wa Njũgũ and all her children. As the nurse continues her admission protocols for them, I am struggling to stay focused. The rich man's money reminds me of his kindness toward me that night. The nurse hands me five hundred shillings change. I put it straight back into her hands.

'Treat that man too.' I say, pointing at Gathuki who is struggling to breathe.

The man with a cut on his head says.

'This is a miracle! It's a miracle. Do you have any money for me too?'

I shake my head putting my fingers into the pocket. To my astonishment there's a five hundred shilling note in my pocket. I hand it to the nurse. The man kneels on the floor and begins to pray.

I watch Wa Njũgũ and her children being taken in behind a door. Mama throws her hands around me and we cling to each other. Kaminde is unsure whether to shake my hand or hug me. He seems relieved to see me. Mama sees the burns on my hands and takes me to a nurse who is dabbing iodine on burns. We have no money left for my treatment, so the nurse gives Mama bandages to wrap my hands.

Mama leads us to the benches in the lobby. I sit down realising how exhausted I am. Kaminde walks over to a small black and white TV and turns it on. The early morning newsreader is doing a news round up. She is reporting on a meeting of world leaders in Milan for the global poverty summit. The world to me is like a horror story and my brain is not engaging. I am only staring because it's distracting me from the wailing and clinical smell of the hospital. We are waiting for the pickup truck to return with more people so we can get a lift back. The camera focuses on a familiar figure. Right there in front of me, I see the rich man, dressed sharp and looking sombre, addressing all the world leaders. I am stunned.

Chapter Forty-Four

The world rises to a calm bright morning. Kīrigiti Hills lies
with the calmness of a boa constrictor, digesting last night's
prey. Even the birds have gone mute in their nests. We are
still reeling from the wrath of the night. Smouldering embers
twitch, reminding us it wasn't a nightmare. Charred remains of
the last burnt-out shells collapse as if to guarantee our obscurity. Not a house is standing nor a fragment of what we once
possessed. Everything gone in flames.

We are crowded by the gate consumed by the sight of our
loss. It's all we can do. We have no plans. Time has stood still
for us, and we are unable to comprehend the night's events,
or process the vanishing of everything we own. How does one
contextualise watching burning children? Or put into words the
feeling of watching those with nothing to lose, lose everything?
We can't mourn we are still in shock. No one is left unscathed
by the fire. We stare into the bleak void of our future.

They say you don't know what you've lost until it's gone. I
think about my room and how much I despised it. But it was
familiar. It was where I did my thinking, staring at beams of
sunlight through nail holes. I had a place to call home. And that
place is somewhere buried in the ashes. There's nothing I would
rather do now than sit on my bed and rest my weary limbs.

I need a drop of water, but the tap is gone. There's nowhere. Where do we begin? Who do we turn to?

Someone is speaking and I turn round to listen. It's a man dressed in a watchman uniform.

'I've opened the gates to Kitch Sarajevo. You can sit in the compound.'

We walk down the marram road to the Kitch Sarajevo development like ghouls. The gates are open but there appears to be an invisible barrier stopping people from going in. The fear of encroaching into the white man's compound, even though there's not a white person in sight. The watchman says we can sit on the pristine lawns trimmed with the rigour of a diligent barber. They say time is a great healer, but the wounds inflicted on me, and the residents of Ministry of Works will take a while. Unable to contemplate our future, many residents lie on the grass wallowing in self-pity.

Counting the aftermath of a catastrophe requires bravery. The severely injured have been admitted to hospital with significant burns and smoke inhalation. My mind wanders back to the hospital and the sight of Wa Njũgũ. I hope she and her children get better. I can't push away the thought of her swollen face and the vacant look in her eyes. When I am less tired, I feel I should go to see her in the hospital. I think of the baby playing with my pocket and of the money. I have no regret of using it to save their lives, but I can't think of mine right now. That thinking space in my brain is closed.

I sit down and let the soft grass take my weight off me. I lean back and fall asleep. I am woken by Mama who instructs me to sit up. There are women handing scoops of *mukimo* to the residents who are eating ravenously. For the first time I realise it's been a long while since I ate. My hands are covered with bandages, and I can't hold the food. The woman serving food is from one of the villages nearby and she promises to bring me a plate and spoon. I'm too hungry to wait so Mama feeds me with her hands like she did when I was a small girl.

The job of nursing the wounded has fallen in the hands of the dying woman. It turns out she used to be a nurse in her younger years, before she gave birth to a stillborn baby. The doctors told her if she ever got pregnant again another pregnancy could kill her, so her husband left her. Without the two most important people in her life, she condemned herself to a death sentence. Until Gĩtonga reawakened her desire to live again.

With renewed rigour she is busy going from patient to patient changing bandages and offering water. When she's done, she walks to the centre of the lawn and commands everyone's attention. She is accompanied by the watchman who begins to speak.

'Two nights ago, I was woken in the middle of the night by a commotion. Well, I had dozed off,' he admits, knowing that falling asleep on his job would be enough for him to lose it. 'I thought we were being robbed. When I checked I saw it was the white men loading their packed possessions into their cars. They left in haste.'

I am struggling to understand why the story of the white men is relevant.

'I have inspected all the cottages, and they are all empty. It's not much but you have had a rough time. I will open the cottages and you can use them for now until you know what to do.'

It takes a few minutes for those words to sink in. Nobody moves in case they are mishearing. The dying woman steps forward. Everyone is focused on her.

'I am very sorry for your loss, our loss. We all arrived at

the Ministry of Works as individuals. Just a group of people co-existing. We lived our lives in the most selfish and despicable ways. It's taken pain and suffering to open our eyes to what real humanity is. Today we move here as a community.'

Firifo walks forward, asks her if he could say a few words.

'Old man Gathuki did not make it,' Firifo says, staring at his thin fingers, his face hollow with sadness.

'He worked hard running into burning buildings saving lives. One of the children was badly injured and he walked him all the way to a neighbour's house looking for a car to take him to the hospital. It was there we found him. He had collapsed as he was leaving. He was admitted. We stayed by his bedside until he went. But before he went, he gave us this message.'

He hands a piece of paper to Kaminde.

Kaminde holds it tight unsure what to do.

'Open it,' says Firifo.

Kaminde clears his throat and burps. Everyone bows.

'*Dear residents of the Ministry of Works, you are brave for putting aside all your differences and working together. Do not be afraid. Every time you have a problem remember; I will be watching over you because you are not alone. I will be your guiding spirit. You are the Chosen Ones.*'

Everyone bows. Firifo wipes tears from his tired eyes. He looks heartbroken. I thought he despised Gathuki. I remember the arguments between them on the night I took the pills from Dr Njaũ, and in the shop during Ndekezie's lynching. He appears humble and a different man.

I think of Gathuki and how distraught he was that night. I barely knew him, but he stood for something. Our old way of life. A way that we young people think is primitive and old fashioned, a way with a decency that with modernity has faded. Maybe the wise people of old knew the concept of rebirth. That it doesn't mean the end when a forest burns to the ground destroying everything in it, because life and time must evolve. The nutrient rich ash nourishes a new life form. Seedlings of hope. In time, the fire that consumed everything is soon forgotten, as the new life form takes on the new era.

I feel wounded. We feel wounded. But I guess healing begins the moment the injury occurs. I'm struck by the generosity, love and care shown by the very people that nauseated me. As in the olden days, we are learning to understand each other, to re-establish equilibrium, for an egalitarian society where no one goes hungry.

A sense of camaraderie has set in, and this is beginning to look and sound normal, but with uncertainty. A move toward cooperation, that never existed before in the history of the Ministry of Works. Maybe our Gĩkũyũ ancestors learnt Gathuki's decency due to shared experiences. Maybe they'd been caught in a thousand fires that drove them to work as a unit not individuals; to become an inclusive society. Maybe they understood the dangers of a fragmented society, weakened by lack of cohesion leading to people stepping on each other's toes, yet there was space for everyone. A space where joy is derived from simplicity rather than material wealth. We too could learn to dance, share, and cherish one another, remembering to thank Ngai Mwene Nyaga. Perhaps a society needs to break and be on the verge of collapse, to ignite togetherness.

Firifo walks away. He sits by his wife Jane and embraces Ruth.

The dying woman steps forward and clears her throat.

'You may remember some time back during our meeting, I was tasked with finding out who owned the land at the Ministry of Works. Although my sister, who works at the town hall couldn't establish that fact, she was able to discover that the land on which we are today, was given as part of ten thousand acres on two thousand shilling yearly rental to a *mzungu* by the colonisers' government in 1904. He took a small section which he allowed his cousin to farm. That *mzungu* was taken ill and rented it to Kitch Sarajevo. The records show that he died in 1986 with no living relatives which means...,' says the dying woman with surprising eloquence.

Everyone holds their breath. She lifts a hammer she had salvaged, heightening our curiosity. She walks over to the fence panelling and starts hammering onto something that falls off the fence panel. Everyone looks on in confusion as the dying woman carries on hammering some more. Finally, she steps back and reveals a sign. It simply reads:

Welcome to The Ministry of Works

Chapter Forty-Five

~

A waitress with harsh kohl pencilled eyes and a beauty spot at the centre of her head, like a third eye, walks towards me. Her red smeared lips, which look like they were applied in an earthquake, twist into a smirk and she tucks her hands into her grubby apron, giving me a quizzical look. Walking into Kīhoto Bar, I've no time for judgemental barmaids. Her eyes drop on my protruding belly.

'Are you looking for someone?'

I say nothing but look around.

'If you are here to harass your husband, I warn you we don't entertain fights.'

I shrug her hand off my shoulder and continue to the corner where a lone figure sits. He stands and walks towards me but halts as he spots my belly.

'Oh Christ. I didn't realise,' he says in astonishment. I'm glad the music is a bit too loud, and no one can hear us.

He stares at my belly then looks at my face. His face is riddled with questions and all I can do is stare back and I too, I'm lost for words. He regains his composure and beckons me to sit at the table tucked away from the glaring eyes of Kīhoto barmaids. He is flustered, embarrassed, shy, and curious and it makes me smile. He asks me, 'Did I do this to you?' and I'm so shocked by the question, I cannot speak.

He goes on, 'I am so sorry. I drank more than I intended to drink that night and had to rush off the following day to Milan. I don't even know your name.'

'I am Mũkami,' I say, my face mirroring the gloom on his face. 'I didn't get a chance to ring you sooner. A lot has happened.'

Please call me Mike,' says the rich man his face fraught with worry.

He beckons a waiter and says, 'What do you want to drink?'

'Fanta *tafadhali*,' I say.

'Make that two please,' he says to the waiter who disappears and returns with two cold drinks, places two wet glasses on the table and pours out the Fantas.

'Sweetheart, I mean Mũkami, I'm a responsible man and had I known that I did this I would never have-'

'It wasn't you,' I say.

I sound more forthright than I intended.

'It was a boy, two boys. I don't know how, they tricked me, into seeing the old woman. The old woman cursed me with her nakedness and because of the *chang'aa*, I don't know how they did it and then Geremani, he's a snitch, I added him to my list of enemies.' Words fall out of my mouth like a biblical flood and tears begin streaming down my face.

'Oh Christ, please don't cry,' he says handing me a silk handkerchief.

'And then the fire, I gave the money you gave me to the woman, vile woman, she's nice now but her baby was going to die.' Just as I inhale deeply, he says with a sympathetic tone, 'Why don't you take a deep breath and tell me everything slowly from the start?'

I sob into the handkerchief some more, then take a deep breath and begin. I tell him of the loan from the crossway tailor and how I made it to school at the start of term. I tell him of seeing Kĩmathi and how he made me feel. I tell him of the school disco and how I upset Kĩmathi with my refusal.

'Mama never told me how else to love a boy, so he got very angry with me,' I continue.

I explain my excitement when he wanted to see me again and how I agreed to go celebrate the end of mock exams. As I tell him of how Kĩmathi and Wambũgũ took me to the *chang'aa* seller and about being spotted by Geremani who reported us to the school, my tears turn to anger. I tell him of the caning by Wamakũbũ and being expelled.

I stop briefly to take a sip of my Fanta then continue. I mention how Auntie Eunice helped me find a new school, only for the toothless matron to force me to the hospital with other hostage girls. I mention the horrible nurse who mocked me and the tirade and expulsion, by the headmistress, from my new school.

'So, I couldn't go back to Auntie Eunice and had to find a solution myself. I tried everything, from the demented Dr Njaũ before finally going to Florida 2000 where I met you and the money you gave me was for an abortion. I meant to use it at the white people clinic but then the fire,' my voice breaks at the memories of the fire that have haunted my dreams to this day.

I am shaking with emotion. He squeezes my hand tighter. I want to stop but I must purge every pent-up anger inside me, so I continue. I tell him of Wa Njũgũ and her children and how they were going to die so I used my money to save them.

'I am so sorry for everything you've been through; I'd have taken care of the abortion for you if I knew you were pregnant and wanted one,' he says, comforting me with tear-filled eyes.

'I didn't want an abortion, I mean I did, but then I didn't because of Ndekezie, when I thought they were going to kill him, I saw the fragility of life which made me realise what I was carrying was precious, so I wanted the baby to live.'

He's confused but strokes my hand tenderly.

'No girl should have to go through what you've been through. Any one of those things would have been bad enough but to go through, all of them is a tragedy,' he says.

The warmth of his fingers fill me with a calmness I haven't felt for a long time. Like I've shed a load of worry. His soothing kindness reminds me of the warm shower in that posh hotel the morning after I met him. We sit in silence. Like the quietness after a storm. I'm too drained. The release of so much emotion has eroded my energy.

'Sweetheart, let me take care of you. Come live with me and I will look after you and the baby and no one will ever touch you again,' he says.

Those words jar me back to reality. I don't want to live with anyone. I am embarrassed.

'But you are married,' I say. I'm shocked at my bluntness, but I am changed now, growing if not quite grown, and I know the importance of being honest, open.

'Oh, it's a long story but my travelling all the time,' he pauses. 'My wife, she found someone else.' For a split second, I detect a hint of sorrow on his face.

I tighten my fingers around his in sympathy.

'I'm sorry for you.'

'It's nothing. It happened several years back, but that's all in the past. I want to be with you more than I have ever wanted anyone before. When you didn't ring me, it filled me with anguish thinking I would never see you again. You will have all my love and everything I own, if only you would agree.'

I close my eyes and let those words rinse the pain away from my soul. I don't know how long I shut my eyes but when I open them, I'm staring into his, kind eyes, filled with love, looking back at me. 'Penny for your thoughts? He says.

'You are the best man I have ever met. Your soft kindness has an authenticity I have never known. Something compelled me to ring you to thank you for that day and the money. And thank you for listening to me. But at this point in my life my heart is closed. I must do this on my own. I want to have the baby first. Then maybe who knows,' I shrug.

'Sweetheart, hear me out. From the moment I laid my eyes on you, I knew you were the one. I have never been so sure and felt so complete, yet you are but a stranger to me,' he says his voice fading.

I close my eyes again and tears roll down my cheeks. This time he can read my thoughts. My heart constricts at the resigned look on his face.

'I know this is not the time but how about we make a deal,' he says as if trying to cheer himself up.

'I shall wait for you. Finish your education, in five years you will be done with school and college, by which time you'll be a grown woman, and, hopefully by then, a geologist.'

I wince at the mention of geologist. I haven't thought about it for a while. The emotion on my face is unmistakable, he leans forward taking both my hands into his, and the room falls away.

'I told you I used to be a headmaster, well I am from a family of educators and my brother owns that school. When and if you ever want to return, there would be a guaranteed place for you there and don't worry about the fees, he owes me. Ring this number. That's my brother's direct line,' he says, fiddling into his trouser pocket, retrieving a colourful business card and placing it in my hand.

My desire for education and my current situation seems like two planets in different orbits. I would have done anything to hear those words a few weeks ago. Maybe some time in the future they'll realign, but for now I have urgent matters at hand.

'If you haven't fallen in love with someone else and you still remember me, please ring me on the number I gave you. I'll never change it. I will gladly welcome you and your little one into my life, and I'll hold onto you so tight, you'll want to stay with me and we will build a beautiful life together, one you deserve,' says Mike.

'Maybe in another time, another place,' I say.

'Here's to the next five years,' he says. He holds up his glass and we clink ours together.

I finish my drink and walk out of the Kĩhoto bar.

Chapter Forty-Six

⌒

I am surrounded by the calmness of the night when my waters break, soaking through my beddings. I mustn't let it get to the Vono mattress donated to us after the fire by the mattress factory. I struggle up, feeling around for a matchstick to light the lamp, then remember in the old white people cottages, where we have been housed, we have electricity. I try to walk to the light switch, but a sharp contraction sends me to the ground.

'Mama,' I yell.

The lights come on as Mama rushes into my room and finds me writhing on the floor. Luckily our new house incorporates the two bedrooms, and a separate living room and kitchen so we no longer need to lock doors.

'My baby is coming Mama,' I say.

She yells to Kaminde to call Salome and Wa Njũgũ. She walks over to where I am. I'm on all fours. Her face brightens with delight. I'd never thought that Mama would have taken the news of my pregnancy with such joy. She's cooked for me and massaged my swollen feet every day. I was certain she'd beat me and throw me out like other girls I've heard of, but she seems to have found a renewed purpose.

She crouches beside me on the floor. She lifts my t-shirt

and rubs oil on my back from my shoulders down to my hips. Her hands are a balm to my tense muscles. She begins to sing a haunting melody. I'm a baby again. I'm reminded of when she'd carry me on her back long past my baby years and rock me to sleep with a lullaby.

'Hush my baby all will be well,' she sings.

I rock my hips in tune with her voice and we fall into a rhythm. I don't hear Salome who walks in carrying a case, wearing a nurse's uniform.

'I never thought I'd ever need these,' she says leaning over her case which she flings open taking out what appears to be a horn and some gloves.

She puts on the gloves and walks over to me. On her knees, she crawls very close to me, places the horn to my belly and brings her ear to it.

'Nice healthy heartbeat,' she says with a wide grin and rigour I would never have thought possible of the old dying woman from the Ministry of Works days.

Wa Njūgū opens the door carrying a lantern. She flicks off the electric switch, toning the harshness of the room with the soft orange glow of the lantern. She looks different. Her face is softer and tender. She's not rushing around anymore, and she seems to have found an inner peace. The wounds on her face are still visible but are fading. It's hard to believe she's the same woman who aroused such fear and dread in me. Something happened that night of the fire gelling us together. She walks out and returns with low stools which Mama and Salome sit on, hurries back out and returns with her own stool and a bundle of towels.

I'm encircled by the women, bringing an aura of love and togetherness. My contractions get stronger and Mama's singing is getting more passioned, her palm rubbing and circling my coccyx. Wa Njũgũ soaks the towels in the heated water and wraps them on my back soothing me. Salome places her palms on either side of my hips applying a little pressure as she begins to rock my pelvis. My body is a vessel guided by the matriarchs around me operating in harmony.

Mama's tone guides me through some mythical land. I'm writhing my way through, rocked by the motion of my hips. It's a wonderland and I am surrounded by tribeswomen, singing in harmony, beckoning me to join them. As the singing gets louder, the matriarchs, imbued with old wisdom and passion guide me through every wave. They are welcoming me.

Rain drums our roof in accompaniment to the singing, heightening the mystics of the night. Mama's voice is distinctive as if programmed into my psyche. She carries me through this wonderland, joining in the choruses of the women. Here there is only pure joy and no sorrow.

I rock my hips faster, and I begin humming their tune. There's a wave emanating from the pit of my stomach, churning its way toward my groin. It's getting stronger and I hum louder as if to overshadow the matriarchs.

I rock faster and there's burning in my lower pelvic floor as my whole body vibrates. There's a piercing cry merging into the ululating women as they welcome my daughter into the world. Salome catches her and I slump back into Mama who holds me tight, crying and singing.

Wa Njũgũ opens the shutters letting in the tranquillity of the dawn, the distant rays of the rising sun. Time appears to stand still as I cradle Gakari my beautiful baby daughter, sipping the ũcũrũ Wa Njũgũ hands me. My world's at peace and it's a world away from all the anger, pain and hurt I've endured until this moment. Everything is irrelevant as I gaze at the delicate little face that so resembles Baba. I wish he would have been here to feel the joy I feel right now. I've found the missing piece of my puzzle, and I feel as if the earth has stopped rotating just for me, to allow me to savour this moment. Just then, the cock crows with gusto as if to announce my joy.

Acknowledgements

I am indebted to the Society of Authors for your generous grant.

About the Author

Njambi McGrath is an award-winning comedian, author, presenter, and political commentator. Her accolades include hit *BBC Radio 4* Series *Becoming Njambi* and *Black Black*. She's had successful Soho theatre and Edinburgh Fringe runs with her numerous one woman shows. She's filmed several comedy specials. In 2019 she won the coveted Hackney Empire New Act Of The Year (NATYS) Award. She's appeared on *Comedy Central*, *Channel 4*, *BBC One*, *BBC Two*, as well as guesting on numerous radio programs like *Front Row*, *Saturday Live*, *Broadcasting House* and *LBC*. Njambi is the author of the critically acclaimed memoir *Through The Leopards Gaze*.

photo credit Steve Ullathorne